I0619586

Echo of a Song

Sher Kyweriga

Silva Publishing
Minneapolis, Minnesota

ISBN-13: 978-0615727875
ISBN-10: 0615727875

Dedication

To Bob who has been my best friend, love, and lifeline since I was 18 years old. Thank you for believing in me.

To my sister, Lori, who has supported me through every crazy endeavor throughout our lives. You give me hope, a push forward when I most need it, and you always have the guts to tell me what you think. You are the best.

To my mom who taught me to laugh and sing and then laugh some more. I wish I could have known you longer.

Writing a book is a solitary endeavor. Publishing it is not, and I would like to thank everyone who provided feedback and expertise to help me complete this book. Kerry Foerster, you were one of my first readers. You read this book from cover to cover and told me to never stop writing. Talia Wagner, I valued your feedback and recommendations very much. Jeanne Munger, you read every word—more than once. Without you, I would never have caught those inconsistencies. Connie Anderson, your wonderful review and editorial expertise gave me the hope and courage to keep going. Bonnie Anderson, your edits were gold—as always. Writing gets into our blood, and although we write in solitude, it is through sharing that the dream comes alive. Thank you all.

Prologue

November 1981

T he bedroom door creaked open, followed by the whisper of small feet.

"Meggie, someone's yellin' at Mama. I'm scared."

I swiveled in the desk chair to see my three-year old sister standing in the doorway, clutching a small rag doll, her toes curled against the cold wood floor. I'd given Jenny the doll for her first birthday, and she never went anywhere without it.

"What did you say, Jenny-Penny?" My mind was still trying to conjugate a whole string of French verbs. No way was I going to get anything less than an A on that blasted midterm.

"Someone's yellin', Meggie."

Now that the door was open, I could hear it too. When I recognized the voice shouting at my mother, I stood up so fast my chair tipped over backwards slamming against the floor.

"Come here, Jen. Now, quick like a bunny."

Jenny scampered across the floor and raised her arms. I tossed her onto the double bed and pulled the blue and gold starred quilt up around her face.

"Stay here until I come back." I leaned forward to give her a quick kiss on the forehead. "Don't move, promise?"

"I promise, Meggie." Jenny nodded so hard her curls bobbed around her face like tiny russet leaves fluttering in a strong wind.

I stepped out onto the landing and pulled the door closed behind me. The angry voice twisted up the enclosed staircase.

Ron Buckman. He was high on something. Based on what my mother had said when she told me to watch out for him, high was his usual state.

"So, what'd you tell my boss, huh Peg? I wanna know what you said, and I wanna know it now." He screamed the words in one big slur. "Hey, I'm talkin' to you, Bitch."

"I can hear you, Ron. I can hear you just fine, but I haven't spoken to your boss. I don't even know who your boss is." My mother's voice was calm and even. I knew she was trying to talk him down from whatever high he was on this time.

"I don't know who your boss is," Buckman mimicked in a high falsetto. "*Liar.* You thought I'd never find out you been talkin' to my boss behind my back, didn't you?"

My mother was the director of the Elizabeth Sheridan Sanctuary, a women's shelter downtown. The shelter had hidden his wife and six-year-old daughter to keep them safe, and since he couldn't get at them, he'd started following my mother around. He would show up at odd times wherever she happened to be, demanding to know where his family was, until Mom asked the court for a restraining order. Big deal. As though a stupid piece of paper could keep a jerk like him away from us if he decided to show up.

I crept down the staircase and stopped four steps from the bottom. I couldn't reach the telephone to call for help, and I didn't know if it would make things better or worse if I went into the kitchen. So, I just stood there, frozen in the stairwell.

"No, Ron, I didn't talk to your boss. Honestly, I didn't, but I'll go with you if you'd like to see him. You know, to straighten things out." As always, my mother was trying to solve the problem, only this time her voice held a note I'd never heard before.

"Don't lie to me. You know it's too late for that. It's too late for everything." I heard him stomping around in the kitchen. "I got canned today. Canned, do you hear me? First, you take away my family, and now you take away my job. But, I'm gonna get you and yours."

"No, Ron, please don't. Put that away. We can talk things out, you know we can." My mother's voice spun around the room, thin as cotton candy, pleading with him.

Something was wrong, really wrong. My mother never lost it. Never. I moved two steps down, hesitating. For a moment, silence filled the old house, and then I heard the patter of small feet on the bare kitchen linoleum.

"Don't you hurt my mama." The voice belonged to my little brother, Jimmy, who was eight years old, and if Jimmy was there, so was Danny.

No decision anymore. If the kids were in danger, it was my job to get them out. I dashed down the steps, pushed open the door at the bottom, and swung around the corner to see my mother backed up against the stove, clutching six-year-old Danny tight to her side with one hand, while she tried to pull Jimmy closer to her with the other. Jimmy wouldn't move. He stood squarely in front of her, blue eyes blazing and not a trace of fear on his face as he stared up at the man looming over them.

Ron Buckman stood in the doorway leading to the hall, his arm extended, holding a small black gun that looked like a toy in his thick, hairy fingers. Before I could say anything, he jerked his finger against the trigger. The gun bucked once, thunder echoing against the ceiling, walls, and floor, engulfing me where I huddled in the entrance to the kitchen. A metallic smell permeated the room. The smell was cordite. I found that out later, much later, and I'll never forget the smell and the taste of it on my tongue.

Without a word, Jimmy fell to the floor like a load of wet laundry, his eyes wide open, the wound on his shirt dead center.

"No," screamed my mother, pushing Danny behind her and

moving forward, reaching for Ron, trying to get the gun.

I opened my mouth to tell her to stay back, to warn her. Before one sound left my throat, Ron shifted the gun toward my mother, who was no more than three feet in front of him. He fired again. The bullet slammed into her, and she spun hard against the kitchen wall, a small red spot blooming high on the left side of her chest.

At first I thought, it's okay, she's not hurt that bad, it's okay. Then the spot morphed into an ugly scarlet inkblot that spread down the front of her white blouse, and with a look of resignation on her face, her eyes met mine. I could see her lips trying to form words as she fell.

I knew what she wanted, and I dashed toward Danny where he crouched by the stove. I could almost touch him when Ron turned the gun in our direction, his face twisted with the kind of rage I'd never seen outside of the movies. He pulled the trigger three more times, and I closed my eyes waiting for the pain to pierce my body. Nothing.

I opened my eyes and saw that Danny had fallen on top of Jimmy, his arms and legs splayed. If it weren't for his head, he would have looked like he was trying to wrestle with his older brother, but his head, his poor head.

Ron raised the gun again, and as he stumbled two steps toward me, I turned and leapt for the staircase, slamming the door shut behind me and taking the stairs three at a time. As I reached my bedroom door, I heard him crash through onto the stairway below.

True to her promise, Jenny hadn't moved from the bed. As I flew through the doorway, slammed the door, and spun to lock it, she turned to me, eyes wide, mouth open in a perfect circle.

I grabbed the edge of my bed and tried to drag it in front of the door. "Come on, move," I shouted in frustration as the heavy brass frame stood firm in the grooves its weight had furrowed over the years in the old varnish and wood. Finally, it began to inch its way toward me across the wooden floor. I pulled harder, panting, expecting Ron Buckman to burst through the door at any moment. Hearing his feet pounding up the stairs, I gave a last desperate tug, and the bed skidded across the door.

The room was so small, that a bare six inches remained between the foot of the bed and the window that led out onto the sloping rooftop covering the kitchen below.

"Meggie," whimpered Jenny reaching out her arms.

My hands were shaking, my legs were shaking, and I couldn't get the images of my mother and brothers out of my mind. Jenny's frightened little voice snapped me into the present. I looked at her. She had no one to depend on but me. I looked desperately around the room, trying to think of a way out. "It's okay, baby. Sit tight just for a minute. I have to think."

"Open the door. Open it now," bellowed Ron, rattling the doorknob. He threw his heavy body against the door, but the lock held. I knew it wouldn't hold for long. The house was old.

"Meggie, I'm scared."

"I know, Jenny-Penny, I know. Hang on. I'm gonna get us out of here." I rolled across the bed so that I could get at the window leading out onto the roof, grunting as I tried to shove it open. It didn't budge, and I groaned in frustration, realizing I had no one to blame but myself. I'd painted the walls last summer to brighten the old, dark bedroom, and in the process I must have painted the window shut. I turned to look frantically around the room for something to break the glass.

"Let me in, damn you." Ron threw himself against the door again and again.

I scrambled across the bed and snatched the chair from the floor.

"Jenny, get under the covers. I don't want you to get cut."

I threw the quilt over my sister, and she huddled down like a pheasant hiding from the hunter. Just as I swung the chair at the window, Ron bellowed again. A shot exploded through the old wooden door and buried itself in the mattress two feet from where

Jenny made a small bulge beneath the bed covers.

I heaved the chair, and as it connected with the window, sprays of glass exploded in all directions, falling across the bed, nicking my face, arms, and legs with slivers of fire. I kicked out the rest of the glass, pulled Jenny out from under the covers, and lifted her through the window onto the roof. Gales of November wind poured through the window, stripping the trees of their leaves. Jenny's nightgown twisted in the wind, and she reached for me.

"Meggie, don't leave me." Tears ran down her face and dripped off the end of her chin. "Don't leave me."

"Don't move, baby. Wait for me, I'll be right there."

I turned back into the room, and as I jumped off the bed, Ron hurled himself once again at the door, and the old lock finally gave. The door burst in only to bang against the brass headboard, which blocked his way into the room.

Desperately, I yanked at the sheet, ripping it out from beneath the quilt, which was covered with splinters of glass. Just as Ron squeezed an eye up against the crack in the door, I leapt back onto the top of the bed and slithered out the window to join my sister on the rooftop, dragging the sheet behind me.

"Meggie, where's Maudie?" Jenny's teeth chattered as gust after gust of freezing wind pounded against us.

"Come on, Jenny, we've got to go. We don't have time to get your doll."

"No, he's gonna get my baby. Please Meggie."

Inside, Ron Buckman grunted and cursed, slamming the door against the headboard again and again. "Get back here, damn you. I'm not finished yet," he screamed.

I pushed the sheet into Jenny's small hands and dove back through the window and onto the bed, landing in the shattered glass, but I didn't feel anything as I groped in the covers searching for the small rag doll.

Just as my fingers closed on Maudie, Ron heaved his body against the door, and it splintered, banging against the bed, causing it to jitter across the floor and jam up against the opposite wall. He was too big to fit his whole body through the six inches of space, but before I could move, his hand reached out and snagged the hem of my jeans.

He started pulling me toward him as he tried to squeeze his bulk into the room. I stared down at his fat fingers, covered with curling red hair, his nails black with dirt and grease. I rolled over onto my back, searching for a piece of glass. I grabbed a long sliver, and in one quick stab, I drove the glass through the back of his hand and into the palm of my own. He jerked his hand back pulling the sliver of glass with it. Before he could grab me again, I launched myself out of the window and back onto the roof.

I knew I had almost no time to get us down to the ground. My hands shook, and I dripped blood all over me, the roof, and Jenny as I pushed Maudie into her arms and twisted the sheet into a rope, jabbering all the while. "This is going to be so fun, Jenny-Penny. I'm going to give you a ride all the way to the ground. We're going to run away and hide, just like on TV, okay?"

My little sister nodded, tears streaming down her face. I tied the sheet in a big knot under her arms, and praying the knot would hold, I moved as close as I dared to the edge of the roof.

"No Meggie. I'll fall. I'll fall. Don't let me go," Jenny screamed.

"I won't let you fall, I promise. I've got you, Jenny." I clenched the sheet as tight as I could with both hands, and swung my sister down over the edge of the roof, letting the sheet out inch by inch until I knew her feet were solidly on the ground below. I tossed the sheet over the side.

"I'm going to get you damn kids. You can't get away," grunted Ron as he tried again to squeeze through the narrow opening into the bedroom.

A crash caused me to spin toward the open window as Ron gave one last enormous heave of the door, twisting and buckling the bedframe and gaining just enough space to force his bulk into my bedroom.

No time, I thought, no time. I dropped to my butt on the edge of the roof feeling the grit of the shingles beneath me, rolled over on my stomach, and inched my way over until I was hanging from the roof by my hands. Willing my body to relax, I dropped to the ground, shocks of pain shooting up both legs. I didn't stop.

I snatched Jenny up into my arms, Maudie, sheet and all, spun, and took off into the darkness. At the edge of the lawn, I turned back to see Ron Buckman silhouetted against the light in my bedroom. He raised his gun, and before I could move, I heard it roar once more.

Part I

June 2001

Chapter 1

Meg

Avoiding Ben's eyes, I pressed my lips together and set the blow dryer down on the bathroom counter.

"You don't understand, Ben. I deserve a promotion, especially with this upcoming merger. I've worked so hard, and this is my chance to be somebody important."

"Maybe it's you who doesn't understand, Meggie. You already are somebody important."

"You just don't get it. I want to be the one in control, the one who makes the decisions."

"Why, Meggie? Why is that so important to you?" Ben fell silent for a moment. "I'm not good at words like you are, but I wish I knew how to help you find whatever it is you're looking for. I wish you could be happy."

For just a moment, I met Ben's eyes in the mirror. I looked away and reached for the frizz-free conditioner, combing it through my hair to smooth out every bit of curl.

"I'm happy," I muttered, staring into the mirror. "I'd just be a lot happier if that executive team took me and what I have to offer a bit more seriously. Ben, you know my goal was to make vice president by the time I was 35, and I'm already 38 years old. I want that promotion, and I've worked hard for it."

Familiar frustration welled up inside my throat, closing off words best left unspoken.

"I know you did, Honey."

Again, my eyes met Ben's in the mirror, my frustration mounting, seeking an outlet—any outlet.

"Don't patronize me." I flashed. "I get it all day long when I'm hanging out with the big boys. I definitely don't need it from you when I get home, okay?" As always, as soon as the words left my lips, I wished I could snatch them back.

Ben stood there for a moment looking at me as he does sometimes, saying nothing. Finally, with no expression on his face, he turned and started to walk out of the bathroom.

I knew I should be sorry. I even knew I *would* be sorry the minute Ben left the room, but what I knew didn't stop my mouth. It never did.

My eyes flew around the room and settled on the sage green, terrycloth bath sheet he'd left in a damp heap on the floor. Aha, I thought with savage satisfaction. Without another thought, I whipped around and spit out between clenched teeth, "Are you going to leave your towel on the floor all day to mildew? Come on Ben, help me out a little will you, please?"

Ben turned back and looked down at me for a long moment. He opened his mouth as though he had something to say, but finally he looked away, carefully shook out the offending towel, and hung it to dry on the edge of the shower door. He smiled, his eyes gentle and blue as a summer sky, leaned over to kiss me on the cheek, and walked out the door.

I turned back to my reflection, heart pumping wildly. I hated it when Ben acted so nice to me when I was working so hard at being rotten. Sometimes, I just wished he'd fight back a little bit so I wouldn't look so bad.

Behind me, French blue designer wallpaper covered the walls

with delicate, cream-colored calla lilies and twining sage green leaves. A wide tile ledge curved around the Jacuzzi, filled with ceramic pots of white and fuchsia orchid sprays dangling from brown, woody stems. I took a deep breath. I had a lovely home, and I had worked hard to get it.

I took another deep breath, wondering why I got so frustrated, and why when I was frustrated, I always seemed to take it out on Ben. Sometimes I even wondered how Ben and I had gotten together in the first place.

Ben was a software engineer, and he supervised a team who wrote code all day long. He pretty much ignored all the politics. In fact, he stopped thinking about work the second he left his desk. I, on the other hand, thought about work from the moment I woke up until the moment I fell asleep. Even then, images of my job saturated my dreams. I used to laugh and tell people that Ben worked to live, and I lived to work.

I reined in my thoughts, anxiety curdling in my stomach. I was late. Usually I was at my desk by 6:30 each morning with a cup of coffee, breakfast bar in hand, and computer humming away.

Because of all the extra communications work for the merger, though, I hadn't gotten home until 10:00 the night before. I was so wired I couldn't sleep, and when I finally did fall asleep, I had one of my dreams. I shrugged the memory aside, refusing to think about it.

A wave of weakness and nausea curled through me, causing me to lean against the counter. Shit, I thought. My blood sugar was low again. I had to be the worst possible personality to be a diabetic. Regretting the extra time it would take me to test my blood and eat something, I straightened all the brushes, combs, and creams on the counter, turned out the light, and went in search of food.

I paused at the top of the stairs as I did every morning to look at one of the photos in a multiple photo frame. The photo was small, showing only the head and shoulders of a pretty teenage girl. She wore a salmon-colored blouse, and her soft brown hair poofed up over her forehead in a style from the fifties. That photo never failed to spark a quick rush of anger.

"Life sure was simple for you, wasn't it Mom?" I whispered. "All you ever did was dream about saving the world and everyone in it, and look where you ended up. Dead at 36."

I turned away, and as I did, a feeling of confidence flooded through me. I was so different from my mother. I never indulged in dreams or fantasy. It was reality all the way for me.

Suddenly, I knew the time was right to meet with my boss and have a serious discussion about why I deserved a promotion. The merger would almost double the size of our company—in terms of people and revenue. With the added scope of responsibility, I was sure my boss would approve my promotion. All I had to do was work the system like all the big boys did. I continued down the staircase in search of orange juice.

Chapter 2

Meg

I put both of my hands on Marty Kazinski's desk and leaned forward. He rolled his chair back a few inches to put more space between us.

"I'm not going to give in on this one, Marty. I'm right, and you know it."

"Meg, listen to me. This isn't about being right or wrong. This is about being a team player. You have excess office space, and since we've closed the Baker Street location, I'm getting ready to stack people two deep in a bay. Global Communications has more than enough space. I don't understand what the big deal is."

"No. Those offices belong to me. I'll be the judge about whether I have enough space. If you need more, go talk to Larry or Eric. Their departments aren't going to grow any time soon."

Normally, I play the political game with a bit more flair, but Marty was so damned annoying. Besides, as far as I was concerned, he had more staff than we needed in his Information Services department.

"Oh, and your department is going to grow? My understanding

is that we have zero head count through the end of the year. So, do you know something I don't?" His eyes brightened, and he leaned closer.

I wasn't about to fill him in on anything I knew. Knowledge was a competitive differentiator. I had big plans, and I wasn't about to share them, at least not until my promotion came through.

"Look, I've got to go. I have a meeting with Richard in ten minutes."

Marty's nose practically twitched, he was so interested in finding out my business. Well, as far as I was concerned, he could take care of his own and stay out of mine. Besides, I didn't really have a meeting with the CEO. I only said so to get a rise out of Marty.

I sauntered down the hallway to my office. Joyce Iverson, my administrative assistant, was not at her desk. Again. I was going to have to talk to her. Again. When people called me, I wanted them to get instant service. I didn't believe in voice mail except as a backup system. When someone has an emergency, they want to talk to a human being—not a machine. Her job was to be that human being from 7:30 a.m. to 5:00 p.m. Monday through Friday, except for lunch and emergencies.

I sat down in my black leather chair and swiveled it from one side to another as I checked through the stack of pink message slips that Joyce had left on my desk. Nan Zablonski. Hmmmmm, interesting. I wondered what she wanted from me. Nan was the national president of the International Association for Business Communicators.

I dialed her number.

"This is Nan Zablonsky."

"Nan, how are you. This is Meg Jacobi calling you back," I used my warm, mellow, aren't-I-just-the-consummate-business-woman voice. I was proud of that voice. I'd practiced until I got it down flat.

"Meg, thank you for calling me back so quickly. I know how busy you are, so I'll only take a few minutes of your time."

"No problem, Nan. I always have time to talk to you."

I heard the pleasure in her voice as she continued.

"Thank you. Well, as you probably know, our annual seminar is scheduled for next February, and we're still in the early planning stages. Meg, you have been such an excellent speaker for us. A speaker, I should add, who has won a steady stream of Gold and Silver Quill awards. I can't even begin to tell you how much we have appreciated you and the expertise you bring to IABC."

"Thanks, Nan. Coming from you, that's quite a compliment."

"Well, it's heartfelt. You are so good at what you do. Last year your team stole the show by winning the Gold Quill award with the excellent communications work you all did on the acquisition of Obitron, Inc., but I'm beginning to ramble. Long story short, the planning committee would be honored if you would agree to be our keynote speaker at next year's international conference. Please say you'll accept."

I smiled, a feeling of power filling me from head to toes. I loved that feeling. I was good at what I did. I knew it, and that was mostly enough, but to have others recognize my gifts was something I never got tired of hearing.

"Nan, I'm the one who is honored. Of course, I accept. Thank you so much for thinking of me. What topic do you want me to cover?"

A clear note of triumph sounded in Nan's voice. "Thank you, I can hardly wait to tell the committee you accept. We'd like you to talk about critical success factors for growing as a communications professional. So many young communicators keep asking for more information about how to be accepted at the executive table, how to gain credibility, how to be accepted as a strategic partner. In my opinion, yours is the shining example of a path that serves as a model for anyone. As I said, the conference is in February. We're getting a bit of a late start here, and yours was the first slot we needed to fill. Thank you so much for accepting."

We chatted for a few more minutes and arranged a time to talk the following week. I hung up the telephone, already thinking about how to spin the story. Success, or rather, the path to success. It sounded almost too easy.

I looked around my office. Nan was right. I was successful. When I'd first joined Educational Software, Inc., that would be ESI for short, the communications manager—manager, mind you, not even director—was located downstairs. When I accepted the job, I not only angled for a director title, I negotiated an office in the C-suite with the CEO, the CFO, the COO, and all the other big boys. I kid you not, every one of them was a guy.

At least my boss seemed to understand how important it was for the communications leader to be an active member of his staff. I even had the office and a few perks to show for it.

I was part of the way there already because I definitely had an executive's office. I could look out of an enormous pane of glass onto a grove of trees for inspiration whenever I wished. My desk was a smooth slab of walnut, and it matched the walnut paneling. Two glass-enclosed bookcases hung over my credenza filled with my collection of business books like *Leading Change* by John Kotter, *The Fifth Discipline* by Tom Peters, and *The GE Way*, sorta kinda by Jack Welch with a little help from his public relations friends.

On the other side of the room, another credenza and bookcase were crammed full of books and mementos from all over the world. No question about it, if offices were a reflection of success, I was definitely successful.

I remembered laboring for hours as a junior communicator, though, in an 8' x 8' cubicle, surrounded by noise I couldn't control. I also remembered having no direct access to company strategy and having to regurgitate what some executive thought was the flavor-of-the-month initiative. So, how had I grown into my current position? How had I achieved success, and what could I share in a speech to fellow communicators?

Really, I thought, tapping my right forefinger against the top of my desk, I attributed a lot of my success to two behaviors. One, I focused on work to the exclusion of all else. I gave up the Friday night gatherings with coworkers over wine at the kitschy little bars cropping up all over downtown Stamford. I also gave up Saturday night dates with Ben. My average workweek was a minimum of 60 hours. Two, I worked the network every chance I got.

So, I guess if you boiled my success down into one headline it would read something like: Meg Jacobi attributes personal success to working harder than 98 percent of all other communicators and making friends with the big boys. Well, maybe that spin wouldn't look so good in a brochure, but, by the time I stood on stage in front of several hundred conference participants, I knew I'd be ready.

Before I could forget, I grabbed my Palm Pilot and tapped a note to myself to begin outlining the speech over the weekend. I saw the entry I'd made earlier that morning to meet with my boss, Richard Jamieson, and so I reached for the telephone to make an appointment.

Before I could pick up the receiver, the telephone rang. I expected that Joyce would be back at her desk by this time, and so I let it ring. It kept right on ringing. Damn. I picked it up. Big mistake.

"Meg Jacobi," I said briskly into the telephone.

"Meg, hello, I never dreamed I'd be lucky enough to get you directly. This is fantastic."

Shit, I thought, recognizing the voice immediately. To others the voice belonged to Marlene Jenkins. To me, it belonged to the Great White Shark, bloodthirsty reporter for the *Stamford Register*, local competition for *The New York Times*. The *Register* was less than two years old, but it was already getting a significant readership. In my opinion, the reason for its popularity had less to do with excellent reporting and more to do with sensationalism.

"Marlene, what can I do for you?"

"Well the rumors are flying about ESI. Sounds like you're thinking about making another acquisition?"

ESI was almost ready to announce the merger with our key competitor, the biggest integration we'd ever attempted. We were calling the potential merger Project Snowball. Information about it was need-to-know only, which definitely did not include bloodthirsty local newspaper reporters.

"Marlene, you know ESI's policy. We do not respond to speculation."

"Oh, so, what you're saying is that you aren't thinking of an acquisition? Funny, that's not what I heard."

"Let me repeat what I said a moment ago," I said speaking slowly and patiently. As much as I wanted to tell her that it was none of her business if we were planning to make an acquisition, I knew I had to stay on her good side. Not that the Great White Shark had a good side, unless you counted teeth-as-sharp-as-butcher-knives-ready-to-rip-you-to-shreds as a good side. So, I simply repeated, "It is ESI's policy to not respond to speculation."

"So you might be making an acquisition after all?"

"All I can say is what I've already said."

"Well, here's the deal. I have a deadline I need to make."

Of course she did. Here comes the blackmail, I thought, squeezing the telephone receiver with all my strength. I wished it was her stumpy little neck that I had my hands around.

"Meg, I need you to help me out here. I want to be accurate about what is going on at ESI, and I'm going to need a formal statement from you. Otherwise, I'll have to print my article based on what I know and say that ESI refused to comment."

Marlene's voice was as sweet as it could be as she so carefully explained her dilemma to me. As if I cared. Here's where I called her bluff. Then, I'd need to wait and see if she followed through on an article in tomorrow's paper. I was 99.9 percent sure she was bluffing.

"Marlene," I said in a calm voice. "I understand, but if I were to respond to speculation, I wouldn't be helping you out at all. You know that if we were planning a major organizational change, I'd prepare a formal statement. You would be one of the first people I'd call."

"I see," said Marlene in a clipped voice. "Well, I'm sorry you can't be a bit more specific. I really hate to print what some of your employees have been telling me."

For a moment, I wondered what the hell our employees had been telling her, but I was too experienced to fall into that trap. One more time. "I understand your position, but as I said, it is ESI's policy to not respond to speculation."

I said goodbye to Marlene and hung up the telephone very gently.

I hated public relations. I liked the investor relations part, and I absolutely loved creating strategic communication strategies to help our employees understand how they could personally contribute to the success of our business, but public relations? Yech! It was a "no win." The best you could do was keep the company out of the paper. The worst you could do was make a misstep that led to a series of articles filled with innuendos and misinformation that got everybody's undies in a bundle, from the mail boy, who was worried about whether he'd have a job going forward, to my boss, the CEO, who just plain didn't want to jeopardize his annual bonus.

I pulled my Palm Pilot closer and punched up my to do list. It was already 4:00, and I had at least another three hours of work. No problem, because the next thing I'd listed was: Go to the gym at 7:30.

I have to say working out was about as appealing as a trip to the Amazon before breakfast. Never mind. I was sticking to my goals. I'd embarked on this fitness plan more than twelve months ago, and so far, the results had been good. I had more energy than I'd had since I was twenty-two. My stomach was flatter, and my mammoth tree-trunk thighs were beginning to look at least a little bit toned. The best benefit of all was fewer nightmares, but I didn't need to be thinking about those nightmares.

First things first. I really needed to set up that meeting with Richard to talk about my promotion. Reaching for my telephone, I punched in the extension for his assistant, Sandy Smith.

"Good afternoon, Sandy. This is Meg Jacobi. Listen, does

Richard have any time for a meeting tomorrow morning? I've got some information I'd like to pass by him."

"Sure, Meg, no problem. How about first thing in the morning, say about 8:00."

"Oh, could we make it later, maybe 10:30 or 11:00? I have a doctor's appointment tomorrow at 8:00."

"Uh, let me see. 10:30? Looks good, I'll put you in and see you tomorrow, okay?"

"Thanks so much, Sandy."

I hung up and decided it was time for a cup of coffee, definitely my drug of choice. As I walked through the entrance to my office space, I could see that Joyce was still not at her desk. My lips tightened. I didn't fail to perform my duties, and I expected everyone on my staff to do the same. I was definitely going to have to talk to her.

I threaded my way through rows of cubicles to the stairs leading down to the cafeteria, pausing at the bottom and reaching into my pocket to be sure that I had the coffee money I'd stashed there. As I pulled out a bunch of quarters, I recognized the voice of one of my direct reports on the other side of the wall.

"Don't get me wrong, Ginny. I think Meg is an okay boss, but my God, the hours that woman puts in. She never stops. If you ask me, it isn't healthy to work so much. The woman doesn't even have a personal life—all she lives for is ESI. I bet she even bleeds ESI green."

"Karen, you know that Meg's been a blessing to our department. If it wasn't for the high profile she helps us achieve, we'd report to Human Resources instead of to the CEO." This was the voice of my publications manager, Ginny Olson. "I don't think she means to be so curt all the time. She's just really busy."

Karen's voice was subdued. "I'm not criticizing, or at least I didn't mean to. I really do think Meg is fantastic."

"You may want to keep your voice down."

"I'm not ashamed of what I'm saying, Ginny. I will never be able to make the commitment to ESI that Meg is making. I want to have a life."

I made a mental note to have a discussion with Karen Richardson within the next day or so. No way did I want someone on my staff who wasn't willing to give the job everything she had. Unless she was willing to change her attitude, I wasn't sure that I wanted to keep her on, and I intended to tell her so.

"Fine, but keep your voice down, will you. I don't think voicing your opinion out loud in the cafeteria is a very wise move, that's all. Besides, you don't know what's driving Meg. None of us does. I suspect she has her reasons for doing what she's doing."

"But that's my point. Meg doesn't seem to have any interests outside of work. No hobbies, no kids, she doesn't even have a dog. Her husband seems so nice, but I sure don't know when they ever have time to get together. No wonder they don't have any kids. She seems to plan every minute of every day around her job. Do you know, I've never even seen her without that Palm Pilot in her hand?"

I looked down at the Palm Pilot I'd scooped up on my way out of my office, put the quarters back in my pocket, and retreated up the stairs. Maybe I didn't really want a cup of coffee after all. The words I'd overheard stung. I had a personal life, and it suited me just fine. Besides, what I did with my time was my business and nobody else's.

As far as kids went? Ben was enough, thank you very much. I'd never wanted any children or dogs for that matter. Why would I foul up my life with a bunch of snotty-nosed little creatures that leached the life out of me or peed on my carpet?

As far as the Palm Pilot went, how else would I keep control over my life? I shrugged my shoulders and waltzed by my administrative assistant who was just getting back to her desk.

"Joyce, I'd like to see you in my office, please. Right now."

Dropping into my chair with a whump, I crossed "get a cup of coffee" off my to do list and added, "set up meeting with Karen Richardson."

Joyce hovered in the doorway, a notepad and pen clenched in

her hands.

"Come in, come in." For Pete's sake, I thought, what did she think I was going to do to her? Yell? I never yelled. Ever. I didn't believe in losing control, but I did believe in giving straight feedback about performance issues.

Joyce came in and sat on the edge of one of the cushioned chairs in front of my desk.

I sighed. Joyce winced. I felt like rolling my eyes, but didn't.

"Okay, I noticed you were not at your desk for a significant period of time this afternoon."

Joyce swallowed, hard. "Uh, I was gone for about forty-five minutes. I'm really sorry, Meg. I know you want me to be at my desk to answer your telephone."

"Yes. I do. I picked up one call that I should not have had to answer." My words were clipped and sharp. I wanted to make sure that she completely understood my disappointment. "Marlene Jenkins called from the *Stamford Register*, and she really put me on the spot, Joyce. If you'd picked up the telephone for me, I could have put her off long enough to miss tonight's deadline and finish the holding statement I'm working on."

Joyce looked down at my desk. "I'm sorry, Meg."

I leaned forward and tried to make eye contact with her. No such luck. She seemed to be intensely interested in the wood grain of my desk and refused to look up. I forged ahead.

"Here's the deal, Joyce. I need to know that you're serious about this job. When I hired you, I explained that I needed a partner who was willing to make a commitment to be present when I needed her. So, I'm going to ask you again. Will you make that commitment?"

I heard her swallow, and she looked up to meet my eyes, her own welling with tears. She nodded and opened her mouth to say something. Since I wasn't really interested in any excuses, I waved my hand at her, and she closed her mouth without speaking, lowering her gaze to my desk top again.

"Enough said. Please, don't let it happen again."

Tears spilled over and trickled down Joyce's cheeks, but she nodded and rushed back to sit in her cubicle.

I sighed. I never liked to discipline the people in my department, and I certainly didn't like to make them cry. As far as I was concerned, though, crying was not professional. I never cried on the job. I never cried at all. It was my opinion that women couldn't afford to cry all over people if they wanted to get ahead. Besides, I'd said nothing that should have made Joyce cry. I'd only clarified expectations. That was my job. Her job was to listen and respond to my feedback.

I glanced at my watch to see that it was 4:30. I thought about calling Ben to let him know I'd be late, but I decided not to bother. He'd figure it out when I didn't show up at my usual time.

Chapter 3

Ben

"Would you like something to drink, Sir?"

Startled, Ben turned from where he was staring out the window to find the flight attendant smiling at him and holding out a tiny packet of pretzels.

"No, thanks. I'm fine."

He turned back to stare out the window again. Wooly mountains of cumulus clouds tumbled in complex patterns below the airplane, looking substantial enough to get lost in. That wouldn't be so bad, he thought, to lie down and get lost in softness.

His thoughts veered back to Meg.

Ah jeez, I should have called her. What a crummy, cowardly act to leave a note on the kitchen counter for her to find when she got home from work.

Ben took a deep breath and let it out. He took another. It wasn't like him to get so angry, but for a while that day, he had needed some space from his wife and his marriage.

Never mind, he'd married Meg for the good and the bad. It was just that lately, it seemed as though she was becoming more and more obsessed about this promotion she wanted so much. Nothing he said or did seemed to help.

Ben shifted in his seat. As he moved, the paper he'd shoved into his coat pocket crackled. He frowned. Carly's note. What the hell was he going to do about Carly?

Chapter 4

Meg

I rounded the curve and our home came into sight. We lived in an upscale neighborhood, and every time I drove into it, I basked in a sense of accomplishment. Each home was custom built on two-and-a-half acres.

Our house, painted a soft grey and adorned with white shutters and trim, beckoned me from within with warm yellow lights. Ben had installed an automatic light system so that I never had to come home to a dark house. He knew how I felt about the dark. But enough about that, I never allowed my thoughts to wander into dangerous places unattended.

I drove into the driveway and parked in front of the garage so that I could walk through the garden and under the pergola to the back door. I had strawberries, blueberries, and pink, yellow, and purple flowers growing in my garden. I didn't know their names, and I never had time to harvest any of them, but I didn't care. They were there, they were beautiful, and they were all mine.

I noticed that the back of the house was unlit. Odd. I walked up to the back door, and pressed the doorbell. I waited, peering through the sidelight, expecting Ben to come trotting around the corner into the kitchen any second. He didn't come, and I rang the bell again. Nothing.

Damnation. The least he could do was open the door. Was that too much to ask? Evidently. I pulled out my key, inserted it into the lock, and shoved my way into the house. Silence surrounded me, and I knew I was alone. Weird. Ben was always home by 6:00.

It wasn't until I flipped on the lights that I saw a folded piece of paper leaning against the telephone. I snatched it up and read:

Dear Meg,

This morning, Jake asked me to go out to the plant in Fort Collins for two weeks. He wants me to work with their engineering team to bring them up to speed on the coding for the new guidance control system.

I hesitated about being gone that long, but actually Meggie, I think it might be a good idea for us to have a little space right now. I understand that you're struggling with a lot of issues. I wish I knew how to help you. I wish that I believed you even want my help, but I'm not sure you're thinking much about how our lives fit together anymore.

I love you Meg. Always have, always will. I'll be gone for two weeks. Let's talk when I get back, okay? We really do need to talk about a few things.

Call if you need me. You have the number—I'm sure it's in your Palm Pilot (that was not a slam, okay?).

Take care of yourself. Don't forget to check your blood sugar.

I love you,

Ben

You know how in books they're always yammering on about how the lead character feels a flood of emotion in this situation or that? Well, I was feeling a whole lot more than a flood of emotion after reading that letter. A full-fledged tsunami was blasting through my mind, hurling debris from so many different places in so many directions that I wasn't even sure how I felt.

The facts? I wasn't going to be any more ready to talk about "a few things" in two weeks than I'd been throughout our fifteen-year marriage. We'd already been there and done that. I loved my work, and I didn't intend to slow down or take time away from it to go on vacations or to putter around the house. I had no interest at all in any of those things, and, in terms of the big, loaded topic? I didn't want children. I'd told Ben I didn't want children when we met, when we became engaged, when we married, and about every six months since. I-did-not-want-children. End of discussion.

Maybe Ben and I really needed to face the fact that we wanted different things out of life. My mind winced away from that thought, but I forced myself to examine how I was feeling.

I started by listening to the silence in the house. I liked how the silence felt, and I liked the way it wrapped around me. I didn't have to make conversation with anyone. I didn't have to eat something unless I felt like it. I didn't have to be on. I didn't have to prove how important I was and how much I knew about anything. I probed a little further, kind of like poking a bruise to see if it still hurt, and if it did, how much.

After a moment, I sighed. What I mostly felt was relief. Ben and I had been heading for something, but I didn't know what it was, and even more important, I didn't even know if I cared. I'd behaved horribly to him over the past months, and it seemed to be getting worse. I didn't like my behavior, but I couldn't seem to stop it either.

I remembered one recent evening when I'd gotten home at about 10:00. I'd been working on the communications plan to close our Baker Street plant. The executive leadership team all agreed that the plant wasn't making enough money and that it made sense to close it down and move the manufacturing to Mexico.

That decision alone would really add to our bottom line. That's a good thing, right? The shareholders want the companies they invest in to make a lot of profit. I understood all that. The problem was that our decision ravaged the lives of 273 people. These were people I knew, and friends and relatives of many of the people at the main plant. My job, of course, was to spin the whole thing in the best possible way for our customers, shareholders, and remaining employees. The operative word was spin. Like a spider.

That night when I walked in the door I could smell candle wax and hear the sizzling of meat on the grill. I knew that Ben had waited to make me a nice dinner because I'd had to work so late on what he called a really stinking project.

"Meggie," he said coming around the corner. "Come on, Honey. I've made you dinner."

Ben put his arms around me, and I stood there stiff as a board. I didn't want dinner. I didn't want to talk. I didn't want any comfort. All I wanted was to go upstairs with a glass of wine, get into the bathtub, and read my latest in a whole series of junky suspense novels. Reading was the only way I could turn off my brain.

Ben steered me into the kitchen. He pulled my purse and briefcase away and stuck them behind the door. I reached for the briefcase and set it on top of the counter next to the spinach and tomato salads. My plan was to get up the next morning at 4:30 or so and start in again. Time was short, and I had a ton of things I had to get done before we announced the closing at the end of the week.

"Bad day, huh?" Ben must have been watching for me, because candles danced with golden light on the dining room table and steak was already grilling on the broiler. He steered me into the dining room, and I sank down into one of the dining room chairs.

Ben poured me a glass of merlot and kissed me on the back of my neck. I wanted to wipe off his touch. "I'll be right back with your salad. You can eat your dinner and relax now, Honey, okay? You can forget all about work until tomorrow."

That was the problem, really. I couldn't forget. I couldn't forget that after Friday, Joe Lawrence, the gnarled little security guard at the Baker Street plant who was always trying out a new joke on me would no longer have a job. I couldn't forget that Alice Johnson, the receptionist who always had a cup of steaming coffee waiting for me, would be out of work with no income to feed her four children. Alice was a single mom.

Most of all, I couldn't forget that Joe and Alice were just two of all the others who would lose their jobs on Friday because a bunch of executives wanted bigger bonuses. I knew most of these people by name and a whole host of personal details. I couldn't forget any of that, somehow, and not all the lovely, fragrant candles and sizzling steak dinners in the world were going to help me forget.

Ben set my steak and salad in front of me and sat down across the table. I could tell he'd gone to some care in making dinner. I stared at my plate. Asparagus nestled next to a perfectly grilled piece of New York strip steak. I poked it with my fork and watched the juice pool up and run down the sides to mix with the vegetables. It looked like blood. My stomach turned, and I pushed back my chair.

"I'm sorry, I can't eat this. It's disgusting. I'm going to take a bath." I grabbed my wine and walked out, leaving Ben sitting alone in the soft candlelight with the bloody fruits of his labor. He never said a word about my behavior. Not that night. Not ever. It is so damned hard to live with a saint. It would have been easier, and so much more satisfying to have had a knock-down, drag-out fight.

Later, he came up and slid under the blankets next to me.

"Meggie? Are you okay?" He put his arm around me and pulled me closer. I felt claustrophobic, as though if I didn't get some space I was going to throw up all over the bed. I went rigid, and he let me go immediately. I slid over as close as I could get to the edge of the bed and tried to relax so that I could sleep.

I got up at 4:00 a.m., went downstairs to make a pot of coffee, and started working again. I was feeling much better. After all, it wasn't a personal decision to close that plant, right? It was a business decision. I was just doing my job.

I pulled my thoughts back to the present. I decided that Ben's absence, was exactly what I needed. Now, I could focus exclusively on my work. With the merger coming up, I had so much to think about and so much to do. I didn't need any distractions. I decided that what I was feeling was relief. Pure and simple.

A wave of nausea flooded through me. There's that flooding thing again. I pulled out my glucometer, jabbed my little finger, and squeezed a drop of blood out onto the test strip. Thirty seconds later, the machine beeped, and I could see that my blood sugar was 325. A normal blood sugar reading was closer to 100. No wonder I'd been feeling nauseated all day.

Oh well, I was scheduled to see my endocrinologist the next morning. I was only going in because I had no choice. He'd cut off any future prescriptions until I came in for a checkup, which really pissed me off.

I'd been feeling really crummy lately, though. I knew I needed to go through the usual battery of tests to be sure my kidneys were working, my blood sugars were more or less under control, and I wasn't about to expire for any reason.

I hit the bolus button on my pump three times to get a jolt of insulin to bring my blood sugar back under control.

I opened the refrigerator door and stood facing into the cool interior. I felt so warm. We really needed to go to the grocery store, but I'd been so busy I hadn't thought about groceries in weeks. Usually Ben was the one who stopped off to pick up something for dinner.

I decided I wasn't all that hungry. I reached for the wine, but somehow the very thought of drinking it turned my stomach. Instead I grabbed a breakfast bar and a box of the orange juice Ben insisted we keep on hand for insulin reactions.

As I headed toward the staircase, I noticed a small shadow on the window next to the front door. Curious, I pulled open the door to find a box addressed to me. I didn't recognize the return address—no name, just an address in Minneapolis, Minnesota.

I shook the box. Hard. I swore I could hear a musical ping. So,

I shook it again. As far as I was concerned, if I broke whatever damn thing the box held, fine. I wanted nothing from Minneapolis. Nothing.

Chapter 5

Meg

I held a hot washcloth against my face. God, it felt good. I could have stood there forever, my face covered in warmth, my mind focused on nothing else. The nothing else didn't last. It never did. I felt the familiar twist in my stomach as I recalled the pile of work I had to complete by the end of the next day. I tried to pull my mind back from the abyss and revel once more in the present.

You know what they say, right? You can't change the past, so leave it alone. The future isn't here yet, so why worry. Simply focus on the present—because that's what it is, after all—a present. Cute, huh? Whoever thought that one up definitely didn't hold a corporate job.

I dropped the washcloth in the sink and opened my eyes to see a reflection of the closet door in the mirror. Inside that closet, the mysterious box lurked like an ugly troll under a bridge waiting to grab me with long scaly arms. It wasn't going to get me, though, because I wasn't going to give in and open it. I didn't care what was in that box. I was not going to open it. Period. End of story.

I reached for my advanced night repair and squeezed out one

drop of the viscous yellow liquid. I smoothed it onto my face and followed up with the resilience face cream. No way was I getting any more wrinkles than I had to before my time. According to the sales clerk at Lord and Taylors, this was the best anti-aging product on the market.

I found myself staring at the reflection of the closet door again. Stop it, I thought, turning out the light and closing the bathroom door behind me. You don't need to worry about anything more tonight. Things are cool. You'll catch up in the morning. Now, you can forget about everything and go to sleep.

Everyone talks to herself like that, right? Besides, I had no one else to talk to because I was abandoned for two whole weeks. I smiled. I didn't have to be nice to anyone. I didn't have to talk about silly, stupid things. I could focus on work, on solving the problems they paid me to solve.

I slid under the comforter sighing in bliss and snuggled up against the mound of feather pillows I burrowed into every night. I got the comforter on sale, and it still cost the moon. I'd have bought it even if it hadn't been on sale. I loved the sprays of plum and orchid irises and the soft green leaves printed on the cream background. I'd been especially daring and painted the bedroom walls a deep mossy green. Ben didn't like it, but it matched the leaves on the comforter, and I liked it fine. That room was my haven, and my breathing slowed down every time I came into it.

I sighed again, reaching for my latest trashy novel. This one was about an FBI profiler who was tracking a serial killer who had a penchant for styling his victim's hair and painting her finger- and toenails postmortem. When I read my novels, I could turn my thoughts off in a way that wasn't possible during any other activity except work. I read like some people eat popcorn. I was definitely addicted and went through at least three novels every week, but it didn't hurt anyone else, so why not?

I opened the book, but before I could stop myself, I turned to stare at the closet door.

If I'd been a bit more fanciful, I'd have sworn that damn box was calling out to me in the voice of that ugly troll: *Meg, come and open me.* No. No way, was I going to go near that box. I dragged my gaze away from the door and settled back against the pillows to read.

As usual, about thirty minutes later, my eyelids felt as though they were encased in lead, and my body relaxed against the feather pillows. I closed my eyes all the way and reached up behind my head to lay my book down on the headboard. I patted around until I found the light switch and clicked it off. I don't remember falling asleep. I'm not sure what time the dream began.

I was so excited to see the new puppies again. Puppies. I'd never had one. Never wanted one before. They were dirty, demanding little creatures that soiled your rug and whined for attention all the time. Even so, my excitement kept building as I strolled along the path toward the barn humming softly, the early morning air whispering against my skin in short feathery bursts.

All around the world was coming alive with the music of the morning. Meadowlarks trilled in the field on my left and robins chirped. Dragonflies entwined iridescent blue/green bodies and buzzing wings in living hearts, clinging to the tall waving grass as they passed new life from one to the other.

I smiled as I thought of the puppies. There were three of them, and now that their eyes were open they tumbled and bit and played with each other as they learned which was the alpha, which was the omega, and which would fit the remaining position between.

I loved to gather all three of the squirming sweet things in my arms, to feel the small, warm tongues against my chin. They were beginning to come to me when I called, and that I liked best of all. I was committed to helping these puppies grow into everything they could be. I was responsible for them. They trusted me to be there for them.

Wait, I thought, caught for a moment on the edges of the dream—not really awake—not completely asleep, but feeling a tiny bit of dissonance. Wait, this can't be right. I don't want the responsibility. I can't have the responsibility. I slid back into the dream, and the anticipation of seeing the puppies once more drove away my confusion.

Squinting against the rising sun, I was surprised to see a stranger enter the barn before me with a large, burlap sack in one hand and a baseball bat in the other. My heart started to pound. A fierce growl followed by a shrill yelp split the morning air. Then silence. The birds were silent, the dragonflies motionless, and the air was so heavy and liquid I could hardly make my way through it to the door of the barn.

Inside, the mother dog lay bleeding from her mouth and ears, her skull crushed, her tongue hanging out like a long piece of liver, her eyes flat and glassy. The pups huddled together against the rough boards of the stall that served as their den.

A low keening filled my mind, but no sound left my lips. I tried to move forward, but it was as though my limbs had no connection to my will. The man stood no more than two feet in front of me, but he ignored me. It was as though he didn't even know I was there. He reached down to pick each pup up by the scruff of its neck and dropped it into the sack. The littlest pup, squirmed away as he reached for her, but with a curse he leaned forward, snagged her by the scruff of her neck, and dropped her into the sack on top of the others. Fastening the neck of the sack with twine, he turned, his sack bulging with squirming pups and left the barn, heading for the river.

Nooooooooo, I tried to scream, and again no sound left my lungs. Suddenly, my legs were my own again, and I ran after the man, reaching for him. My hands went right through his thick, hairy arm. He reached the river, swung his arm back, and sent the sack sailing out into the middle of the water.

With no thought at all, I ran into the river and dove beneath the surface, eyes open and straining against the murky water, rays of sun filtering down into the green, brown gloom. There, three feet ahead of me. The sack was sinking. I reached for it, but it slipped out of my fingers. Too much time was passing. I had to get them out. I kicked harder, lungs bursting with the need for air. I reached and missed again. My lungs screamed for air, but I kicked harder and flew down through the water like an arrow.

The lower I dove, the darker it got, until I had trouble seeing anything. I thought I knew where the sack should be, but no, my hands connected only with waving riverweeds. Silver bubbles began to stream out of my mouth. I knew I'd run out of time and had to take a breath, but I also knew that I was too far from the surface. Then, with no warning, I was back on the shore of the river, cold and covered with mud and slime. The river was calm before me. Not a ripple disturbed its surface. All around me the music of the morning began again as I sat by the side of the river with tears streaming down my face. I had failed.

I awoke with a gasp, covered with sweat, my heart pounding between my ribs. I pushed back the covers and staggered into the bathroom. I barely made it to the toilet, before I lost the breakfast bars I'd eaten earlier. I was trembling from head to foot, sweat trickling between my breasts and down my forehead.

I rinsed out my mouth and reached for my glucometer, inserted a test strip into the small machine, and pricked my finger. While I waited to see the results of the blood test, I leaned against the counter waiting for my heart to slow. The machine beeped. The glucometer read forty-eight. Far, far too low.

I reached into a drawer and pulled out the box of juice I'd stashed there earlier in the evening. I tried to insert the straw, but my hands were shaking so badly it took me three tries to break the seal. I sucked six ounces of juice down in less than three seconds.

Staggering back into the bed, I pulled the comforter up high beneath my chin and wrapped my arms around a couple of pillows, waiting for the icy cold that always shot through me as my sugar soared back to where it needed to be. As my limbs turned to ice, I rolled over, shaking with cold and curled up as tightly as I could to get warm again.

For the first time since he'd left, I wished Ben were there so that I could ease up against his warmth. Slowly, gradually, I stopped shivering. It was a long time before I could close my eyes again and try to sleep.

Chapter 6

Pete

Miles away, in another time zone, a child of eight years lay awake staring at the ceiling. His name was Peter Kazmarik, and he was far too excited to sleep. His mother was coming to visit tomorrow, and she was going to take him to the Como Park Zoo. He'd heard the zoo had Siberian tigers, an elephant, ostriches, and ponies that you could ride. The child had never ridden a pony before, but it was definitely high on his list of things to do.

Pete shivered in excitement. He hadn't seen his mother in a very long time, but he thought he could remember what she looked like, and how she smelled. He remembered climbing into her lap when he was very small and how good it felt to lean his head against her while she read to him. But, that was before.

That was before, thought Pete, clenching his fists into tight balls at his sides. Tomorrow would be okay, though. He was sure of it. His mother had sounded fine on the telephone. He relaxed into the warmth beneath his old blue comforter, and turning on his side, he stared out the window. The moon was rising, and Pete tried to see the face of the man in the moon. He smiled. He knew there really was no man in the moon. After all, he was going on nine years old. Still. Sometimes, when the moon was full, he was sure he could almost see a face.

Smiling, and filled with hope, the child fell asleep in the small yellow room, high under the eaves of the old house.

Chapter 7

Genna

Good God, Genna, what on earth are you doing? It's two o'clock in the morning." Sylvie padded into the kitchen yawning.

Genna stopped dipping small scoops of dough out of a blue ceramic bowl and onto a cookie sheet. She smiled at her sister, noting that in spite of the hour, Sylvie had still taken time to smooth a lipstick across her lips, pat a bit of powder over her nose, and slide her feet into a pair of ridiculous yellow satin slippers complete with feather puffs on each toe. The slippers matched the pale yellow satin robe, which matched the pale yellow satin nightgown.

"Cookies? You're baking cookies in the middle of the night?"

Genna's smile grew as Sylvie shuddered and draped her satin folds just so as she sank down onto one of the kitchen chairs.

"Oh Sylvie, look at us," laughed Genna, catching their reflections in the kitchen window. "It's the middle of the night, and you look like you're dressed to greet the king, while I look like a big, old mattress dressed in this blue terry cloth robe. What a pair we make." Noticing Sylvie's confusion, Genna nodded toward their reflections in the glass.

Sylvie followed her glance. Tilting her head back, a trill of laughter burst from her throat.

"Mattress? I don't think so. Give me a break, Genna. I think you look like one of those beautiful Rembrandt models. You know, they have that wonderful excess padding, but it's in all the right places, so they look all curvy and soft. What's the word I'm looking for? Zaftig?"

"Fat. That's the word you're looking for, Sylvie, fat. Now, here, have a cookie. You could use some of that, uh, what did you call it? Excess padding? You're turning into skin and bones, and you need to eat more. Oh, it's so good to have you home again. I've missed you since last summer."

The stove alarm sounded, and Genna turned to pull a tray of cookies out of the oven. She set it down on top of several blue and yellow hot pads and with deft movements slid a spatula beneath each hot cookie, depositing it to cool on a strip of aluminum foil.

Sylvie wasn't really skin and bones, but she was a tiny, fine-boned sparrow of a woman. In 1961, she'd been voted the prettiest girl at Sibley High School. Forty years later, with her sapphire blue eyes as bright as ever, her high forehead, and a tangle of silver-blond curls pulled up high on her head to form a tiny cascade in back, Genna thought she looked like a lovely, aging fairy.

Genna caught another glance of the two of them in the window and chuckled again. What a sight the pair of them made. At 5'10" in her bare feet and with all her excess padding—even if she did curve in all the right places—she was certainly not skin and bones. Genna liked to cook, and she liked to eat. Always had, always would.

"So, have you started to bake cookies in the middle of the night on a regular basis?" Sylvie picked up a warm cookie and started nibbling around the edges. "Hey, these are good."

"Of course they're good, and of course I don't. Bake cookies on a regular basis in the middle of the night, I mean. But chocolate chip cookies are Pete's favorites, and I thought I'd bake him a few for tomorrow."

"Just in case that mother of his doesn't show up, right?" Sylvie reached for another hot cookie and watched as Genna continued depositing dough in neat uniform scoops on the cookie sheet.

"I hope you're wrong, Sylvie, but yes, I probably wouldn't be baking these cookies for Pete if I wasn't thinking the same thing you are." Genna sighed. "I also packed him a sandwich, because I suspect he'll be out on that back step waiting for her at the crack of dawn."

Sylvie leaned over and gave Genna a hug. "You're too good for all of us, dear. What would we do without you?"

Genna never knew what to say when someone praised her, and so, as she usually did, she changed the subject. "Would you like a cup of chamomile tea to go with these cookies?"

"Sure," replied Sylvie absently. "Hey Genna, do you think Meg's gotten the package by now? You sent it, right?"

"Yes and yes. I sent it yesterday, and she would have gotten it today, because I sent it registered overnight mail as Marion asked."

"But why did she ask you to wait so long to send it?"

"She wanted everything to go through probate so that Meg owned the house free and clear."

Genna dumped some loose tea into a blue ceramic teapot and poured boiling water on top. She swirled things around for a bit and poured a steaming stream into a matching blue mug.

"I'm guessing that Meg will be here within the next few days. Do you know, Sylvie, I haven't seen her since Peg's funeral. I wonder if she still looks like Peggy."

"Hmmm, I wonder." Sylvie reached gratefully for the tea, took a sip, and set her half-eaten cookie down on the dainty yellow plate covered with bluebells that Genna slid in front of her. "You know, Genna, I don't think she'll show up. She blew this pop stand a long time ago, and I have to say, if I were Meg, I'd be pretty hard pressed to think of any good reason to come back now. Everyone's dead."

"Everyone is not dead, Sylvie. Look at us; we're still here, aren't we? She'll come. Don't ask me how I know, I just do.

"Poor Meg, I know she never forgave Marion for what she did. As far as that goes, Marion never forgave herself. Anyway, as I recall, you also blew this pop stand a long time ago yourself, and I still get you back all to myself every summer. So, if you come back, why shouldn't Meg given the right timing?" Genna smiled her crooked smile and raised one eyebrow. "Enough guessing, what will be, will be. Talking about it won't make it so."

Sylvie propped her head on one hand and watched her sister moving to and fro at the counter.

"But Genna, talking about things is part of the fun, trying to understand why people do the things they do, why they behave the way they do. At least that's what I think." She took another dainty bite of cookie and stared out the window.

"Hmph, I like to deal with facts—what I know to be true. You could spend your life trying to guess what's going to happen, but when you come right down to it, Sylvie, people aren't so very complicated. We all behave the way we do because of who we are, where we come from. It's as simple as that."

Moving like a dancer with purpose, Genna pulled another china plate and mug out of the built-in kitchen buffet with the barest economy of motion, swung the cupboard door shut with a decisive bang, and poured herself a cup of tea.

"It's never as simple as that, Genna. There's so much more to it. When I think of what happened to that poor family, it makes my heart break."

"It was a horrible thing. Peggy was my best friend, and I'll never forget her. Not ever." Genna took a deep breath and pressed her lips together. "But it was twenty-one years ago, Sylvie, and I'm sure Meg has had to deal with things by now. People do, you know, deal with things. In the end, we have no choice, really."

Genna felt the sharp glance Sylvie shot her way. "Have you gotten over things, Genna?" she asked gently, taking another tiny bite of her cookie and keeping her eyes focused out the window in front of her.

Genna plopped down onto a sturdy chair next to Sylvie at the scrubbed pine kitchen table. She reached for a cookie, added a liberal spoonful of sugar to her tea and took a hearty sip, turning lazy gray eyes in Sylvie's direction. She smiled a very small crooked smile this time as she munched her cookie. "Me? What would I have had to get over? I've led the most boring life of anyone I know."

Sylvie sniffed and kept looking out the window.

Genna ignored her, taking another large bite of her cookie. Even after forty years, she was not willing to share her secrets. "And that's the way I like it, you know. No surprises to deal with. No trauma, no drama. I save the surprises for you, Sylvie. I just do my thing all year long, one boring day after another, and wait for the excitement to begin when you come to visit me."

"Oh give me a break. One boring day after another, sheesh, you're the Superwoman of Northeast Minneapolis."

Sylvie was off on another tangent now, which suited Genna fine. She started counting all of Genna's commitments on her fingers. "You organize the entire Minneapolis Meals on Wheels program—and you even deliver three times a week yourself. You tutor English as a Second Language, and you're the first person everyone from Hope Lutheran Church calls whenever they need anyone to do anything."

"But come June of every summer, I know you're going to show up, and we'll have enough surprises to last throughout the rest of the year." Genna's chuckle started in her belly and moved up across her ample bosom and out her mouth with an infectious gurgle.

Sylvie seemed to hesitate, and then she joined in Genna's laughter.

"Well, do you want to know what I think, Genna?"

An enormous smile created fascinating lines and dents across Genna's broad face "Of course I do, which is a lucky thing for me, isn't it, because I'm not sure I could stop you once you get going."

Sylvie grinned back, dimples quivering. "Probably not, so here goes. My own personal theory is that we're shaped by what happens to us, and if we're not careful we can let the past impact our ability to move forward in the present."

For a moment, Genna stared at her own reflection in the kitchen window, seeing an old woman with graying hair curled wildly around her face and a lost, lonely look in her eyes. With a visible shrug, she turned away, saying in a grumpy voice, "You sound just like Oprah. Here, have another cookie."

Chapter 8

Meg

My pillows felt like lumpy wads of old cotton instead of down. I rolled over again, trying to fall back to sleep. No dice. I tried my mind-drifting trick, where I let my mind wander through pleasant images and sounds. No dice, twice.

I always thought of my mind drifting as a form of meditation. Of course, I'd never taken any formal meditation classes. I didn't have the time to waste on things like that. So, I'd come up with my own version.

Lately, though, I was unable to turn off my worry and anxiety about the work piled up back in the office, and my mind drifting was working less and less. No matter how hard I tried, I couldn't conjure up a single tropical image with or without a hammock by the edge of an aquamarine ocean.

I turned over on my right side, squinting up at the alarm clock. It read 2:15 a.m. Not good. It was definitely too early to get out of bed, but if I didn't get back to sleep pretty pronto, I was going to be exhausted when I finally did have to get up.

I took a deep breath and emptied my mind, seeking an image,

any image, but preferably one with the hammock and me in it. Nope. Instead, what do you think slithered into my mind? That damn box. Adrenalin started coursing through my body, and I knew I was awake for the duration. Okay, enough with the meditation. I sat straight up in bed, and flipped on the light.

Marching over to the bathroom, I did my business, washed up, and yanked open the closet door. The box was about two feet square, and it sat where I'd stuffed it earlier. I grabbed it and marched back to my bed to sit cross-legged in the center. I stared for a moment at the box, took an enormous breath, and ripped off all the wrappings. Inside, I found a plain white packing box taped shut all around the edges.

I smiled. Only one person I knew had ever taped up a box like that. My Aunt Marion. I remembered the magic packages she'd sent through the mail when I was small. The packages never really contained anything big or expensive, but their contents were gold to a child. Once, she sent me a tin filled with 100 small cakes of watercolor paint in every color I could ever imagine. Just looking at those paints made me want to be an artist. Of course, I had absolutely no skill, but that didn't stop me from experimenting and trying to paint everything in sight.

Somehow, though, I didn't think the box before me held a tin of watercolors. I shivered. I hadn't spoken to my aunt in more than twenty years. I held her responsible for what happened after the accident, and I'd refused to have anything to do with her. The accident. I always thought of that night as the accident, that is, if I allowed myself to think about it at all.

Marion had tried to reach out a couple of times every year for a long time, but even a determined person will eventually realize her efforts are not appreciated. I hadn't heard from her even in the form of a birthday card for years. I wondered what lay inside the box.

I reached for it and stopped. I decided what I really needed at that very moment was a cup of coffee. I picked up the box and lugged it downstairs. It lurked on the counter behind me the entire time I was measuring, pouring, and listening to the water drip through fragrant, rich coffee grounds and down into the stainless steel carafe. I didn't want to touch it.

My eyes drifted across the counter, and I spied a stack of mail I hadn't yet sorted. Hmmmmmm, I immediately felt as though I should take a look. What if someone had sent me something time-sensitive and important, and I didn't see it? No one had, unless I counted the pizza flyer.

The box sat there in front of me. Lurking. Waiting. I sighed, tossed the mail down on the counter, snagged a mug out of the cabinet, filled it with coffee, and took a long, satisfying sip. Yes. I swear I could feel the caffeine coursing through my veins.

I decided I might as well open the box, unless I could come up with something else to do at 2:30 in the morning. Like cleaning the house—which I never did, that's what Merry Maids were for, or gardening in the moonlight—which I never did, that's what Growing Things was for—not in the moonlight, but you know what I mean.

My head started to pound, but I reached for the box, sliced through all the tape with a paring knife, and pulled off the lid.

"Oh no," I said softly. It had been more than twenty years since I'd seen the maroon leather jewelry box that lay inside, cushioned by Styrofoam packing peanuts. I pulled it out and set aside the letter that lay on top. I traced my fingers across the gold design stamped around the lid in a border of diamond shapes, reluctant to open the jewelry box, and at the same time yearning to see if all the pieces I remembered so well still lay in their appointed slots.

Yes, by the way, yearning is a real emotion, and even if it sounds dramatic, it describes exactly what I felt at that moment and at that point in time. If you've ever felt it—and who hasn't—I'm talking about that tug that starts in the middle of your stomach and wraps around your heart squeezing and squeezing until you could almost die longing for something you know you can never have.

I looked down at my hands, surprised to see them shaking. I

opened my right hand and turned it palm up, staring for a moment at the thick scar in its center. After all these years, it was faded white and puckered, but it was still visible, still ugly.

I sighed as I reached for the small gold clasp, focusing on the jewelry box once again. The box wasn't real leather, of course, and the clasp wasn't gold, just some cheap, gold-colored metal. My mother never had the kind of money it takes to buy something as frivolous as a real leather and gold-trimmed jewelry box.

I closed my eyes, pushed the clasp, and gently lifted the lid. The smell of old material and that coppery smell of cheap metal wafted up to me. I took a deep breath of all the dead memories and opened my eyes. Everything was still there, and I laughed out loud just as I had as a child.

"Mama, you're really rich aren't you. Look at all your jewels."

We had a ritual. I'd always tell her how rich she was, and I'd reach in for the jewel of my choice and pretend I was the princess of a far-off kingdom my mother and I called Shalalaland.

My mother would pull me close, wrap her arms around me, and plant a big kiss on the side of my cheek. Then, she always, always said, "Meggie, you are so right. I am the richest person I know." Only, she wasn't looking at the cheap costume jewelry. She was looking at me.

I realized that tears were running down my face and dripping off my chin. Damn. I never cried. I hadn't cried twenty-one years ago, I hadn't cried since, and I wasn't about to begin crying now. It was a waste of energy, and in the end, crying never changed anything. I wiped my face on the bottom of my nightshirt and sniffed hard. No one was around to hear me being a slob, so what did I care?

On the inside lid, a small square mirror balanced on one point in a diamond shape, reflecting all the bright colors in the box. The bottom half divided into large squares for necklaces, beads, and other jeweled treasures. The top row was only half as wide as the bottom and contained slots for rings and small open squares for earrings and smaller pieces of jewelry.

My mother never wore any rings other than her wedding and engagement rings, and there they were, fitting snugly into the ring slots. I pulled out her engagement ring. It was no more than a tiny diamond chip in the basket setting so popular in the 50s and 60s. I looked at my own engagement ring, which was a full carat and designed by Gabriel to reflect more than twenty-eight facets of light and fire. My ring was the most beautiful engagement ring I'd ever seen. Of course, I'd planned my life better and could afford the best.

I slipped my mother's engagement ring back in its slot, pulled out the wedding ring my father had given her, and tried to put it on. It fit my smallest finger. Even after all these years, the ring shone brightly. Carved orange blossoms twined around the tiny gold band, and when I pulled it off and tilted it, I could see *TH to PL forever, 8-17-61* scripted inside. Yeah. Right. Forever. Nothing was forever. I slid the ring back on my finger.

A flash of pink fire caught my eye, and I laughed out loud again, pulling my two favorite pieces out of the box. The first was a magnifying glass. The handle was imitation gold and encrusted with topaz, ruby, sapphire, and emerald stones. When I was eight years old, I'd spent three whole dollars on that magnifying glass for my mother's birthday present.

I smiled again as I picked up the second piece, a necklace made of round, quarter-inch, gold links with a rectangular pink topaz dangling from the end—imitation of course. That topaz was the height of vulgarity or ostentatiousness, take your pick. It was at least an inch square and bordered with seed pearls. I'd loved that necklace above all the other pieces in my mother's jewelry box. Even as a child, I'd loved the biggest and brightest jewels.

I carried the box and my cup of coffee over to the soft leather couch that faced my marble fireplace. Turning on the fire, I curled up in a corner of the couch, and continued to dig through the jewelry box. I gulped when I found the tiny golden heart suspended from its fine gold chain. I couldn't remember a time when my mother didn't have that heart suspended around her throat. Jenny loved that necklace. She used to call it Mama's heart, and she would beg and beg until my mother took it off and let her wear it for a few minutes. Tiny as it was, that heart was one of the few good pieces of jewelry my mother had. My father gave it to her on their six-month anniversary. He told her that whenever she looked at that little heart she would know that his was beating just for her. Hokey, huh?

Well, the little heart must have meant something to her because she never took it off, even though my father's heart quit beating a few days later when a drunk driver slammed head-on into his car. I never got to know him, but my mother always said I would have loved him. Who knows? Maybe I would have, and maybe he'd have turned out to be a jerk.

I poked the little heart with one finger. My mother never stopped wearing that heart even when she married my stepfather. Jim was always really good to all of us, even me, and I was only his stepdaughter. It was a shame he had a bad heart. He was only around long enough to get my mother pregnant with Jenny before he died. My mother just had no luck with men.

As always, I tried to shrug away thoughts of my mother and the accident the instant they entered my mind. I reached for my coffee, bumping the jewelry box. Something inside pinged, and my heart pinged in response.

How could I have forgotten this was a musical jewelry box? I felt for the turnkey underneath and twisted it. Nothing happened except another small ping. I fished inside the bottom half of the box, pulling out a long strand of purple, maroon, and clear beads that had wrapped themselves around the music box mechanism.

Tinny music tinkled into the room as I pulled the beads loose. The notes brought with them an echo of the accompanying words, branding them against my mind.

> *Live well, love deep, and give your heart.*
> *Your dreams are safe and true.*
> *Shed pain, my darling, no regrets.*
> *Your life belongs to you.*

My mother used to sing all the time, that song and so many others. This particular song had more meaning than most, though. *Live well, love, deep, and give your heart* along with that bit about dreams just about summed up my mother's philosophy to life. I still could not bear to remember how those dreams ended for her—and for the rest of us.

I laid my head back against the soft leather arm of the couch, trying with all my energy to stem the flow of memories. I should never have opened the box. I should never have allowed myself to remember.

Chapter 9

Meg

The doorbell rang, scattering my dream like dandelion fluff in a strong wind. Disturbing emotions, surely a remnant of the dream, bounced around in my mind, but I couldn't capture a single, solid image. All I knew was that the dream had not followed the pattern of any of my previous dreams. I stretched, realizing that I still held my mother's jewelry box clutched in my hands. Before I could suppress them, a few lazy curls of music drifted through my mind. *Love well, love deep, and give your heart . . .*

I shook my head to dislodge the troublesome notes. The doorbell rang again. Odd. No one ever came over in the morning. As far as that went, people rarely came over at all. I had no time for socializing.

I sat up, pulled my nightshirt straight, swallowed down a twinge of nausea, and went to answer the door. A tall, slim woman dressed in jeans, a white oxford shirt, and tweed jacket nodded her head at me. She didn't smile, and her dark brown eyes didn't quite meet mine as she spoke.

"Hello Meg. I'm Carly Roberts from GSC. I'd like to talk with you. It's important. Can I come in?"

I stared at her. It was practically dawn, I wasn't even dressed, and this Carly Roberts person—who I'd never even seen before—from GSC, that would be Guidance Systems Controls, showed up out of the blue, asking for an audience.

All of a sudden, a chill chased up my spine and back down to my toes. GSC was Ben's company, and I seemed to remember that Ben's administrative assistant's name was Carole, or Carla, or . . . Carly, as in Carly Roberts.

My heart started pounding its way out of my chest, and I blurted out the first thing that came into my mind.

"Something's happened to Ben." I couldn't move. I couldn't think beyond the words I'd spoken. All I wanted was to talk to Ben, to tell him I was sorry for how rotten I'd been over the past few weeks. No. That wasn't true. I'd been pretty rotten whenever I felt like it throughout our marriage, and Ben never got angry. He just stood there and took it.

"Oh no, Ben's fine. That's not why I'm here. At least, I'm here to talk about Ben, but nothing bad has happened to him."

Carly smoothed a tendril of shining brown hair, which hung artfully to her shoulders. She tilted her head so that all of her shining brown hair swung in perfect synchronicity around her pointed little face.

"When I spoke with him last night he sounded really relaxed for a change, probably because he was out of town."

Well, what the hell was that supposed to mean? My heart dropped back into its normal rhythm, but now I was feeling a bit peeved. No. A bit peeved is not how I was feeling at all. I was pissed. Pissed as in I wouldn't have minded ripping off someone's head at that particular moment in time. Carly's? Ben's? I wasn't sure yet. I needed more information. When I had it, I'd decide.

Who was this Carly person, and why was she standing on my doorstep, uninvited, at dawn? Oh, and another thing? What was she doing having a conversation with my husband when he didn't even call me last night? Not that I'd wanted to talk to him, but what if I had. Huh? I couldn't think of one single, solitary reason I should listen to a word she had to say.

"Look, I don't even know you, and I definitely don't have time to talk to you or anyone else for that matter right now. I have an important meeting I need to get ready for, and I can't possibly be late." The fact that my important meeting was with my endocrinologist was none of her business.

I started to close the door. She moved two steps forward so that if I continued to close the door, I'd first have to push her out of the way. Carly's face was a study in determination. I wanted to take my fist and punch her pointed little face right in.

"I know you're busy. Ben says all you do is work. That's why I've come so early. Look, it's only 6:30, and this won't take long. At least I don't think it will, but I need to talk to you. It's really important, and I think it would help all of us if you'd listen to what I have to say."

So, Ben talked about me with this Carly person. Now, I was beyond pissed. I was standing in my doorway at dawn. I was barefoot, wearing only one of Ben's oversize yellow polo t-shirts, which made me look like a walking sunflower, and I wasn't wearing any underwear. It's amazing how vulnerable you can feel without your underwear.

I pushed my feelings of vulnerability aside. She didn't need to know how I was feeling. I'd learned a long time ago, that no matter how insecure I felt inside, no one would ever know unless I betrayed my feelings with words or nonverbals. I didn't know who she was or why she was here, but I was pretty sure I didn't want to hear anything she had to say.

She pushed past me into the hallway, her oversized chest—at least in my opinion it was oversized—bounced against my shoulder as she headed toward the kitchen, her narrow hips and her shining brown hair swinging right along in rhythm.

I pulled the screen door shut and trotted after her, feeling like a mixed-terrier mutt trailing a well-groomed Afghan Hound on its way to winning the best-in-breed blue ribbon at Westminster.

Lord, that woman moved fast. Before I could get out in front of her, she was standing in the middle of my kitchen, examining everything she could lay her eyes on. She acted as though she was thinking about buying—or taking over—my home.

"Hey, I said I don't have time to talk right now. Why don't you call my admin and set up a meeting like a normal person would do? I'm sure I can fit you in next Thursday or Friday, provided I juggle a few things around."

I may be little, but I can definitely be mean when there's a need.

"Oh, I don't think you're going to want to have me anywhere near where you work. This is quite personal." She perched on a stool and looked around, those dark brown eyes lighting on my coffee maker. "How about a cup of coffee?"

By now that coffee had to be bitter sludge. I was more than happy to share it with her.

"Of course, let me get you one."

I reached into the cupboard and yanked out an old chipped mug. Maybe she'd slice a chunk out of her perfect little bee-kissed lips. Savagely, I wondered who'd kissed them last. I grabbed the coffee carafe and poured a long stream of the tar that had been brewing since 2:30 that morning into the mug. I plunked it down on the counter and waited for her to drink her coffee, say her piece, and move her little patootie right on out the door.

The smell of burnt coffee filled the air between us. I inhaled with deep satisfaction.

"You wanted to talk. So talk. You have five minutes, and then unless you want to watch me shower and dress, you're out of here."

"Wow, that's a bit abrupt," she shook her head. "I've heard the stories, but somehow I never really believed them. Anyway, it makes it easier to say what I have to say."

Stories, what stories? Was Ben telling his admin stories about me? I pulled my sunflower yellow nightshirt down and hopped up on the other stool. Cool, in charge, and visibly letting her words wash right off my shoulders. She didn't know that her words had sliced right through my heart—and not because I thought they were untrue.

"Well, you have my undivided attention—for the next five minutes. So go."

She swirled her coffee, took a sip, grimaced, and set the cup down. She smoothed her fingers across the Corian counter and turned to peer into the family room. Her gaze seemed to linger on the bookcases filled from floor to ceiling with everything from hydroponic gardening to beekeeping to the latest Ken Follett novel. She took a deep breath.

"Look, this isn't easy. All the way over here, I kept trying to think of the best way to talk to you." Long, perfectly manicured fingers tapped the edge of her coffee mug.

I folded my hands with my own bitten-to-the-quick fingernails in front of me on the counter and tilted my head, no longer abrupt, merely waiting for her to continue.

She took a deep breath, and looking over my left shoulder as she spoke, she spilled her guts.

"Here's the deal. Ben will never leave you, not unless you let him go. The thing of it is, he is so miserable. I've tried to do what I can to help him, but he thinks it's his fault you're so unhappy, and he doesn't know what to do."

For a moment, she looked into my eyes, and then hers slid away. "I'm asking you to let him go. I can make him happy, and you don't really want him. All you do is work. He wants a family, and so do I. He wants a partner to love, and so do I. All you want to do is work. I don't want to hurt you, but unless you let him go, he won't ever leave you, and he'll be stuck in this marriage."

I was stunned. I was humiliated. I was—oh, for Pete's sake, I don't know what all I was. How could Ben have confided in someone else? Why didn't he talk to me? But, I knew the answer. I never listened to him when he tried to talk about us. I was always too busy, with things to do and people to see. Carly's words ate through my heart like acid through toilet paper.

"How long have you been seeing Ben?"

"I've been his admin for the past three years. Surely, he's mentioned me to you?"

I wasn't going to feed her ego in any way, shape, or form. "Sorry, he's never even said your name."

Something flickered across Carly's face, but it came and went so fast, I couldn't recognize what lay behind the expression.

"Well, we've grown to know each other very well. After all, we see each other every day, and whenever we can, we meet for lunch, and well, you know." At this point, she was looking everywhere in the room but at me.

Yeah, well, I did know. Even I had time to watch television every once in a while, and I read trashy romances in between the trashy suspense mysteries I devoured like chips and salsa. So, even without any details, I had a pretty clear understanding about her implications.

I cleared my throat. "I need you to leave now. I have to get ready for work."

She looked at me. "That's all you have to say, that you have to get ready for work? I can't believe you. No wonder Ben is so sad all the time."

Ben was sad all the time? A funny feeling tugged against my heart. I stood and raised my chin. At that point, I didn't care if I was half her size and dressed like a sunflower. She didn't know how I felt. No one knew how I felt—not even me.

I walked around the island, picked up her purse, took her firmly by the elbow, and yanked her off the stool. Then, in spite of the fact that I had to look like a tugboat pulling along a luxury liner, I continued down the hallway, opened the front door, and pushed her out onto the welcome mat.

"Good day. I appreciate your time. If you ever need to speak to me again, set up an appointment with my administrative assistant. Oh, wait just a moment, please." I marched over to the coat closet, pulled out my briefcase, and snatched out a business card. Whirling carefully, I definitely did not want to show bare butt at that particular point in time, I slapped the card into her hand. "You can call that number for an appointment."

I shut the door in her face and went upstairs to dress for my appointment.

Chapter 10

Pete

Pete sat on the back steps waiting for his mother to drive up the alley. He'd been dressed and waiting since dawn. He knew she wasn't coming to pick him up until 9:00, but he had nothing better to do, and he was too excited to stay in the house and wait. Outside, he could listen to the birds sing, breathe in the smell of wet earth, and every once in a while, the breeze would catch the scent of Mr. Regnier's roses and blow them his way. Pete liked the smell of roses.

He hadn't seen his mother for so long that he had trouble remembering what she looked like. He knew she had blue eyes, while he had brown like his dad's. He seemed to remember long blond hair pulled up in a ponytail. He supposed she might have cut her hair though. His friends' mothers were always cutting their hair.

The hardest thing was that he couldn't really remember what her face looked like. That's when he would wonder if he'd ever see her again. His dad said that, of course, he would, but the boy wasn't sure if he could believe everything his dad said anymore. After all, it was his dad's fault that his mom moved out in the first place. She'd told him so once when they were talking on the telephone.

A squirrel chattered at him from the old oak tree that sat in the middle of the back yard. The boy stood very slowly and walked over to the base of the tree. He ripped off a piece of the peanut butter and jelly sandwich Genna had brought him and shredded it into tiny bits in the grass. Just as slowly, Pete backed up to the porch steps.

The squirrel chattered at him for a moment, its small black eyes flitting between the bits of bread and the boy. Finally, when Pete was seated on the steps once again, the small creature scurried down, and sitting upright, tail twitching back and forth, it snatched up a piece of bread with a tiny paw and inhaled it. Chattering in delight, the squirrel snatched up another and another bit of bread.

Pete smiled, watching every move the squirrel made. When he grew up, he was going to work with animals. All sorts of animals.

Inside the telephone rang. Pete tensed, his head jerking toward the door. A few minutes later, his father appeared, and after one look at his face, the boy put his head down on his knees, tears soaking into his new blue jeans.

Chapter 11

Meg

I would like to do a few more tests, and I'd like to do them today, Meg." Dr. Kemper looked up from his notes. "I don't like the pattern of your blood sugars, and I don't like the fatigue and nausea you've been reporting."

"Okay, no problem. Will this take long, though? I've got a meeting this morning."

"I'll have you out of here in 30 minutes, tops. Take this slip and go on down to the lab. Come back up here, and when the results are in, we'll talk."

I wandered down to the lab, let them dig around in my arm for a vein that wasn't too scarred to spurt blood into their little test vials, peed in the cup, and came back upstairs to sit in a chair and leaf through *Ladies Home Journal*.

It was pleasant to have a break in my schedule. Besides, my head was reeling with the images that Carly person had thrown at me. I stuffed them away to think about later. My focus was on finishing up this appointment, getting to work so that I could talk to my boss about my promotion, and . . . and . . . I looked down at the magazine I held open on my lap and finding out How to Make Martha Stewart's Chicken Fricassee in 30 Minutes or Less. Yeah right. I avoided cooking at all costs. I thought cook was a four-letter word.

I jumped at the knock on the door.

Dr. Kemper came in and closed the door behind him. I looked at his face, and thought, oh no, now what? Are my kidneys failing? He sat down in the chair in front of me.

"Meg, how long have you been feeling nauseated?"

"Well, I'm not sure. I've been working 24x7 lately. Let me think." I closed my eyes for minute. "I guess, maybe the last few weeks or so? Are my kidneys slowing down or something?"

"No. It's not your kidneys. You're pregnant, Meg. If I were to guess, I'd say you are anywhere from 6-8 weeks along, but, I'm only guessing. I want you to make an appointment with your gynecologist within the next few days. With the diabetes, I want to take extra precautions during your pregnancy. I don't want you to worry, though, because as long as we're carefully monitoring everything, you and your baby should be fine. No problems at all."

I stood and began to gather up my purse and coat.

"Meg, are you okay?"

I didn't answer him. I smiled politely and continued on my way. After all, I was late for work, and I had things to do and people to see. I'd worry about this pregnancy thing later.

Chapter 12

Ben

Meg, hi, it's me again. I guess you've probably already left for work by now, but I wish you'd called me back this morning. I miss you. Look, I'll try again tonight. Take care. I love you."

Ben hung up the telephone and stared out the window of the conference room. His meeting was due to begin in about ten minutes, and he needed to get his thoughts around his presentation before everyone arrived. The problem was that he couldn't stop worrying about Meg. He'd left her two messages the previous evening, and another message this morning, but she hadn't picked up or called him back.

Her dreams had been more violent and frequent lately, and she may have slept right through the ringing of the telephone. On the other hand, she might have just ignored his calls if she was still angry. She did that sometimes. Today for some reason, though, he was worried about her more than usual. He couldn't shake off the feeling that she needed him.

"I may be little, but I'm really mean. Besides that, I know how to take care of myself. I don't need anyone."

Meg must have said that to him hundreds of times over the past fifteen years. It was a joke. Mostly. It was the first thing she ever said to him.

Sixteen years ago, right before graduation, Ben was walking across the University of Minnesota footbridge high above the Mississippi River late one night. He'd been sitting for hours with a bunch of his friends at Stub and Herb's in Stadium Village. Ben wasn't much of a drinker, so he was in total control of his faculties, and he didn't fail to notice the small woman standing in the center of the bridge, both hands clinging to the railing, as she stared down into the water. Something about her stance concerned him, and he paused to see what she was looking at.

The moon hung like a silver beacon high in the sky, drenching the surface of the river below with dancing, shimmering patterns of light and shadow, chiaroscuro in real time. Ben hesitated, wanting to say something and yet not having a clue how to begin.

"If you come any closer, be aware that you will be in danger," said the small woman without turning her head. "I may be little, but I'm mean, and I definitely know how to take care of myself."

"So, I should be afraid of you?" Ben turned, placing his own hands on the railing and pausing about eight feet away from her.

She'd turned in suspicion to see if he was laughing at her. He wasn't. He was curious and in true Ben fashion, he was saying what was on his mind. He did it again.

"Look, are you okay? I don't mean to pry, but you seem upset or something."

"Yeah, well you'd be upset too, if you were about to move away from everything you know. Besides, you can't possibly care about what's going on in my life. Quite frankly, I'm into some pretty heavy thinking here, and I could use a little solitude. Besides, you're in my space. Don't you have anywhere to go?"

"Not really," he said in his quiet, deep voice. Ben wasn't good with words. He so wanted to say something that would matter to her, but for the life of him he couldn't dredge up one clever phrase, so he turned to her and held out his hand, not moving, waiting for her to come forward or not as she chose. "Hi. I'm Ben Jacobi."

Later Meg told him that if he'd offered even one come on—no matter how clever—she'd have turned her back on him and walked away. Since he just stood there looking at her with a goofy smile on his face, she said she took pity on him and decided to let him stay.

"Okay, you can stay."

Abruptly, she backed up and sat down on one of the concrete benches that faced out toward the water. She patted the bench, and only then did Ben move forward to sit beside her.

All these years later, Ben smiled to himself. Meg had decided to let him stay. As though she could have stopped him, but that was Meg all over. She really thought she had total control over her world, and except for that one time with her family, she did a thorough job of controlling every aspect of her life.

Ben understood that Meg was a control freak because she'd had no control, none at all, over that one time. He also knew she'd never forgiven her mother or anyone else who'd been involved, especially herself.

The night Ben met Meg, he learned three things that would affect him for the rest of his life. The first? Meg was as hard as a nine-inch nail on the outside—make that a three-inch nail because the top of her head barely reached his shoulder—but even so, she was the most vulnerable person he'd ever met. How he understood all that he could never have articulated, but he had no doubt about his assessment.

The second thing? Ben learned about the tragedy Meg tried and tried to forget. Maybe it was the moonlight. Maybe it was the fact that she didn't know him. Maybe it was just meant to be, but she spilled her guts that night. Ben stayed there and listened as she talked on and on, and his heart ached for her in a way it had never ached before.

The third thing? By the time the moon set and the sun started sending up apricot rays promising a new dawn, he knew that Meg was going to become part of his life if he had any say over the matter at all.

"Hey, Ben old man, how're you doing?"

Startled, Ben looked up to see one of his colleagues bearing down on him with a big smile and an outstretched hand.

He stood. "Sam, it's good to see you again."

"Well, it's sure taken you long enough to get your busy butt out here to Fort Collins. What do you say we go down to Old Town and tip a few tonight?" Sam Rivera stuck out a big hand and shook Ben's ferociously.

"No can do," said Ben making up his mind. "I've got to catch a plane this afternoon. Sorry. Rain check?"

The hell with it. He would finish this meeting and leave for the airport. He could just as easily work with these guys long distance. That's what teleconferencing was all about.

Meg needed him. He was sure of it. Maybe he could convince her to take some time off. Maybe they could go away for a while. He wanted to talk about children again. He'd married Meg knowing how she felt about having a child, but he'd always thought she would change her mind over time. Unfortunately from a biological standpoint, time was running out. Ben shivered. He felt as though time was running out from a number of perspectives, and the worst of it was that he had no idea how he was going to get through to Meg.

Chapter 13

Meg

Shoving all emotion to the back of my mind, I walked confidently down the hall. I was at work now. I knew exactly how to behave and what my role was. Today was the day, I just knew it, and no way was I going to let any ancient memories, the Carly person, an unfaithful husband, or unwanted pregnancy get in my way.

I held a small PowerPoint presentation in my hand that summarized all the points I'd been making with my boss over the past few months about the value of consolidating marketing and corporate communications under one leader. In other words, under me. I'd be responsible for all internal and external communications. My staff would double, and since I would be taking on more responsibility, my promotion from director to vice president would be logical and timely—particularly in view of the upcoming merger.

At the VP level, in addition to a higher salary, I'd finally have stock options and other perks like a car allowance. Most important of all, I would finally have arrived right up there with the big boys.

I took a deep breath. As always, when I was at work, I didn't have to worry about anything else going on in my life. It was so strange really. I was an introvert outside of work. I wasn't a joiner of anything, and I absolutely hated parties because I never knew what to say or do. I usually headed for a corner and stood there smiling and trying to look engaged. The older I'd gotten, the better I was at hiding my uncertainty, and no one ever believed I was an introvert. I was though. I was shy in almost every social situation except work. When I was at work, I knew exactly what to say and do. I felt like I belonged, and that I had a special place in the world. I felt as though I was somebody.

If today went well, I'd get that promotion, and I'd really be somebody important. Ben's words from yesterday went through my mind. "But Meggie, you already are somebody important." He didn't understand. He'd never understood, but I knew what this promotion would mean to my career.

My spirits immediately began to rise. I was confident and in charge once more. I didn't need to worry about any Carly person, or Ben, or my mother's failures, or anything except the matters at hand. The pregnancy? Well, that could be dealt with. I had no time for it.

I walked through the CEO's reception area, pausing to say hi to Sandy. That reception area looked better than most homes. The walls were covered in solid walnut paneling, a pair of photographs by Ansel Adams, not prints but the real deal, hung discretely on walls, local examples of Raku pottery rested on highly polished oak tables, and everywhere green plants flourished, softening the work space and turning it into a sanctuary.

"Good morning, Sandy, how are you?" I smiled my most brilliant smile and received a less than brilliant smile back, which was unusual. I wondered what was up.

"Good morning, Meg. Can I get you a cup of coffee before you go in to see Richard?"

"No thanks, I'm good. If I drink any more coffee, I'll start twitching."

I swept past the reception desk and into Richard's office. I stopped short when I saw that he was talking to a man I'd never seen before.

"Meg," said Richard in a hearty, but oddly cool voice. "Come in. I'd like you to meet Tim Rutherford from Innovation Software. He's your counterpoint, and I thought it was time the two of you met."

Tim Rutherford from Innovation Software, more commonly known by its code name Project Snowball for those with the need to know, stepped forward immediately. He stuck his hand out with a jerky movement as though someone were operating his limbs a la marionette. His face turned scarlet. How strange, I thought. With his navy blue suit, red power tie, and salon cut do, which created just the right amount of mess and texture to his dark brown hair, Tim looked like my notion of an up-and-coming YME (that would be Young Male Executive). Oh good. That's what I needed, another one to deal with.

"It's good to finally meet you. Meg, is it?"

Well, give me a break. Richard had introduced me less than three seconds earlier. What was wrong with this guy? Maybe he suffered from some sort of emotional disorder. He was acting as nervous as a mouse in a room full of hungry cats. Oh well, when he reported to me, I'd work with him. A communicator couldn't afford to be sloppy or nervous in any way that showed. I stepped forward smoothly and spoke in a warm voice as I shook his hand with the right amount of firmness. You know, women in business can't afford to have either a wimpy handshake or a killer handshake.

"Tim, it will be good to have you on my team. Let's get together later this week and talk."

Tim turned and looked at Richard, and I saw a look pass between them. I didn't like the look. Tim turned back to me, the red fading from his cheeks and the tips of his ears, and a certain amount of smoothness oiled his voice.

"Tough break about that *Register* story this morning."

Shit. I always read the headlines first thing every morning to be sure we weren't in any of them. I was especially careful after a run in with the Great White Shark, but with my lack of sleep, early morning visit, and trip to the doctor's office, I'd totally forgotten to look. So, of course, I had no idea what the article was about.

Based on the tightening of Richard's lips and the carefully unexpressive look on Tim Rutherford's face, the news wasn't good. I would have sworn though, from the expression in the back of his eyes or something, that whatever the story was about, Tim was pleased as punch about it. The two of us were definitely going to have a meeting—and soon.

Tim pulled his hand loose, and I realized with horror that I was still grasping it in mine, immobilized by his words.

"I've got to go. I have to interview all your key executives by the end of the day."

Richard clapped him on the back. "I'm going to like having you on my team, Tim. I'll talk to you tomorrow."

Tim Rutherford had to interview all our executives? What was that about? Tim pulled his cuffs down, smoothed his flawless navy blue lapels, and sauntered on out of Richard's office.

Richard sat down behind his desk. He did not ask me to sit, but I sat anyway, knowing that something was wrong. Something was definitely wrong.

Richard folded his hands on top of his executive leather blotter. As usual, his desk was spotless, holding nothing more than the blotter, a silver Mont Blanc pen, a single folder, and a copy of the *Register*. How these guys did it, I'd never figure out. If their offices were any indication, they did no real work. My own office was a mass of papers and folders and partially read journals and books.

Richard looked me right between the eyes, his own eyes cloaked, the lids drooping slightly as though he were taking care not to let me see inside his head. "I understand Marlene Jenkins called you yesterday."

"Yes, she did," I answered easily. "I gave her our usual nondisclosure policy statement, which of course, she didn't like, but that's our policy and the statement we all agreed on."

"Well, when you refused to speak with her, she went around you to one of the product managers who was all too happy to explain everything he knew—or at least everything he thought he knew."

"Richard, I didn't refuse to speak with her. As I just explained, I gave her our nondisclosure policy." I kept my voice low and even.

"Well, that wasn't good enough."

I tilted my head, trying to discreetly read the newspaper that lay open to the front page. I could feel the blood draining from my face and pooling somewhere around my ankles. Above the fold, in 48-point type, the headline read "ESI Engaged in Merger with Mystery Software Company." The accompanying sidebar listed all our executives along with their annual base salaries and bonuses. Whenever the *Register* didn't have all the facts, they printed a bunch of crap and put the facts they did know in a sidebar.

I opened my mouth and closed it again. I could think of nothing to say.

"I have to tell you Meg, this is a potential disaster. This article could blow the whole deal. We're not in any position to be talking about anything at this point in time."

"Richard, I'll get on the telephone right away and set up a meeting with Marlene."

"It's too late. Tim has already taken care of things."

"Tim? What exactly has Tim taken care of?"

"Well, Meg, because you were late this morning, I called Tim and asked him to take care of the issue. He promised Marlene an exclusive interview if she would let the issue drop for two more days. She has agreed. We'll send out the news release on Thursday, but the first thing we'll do afterward is meet with her. She'll be able to scoop the other local papers with quotes and extra details they won't have. Tim even promised to set her up with a few schools so she can take a bunch of photos showing children using Innovation Software."

"That's not the right approach, Richard. By agreeing to meet with her, you gave her advance notice about the merger. That's against all regulations. Besides, her goal isn't to scoop the local papers, her goal is to scoop *The New York Times* and *The Wall Street Journal*, and you can't afford to let her do it. Tim doesn't know her. She'll never keep her word about printing nothing until Friday. She'll be all over you like honey on a biscuit."

"She'll hold off if she wants that exclusive interview. Besides Meg, you don't have to tell me how to play the game. With my experience I think I can be the best judge in this particular situation, and I have to say, that given this article, your own track record isn't what it might be."

Richard was too smooth to sound overtly sarcastic, but he was so close it made no difference. I felt the sting. Before I could open my mouth in response to Richard's comment, he picked up his telephone and asked Sandy to send in Marc Stephanis.

I froze. Marc was the VP of HR. I could think of only one reason Marc would be joining us now.

"Hello Meg." Marc walked through the door in his quiet way. He rested his hand on my shoulder for a moment and sat in the other chair next to me, both of us facing Richard across the breadth of his desk.

If I'd felt nauseated earlier that morning, it was nothing to how I felt at that moment. All my concentration immediately centered on how I was going to avoid tossing my cookies on top of Richard's executive blotter.

Live well, love deep, and give your heart. Your dreams are safe and true. I blinked hard, once, to free my mind of the stupid words to that stupid song.

Richard looked at me with his oh-so-sincere expression.

"Meg, you've done a good job for ESI for the past few years, but now, I need someone who is in a different league. I need someone who can talk with all the executives, to the press, to shareholders; someone who is proactive and more experienced in terms of not only public relations but investor relations as well. I need a VP of Communications who will merge all the disciplines beneath him into one integrated department. As of this morning, I've made the decision to promote Tim Rutherford."

Richard stood. His part of the speech was almost over. I knew the drill. He'd deliver the news and walk out the door leaving the rest to HR.

"I'm sorry to have to tell you that today will be your last day of employment with ESI. Good luck, Meg."

Sorry, my ass. I turned with absolutely no expression on my face and watched the walking weenie exit the room.

"Meg, are you okay?" Marc reached out and touched my shoulder again.

I looked at him. I didn't move one single, solitary muscle. I was a rock. *Shed pain, my darling, no regrets. Your life belongs to you.* Yes, I thought. I was okay. No matter what it took for the next ten minutes, I was going to be fine. I took a deep breath, willing away the nausea. It helped a little.

"I'm sorry, Meg. I was not part of this decision, and I have to tell you it was made several days ago, not this morning for whatever that's worth."

I felt a spark of gratitude. I'd always enjoyed working with Marc. He was a straight shooter. For the next ten minutes, he explained that my severance package was six months' salary and outplacement benefits. I could take it in a lump sum or in monthly payments. I told him I'd think about it and get back to him, and that was that. My husband was cheating on me, I was pregnant, and I was out of a job.

Chapter 14

Carly

"You went to their house? Carly, I can't believe you did that. If you had balls girl, they wouldn't be brass, they'd be pure steel." Toni Grabowski took a bite of salad and chewed fiercely for a moment shaking her head in disbelief.

"What's the big deal? I just told her how it is."

Carly Roberts tossed her long brown hair and lifted her chin. A small David Yurmen pin added a splash of color to the lapel of her tweed jacket. She wore plain silver earrings because she couldn't afford the earrings that matched her pin, not yet, but someday, she would. Someday, she'd be able to afford anything she wanted.

"Hmph, wanna know what I think? Ben Jacobi's gonna fire your ass, girl. Besides, he's never given you one single reason to believe he would be interested in a relationship with you." Toni shook her head, dark brown eyes knowing and confident that what she said was God's truth and nothing but.

"Toni, you are so full of shit. No, I really don't want to know what you think." Carly glared at her friend. "Besides, you don't know everything you think you do. Ben has so given me reason to believe he is interested. Do you remember the company Christmas party a few months ago? Ben was all by himself, and we talked for a long time. And, that was really only the beginning, because . . ."

"Get a grip, girl. I was there, and Ben wasn't all that lonely. He was surrounded by his department, and no way was he just talking to you." Toni stabbed the last bit of lettuce on her plate. She reached for her yogurt sundae with a slim brown hand.

Carly pushed away the lunch tray, her own salad barely touched. "Yeah, well, his wife didn't bother to come to our office party, and so he was alone as far as I was concerned. Besides, he did talk to me. Kind of confidential like, you know?"

"I don't think so. He talked to anyone who wandered by. Besides, Ben is friendly to everyone. That's why we all like him so much. Look, Carly, I'm not saying Ben doesn't like you, but get real. You're his admin—not his friend and definitely not his girlfriend—in any sense of the word. What makes you think he's going to look twice at you? I've heard him on the telephone with his wife. I've also seen them at company functions. He's crazy about her." Toni took a careless sip of her coffee and choked. "Whew, is that hot. Watch out you don't burn your tongue."

Carly ignored the warning and started shredding her napkin. "Yeah, well, I hear a whole lot more than you when he's on the telephone. I sit right outside his office, you know."

"Big deal."

"Oh yeah? Want an example? I hear firsthand every day how he comes back from lunch or a meeting and asks if his wife has called. Only guess what? She never does."

"Well that doesn't mean anything. Roger never calls me back even when it's an emergency," said Toni, spooning frozen vanilla yogurt covered with multi-colored sprinkles into her mouth.

"But Toni, that's not the only thing." Carly leaned forward. "I know for a fact they're not getting along right now. No way does she deserve him. Do you know I've heard Ben on the telephone inviting her out to dinner, like on a date? Only she's always too busy to go anywhere. Oh, and another thing, I heard him on the phone one day ordering 29 roses. He told the florist to be sure that the bouquet had exactly 29 roses. He said it was a special code."

"Yeah, so what's your point? Ben's special code is for his wife not for his admin. That would be you, of course." Toni licked the spoon clean and waggled her eyebrows. "Hey wouldn't you like to know what the 29 stands for?"

"No, I would not," said Carly standing up. "I thought that as my best friend you might be a little bit interested in my love life."

"Carly, that's the point. No way is Ben any part of your love life . . . " sputtered Toni.

Carly cut her off, sitting back down and hissing. "You think you know everything, but you don't. You don't know what happened night before last when we both worked late. Guess what? I'm not going to tell you, so there. You also don't know how he keeps asking me for advice. Well, I'm going to be there for him whenever he needs me. It won't be long before he realizes that I love him more than his so-called wife will ever love him. Just you wait. When he figures out that Meg is never going to settle down and give him the kids he wants, he's going to look for someone else. I'm trying to help move things along in the direction they're already headed, that's all." Carly stood up again, collecting her dishes and napkin on her dinner tray.

Toni rolled her eyes. "I suppose that someone is going to be you."

"You betcha." With that, Carly turned her back and started to walk away.

"Hey, Carly," called Toni in a low voice.

Carly turned and raised one eyebrow.

"So, like what happened between the two of you the other night."

"In your dreams, girl." Carly turned her back and walked away.

Chapter 15

Genna

Genna, look. Your new neighbor is working on his roses again. I can't believe how far he's come with his garden since last year. So, what's his name again? Jean-Pierre?"

"Jean-Louis. Jean-Louis Regnier," corrected Genna, busy whipping batter in a bowl at the kitchen counter. She looked up to see Sylvie standing in the back doorway of the porch, leaning out so that she could see two yards over to where their neighbor was digging in his garden. "Sylvie, you look like you're ten years old the way you're spying on that poor man."

"I'm not spying on him. I came to check out our backyard, and voilà, there he was working on his garden. So, how well have you gotten to know this guy over the past year? He's quite nice to spy on, you know." Sylvie's voice was light and barely interested, but Genna turned on her like a hawk.

"You think he's good looking?"

Clearly startled, Sylvie slanted a glance at her sister. "Well, don't you?"

"Me, I haven't noticed." Genna looked deeply into her sister's eyes. "Sylvie, would you like it if I asked him over for coffee?"

"No way, José," a trill of laughter spilled from Sylvie's lips. "For God's sake, Genna, you don't have to serve coffee to every eligible man in sight just to find me a date. I can find my own dates, you know."

"Sylvie?"

"What dear?"

"So, what do you think of Mr. Regnier?"

"Genna, you are too funny. I can't believe you're trying to set me up," Sylvie grinned, but when Genna just looked at her waiting for a response, she sighed dramatically. "Okay, here's what I think—for what it's worth. Jean-Louis Regnier is a lovely man if we're to go by looks alone." Sylvie started to count off points on her fingers. "First of all, he's tall, he's handsome, I've never seen such a beautiful mane of silver hair before in my life, and if on top of all these wonderful attributes you tell me he has a French accent . . ."

"He does."

Sylvie looked at her sister with curiosity. "Hey, I thought you said you didn't know him."

Genna's face turned an interesting shade of pink. "I don't. Not really. I've heard him speak before, that's all."

"Well, okay. Let's add in the French accent, and I'd say . . . oh, based on just these few physical attributes, that on a scale of 1-10, Jean-Louis Regnier—God, it's fun to say his name out loud—is probably a 15."

All of a sudden, words began spewing from Sylvie's mouth.

"But, and this is a very big but, Genna. I spent almost twenty years of my life married to a man who was also good looking. That bastard sucked every bit of life out of me. So, I'm not interested in a relationship, okay? My marriage was a disaster. Do you want to know the worst thing of all, though? I believed everything Phil told me. He told me I was stupid, and I believed him. He told me I would never be able to hold down any sort of job. I believed him. Whatever he said, I believed, Genna. I lost myself for so many years. I lost who I was and who I could be, and I'll never, ever put myself in that position again."

"But Sylvie, you've been single for more than eighteen years. Aren't you lonely? Maybe you'd really like this Jean-Louis."

"Genna, you're not listening to me. I'm not going to get married again, not ever." Sylvie's voice shook, and she gulped, dashing a hand across her eyes. "Sorry, I'm sorry, but there I go, and I never cry about this anymore. I stopped crying about it a long time ago."

"I'm sorry, Sylvie. I'm so sorry. I didn't mean to make you think of Phil." Genna reached out and hugged her sister, bumping her forehead gently against Sylvie's.

Sylvie hugged her back, smiling her brilliant smile, dimples showing on both sides of her mouth.

"Genna, the real truth? The truth that matters? I don't think I ever thanked you. If you hadn't invited me home to stay with you when I left Phil, I don't think I would have made it through that time. You've taken care of me ever since we were little kids. You're doing it again, by letting me come home to bask in the sun every summer while you try to fatten me up."

Genna gave her sister a powerful squeeze. "You're my best friend, Sylvie. I love you, and I love having you around every summer. I want you to be happy, that's all."

"I know. The feeling is mutual, you know?" Sylvie pronounced the word "mootual," to make Genna smile at the reference to the old movie, *Young Frankenstein*. Sylvie sniffed, pulled a tissue out of her sundress pocket, and vigorously blew her nose. "There, I'm done whining now. I promise. I'm really done."

Sylvie's voice stayed light, but Genna's eyes searched her face for a moment. "It was a long time ago, you know Sylvie. You deserve to have someone love you. All you do is work, and I worry about you."

A funny look passed quickly over Sylvie's face. Genna recognized the look, having seen it often enough throughout their lives. She'd always known when Sylvie had something she wanted to get off her chest. "Sylvie? Is everything all right with you?"

The look evaporated as though it had never been.

"Enough already, or I'll be forced to leave immediately and go back to my job as a faculty drone at the university before you fatten me up." Sylvie snorted. "But don't you think for even one minute that I live like a nun, Genna. I don't. I get around fine and have ever since I dumped that jerk. I like my life the way it is, thank you very much. As a professor, I get to teach stories and writing skills to all kinds of wonderful people all year, and every summer I get to come home and be fussed over by you."

Another trill of laughter escaped Sylvie and she backed abruptly into the house. "There, now, you made me stand here so long, Jean-Louis has noticed me noticing him. Poor man. He can't even go out to work in the garden without all the neighborhood women ogling him. Oh well, maybe it'll make him feel good to be ogled." She laughed, not in the least embarrassed. "So, how well do you know him? Maybe we should entice him over for a cup of coffee and get the two of you involved, eh?"

Genna's face turned scarlet. "I don't think so."

"Why not?" said Sylvie in a flippant tone. "You talk about me working. That's like the pot calling the kettle black, Genna. You're the one who worked for the same company for more than thirty-five years, and you're the one who moved home to take care of Mom when Dad died. I didn't. I kept gallivanting all over as I always do. You're the one everyone comes to whenever something needs to be done. It's your turn to have a life." Sylvie giggled. "I think we should try to set you up with this Jean-Louis guy."

Genna looked at Sylvie, saying nothing.

After a moment of silence, Sylvie threw her arms up in the air and danced across the kitchen to wrap an arm around Genna's waist and bump her in a gentle hip check. "Oh, so it's okay for you to set me up, but the instant I suggest setting you up, it's hands off. Hmmmmmm, that doesn't seem quite fair to me. Even big sisters need boyfriends."

Finally, Genna started to laugh, deep belly laughs, and Sylvie joined right in. "Oh, you are so funny. Men don't look at me, and I don't really care. Listen to us. Two old . . ."

"No, stop with the old routine," broke in Sylvie batting her eyelashes and bumping hips again. "Not old, Genna, two beautiful women, wise and a little bit soft around the edges. So, how well do you know this Regnier guy? You never did answer my question, did you?"

"I don't really know him, except to wave to in passing. He moved in last spring and seems to spend a lot of time in his garden. It shows." Genna, still chuckling under her breath, changed the subject. "Remember when the Lofgren garden on the other side of us used to look like Jean-Louis's?"

Sylvie smiled again, more gently. "I remember. It was even more magnificent than Mr. Regnier's garden, and that's saying quite a bit. Oh Genna, do you remember how Peggy's father grew the most beautiful roses, tulips, and sweet peas? Oh, oh, and do you remember how he always presented each of us with an enormous bouquet on our birthdays when we were young? I used to feel so grown up. Carl Lofgren was a good man. I wonder if anything he grew is left in that jungle of a garden?"

Genna sidled in next to her sister so that she could see out the porch window too. She saw their neighbor turn and look at her, and she backed up a bit so that he wouldn't think she was gawking at him.

"I wonder. Can't really see any evidence of flowers in that old green tangle any more, can you? Maybe Meg will have a green thumb like her grandfather. When she comes, we'll find out what's left in that old garden. I'm glad Marion left the house to her."

"Genna, do you really think she's going to show up? She's never been back, not even once, since the accident. Based on what you've said, Meg did everything she could to avoid coming back and having any contact with Marion at all."

"Like I said yesterday, she'll be here, in her own time." Genna's smile was serene. She broke into laughter. "I wonder how much like Peggy she is."

Sylvie laughed, her eyes dancing. "Oh Genna, do you remember how much mischief Peggy was always getting into? She was never malicious, but oh that girl could think up adventures. Not only for herself, but for all of us."

Genna laughed again. "I remember all the trouble the three of us would get into. I will never forget how we would tell our parents we were going to youth group at church, but instead, after they dropped us off, we'd go up the street to the movie theater and flirt with the ushers so they'd let us in for free. Oh, and what about the time we all skipped school and took the bus downtown for the day and were stranded because we didn't have enough money to get home again. I don't know what possessed us that we didn't think ahead."

"We were kids, that's all, but while you and I were moaning and groaning about never, ever getting home again, Peggy walked up to this nice-looking man in a suit and asked him for bus fare. She was so cute, he gave it to her, and he didn't even ask us any questions."

"Well, I'm pretty sure he knew exactly what was going on," said Genna chuckling at the memory. "You know, Sylvie? We were really lucky we never got into any real trouble."

Sylvie turned back toward the porch windows, her face alert.

"Genna, look. Jean-Louis's coming over. He must want to have a cup of coffee with two beautiful, wise women. Now remember, I'm not the one who is interested. You are."

Genna turned to look out the window again as Jean-Louis Regnier climbed up their front steps, two sun-colored roses in one large hand. Her face flooded with color.

"You stop that right this minute, Sylvie Johnson. I am not interested."

Genna whirled toward the counter, keeping her back to the door, fussing with the old silver percolator, and rattling cups and saucers.

"Good morning," sang Sylvie in a happy voice as she greeted their neighbor. "I don't believe we've met, but I'm Sylvie Johnson, here for the summer to be pampered by my sister Genna who I believe you have met."

"Good morning to you, Madame. I am Jean-Louis Regnier. Although I have seen your sister, we have not yet been formally introduced. This is why, when I saw you looking out your door this morning, I thought to myself, Jean-Louis, it is time to go and meet your beautiful neighbors."

"Good morning, Mr. Regnier," said Genna who had still not turned to greet their guest.

"Oh Madame, please, no more Mr. Regnier. We have been neighbors now, oh how long has it been? Almost a year I would say. I would so very much like it if you would simply call me Jean-Louis. That would mean to me, you see, that we are on our way to becoming friends, eh?" His voice was mellow and warm. "And me? I shall call you, Genevieve, eh? It is such a beautiful name."

"Oh, Jean-Louis, I love the way you pronounce Genna's name in French," said Sylvie, "Jshan-a-vi-ev, with a soft "j" sound instead of Jen-e-veeve.

Genna finally turned around, hoping that her cheeks were no longer flaming. Really, she was too old to be blushing in front of a man, no matter how beautifully he pronounced her name. Jean-Louis bowed to her with a smile and twinkling eyes and turned and bowed toward Sylvie.

"I have brought you some of my finest roses in the hope that you might grant an old man a cup of coffee, eh?"

"Jean-Louis, you have definitely come to the right place," said Sylvie with a lovely smile, pulling him over to the table so that he could take a seat. "Come right on in, and sit down."

Chapter 16

Meg

The sun stretched golden beams across ripples of water, and the afternoon breeze picked up slightly. Shivering, I wrapped my arms around myself and leaned against the old gray wooden bench nailed to the end of the public dock.

I'd been sitting on that dock for hours. I couldn't seem to move. What's more, I didn't care if I ever moved again. It was an odd feeling really. I never sat still. I was always doing.

On top of everything, that damned song kept running through my head, and I couldn't get it out. At that moment, I couldn't even remember all the words, just, *"da, da, da, da, da, da, da dah, your life belongs to you,"* which was ironic. At that moment, my life was so far out of control that I didn't even know where to begin to make things right again. I was Meg Jacobi, master planner of the universe, and I even had my Palm Pilot to prove it. Big deal.

This was a busy public dock, and I'd gotten quite a few odd looks as people jumped in and out of their expensive toys. I could only imagine what they thought about the tousled woman sitting with her feet in the water, her shoes and purse plopped next to her in a tidy pile. I didn't care. Screw 'em all.

My mind kept rehashing the events of the morning, and I kept trying to jerk it back into the now, to concentrate on the smell of the water, the feel of the breeze, the sparkle of the sun.

I stared down into the water, watching the waterweeds dance below the surface, wondering what it would be like to roll off the dock with a little splash and let the water cover my body. It would be so nice to forget about everything and float for a while on the surface of the water before sinking down into the depths to sway back and forth beneath the surface just like those waterweeds. I too could do the waterweed dance.

"I'm in big trouble." I spoke aloud and then looked around to see if anyone had heard the crazy woman talking to herself, but I was alone. It must have been late afternoon, and people had either gone out for their sail or they'd already gone home. I never wanted to go home again.

I looked down at my left hand, bare of my wedding ring and the enormous engagement ring I'd always worn so proudly. I'd taken them off and left them in the ashtray of my car. I never wanted to wear those rings again.

A sea gull swooped down over the water in search of a snack. The breeze picked up again, and as I squeezed my arms around my middle, huddling into my suit coat jacket, I heard the crackle of paper.

The crackle was the letter from my aunt. I'd forgotten that I'd scooped it up on my way out of the house that morning. I pulled it out and stared at it for a while. I stuffed it back into my pocket. I didn't want any more surprises. I'd already learned more things than I'd ever wanted to know.

The thing that bothered me the most, was that I didn't even know who I was anymore. I'd always had such a clear image of myself, about how I was supposed to behave as a business professional. Now I didn't even have that role to keep me safe. I tilted my head. That was an odd word to have passed through my mind. Safe from what?

My cheeks burned as I remembered the conversation I'd overheard that morning.

I'd gone into the bathroom after my conversation with Marc. As I said, I knew the drill. He would sit with me as I packed up my belongings, or he would have someone in human resources pack everything up and send it to my home. The second option was fine with me. No way was I going to sit in a glass-walled office, packing my stuff as everyone walked by, watching me, and knowing I'd been fired. Of course, by now, everyone probably knew, but I didn't have to watch people watching me, wondering how I'd failed. I didn't even know how I'd failed.

I told Marc I'd appreciate it if he'd send on my stuff, and I ducked into the bathroom. I knew he would hover until I came out, but I needed a few minutes alone.

Human resources had such a fun job. They had to make sure everyone was paid on time. They had to design and provide benefits, although God knows, companies were cutting back on those. They even had to accompany us on every step of our way out of the building so we didn't cause a scene or slip a nasty computer virus into the system as we slipped on our coats to leave our jobs forever.

Well, I still wielded a bit of power. Short of following me into the bathroom, Marc was stuck outside and I was alone in the peace of an aluminum stall for a few minutes at least so that I could get my feelings under control. I wasn't going to let my coworkers see anything I didn't want them to see. That small part of my life I could control at the very least.

I heard the bathroom door swish open.

"Did you hear? Meg Jacobi got fired this morning." It was Kathy Baker, administrative assistant to the CFO. I didn't like Kathy Baker.

"No way. I thought she was in like Flynn with Richard." Christine Joseph was a tall, willowy redhead who could easily have been a model instead of administrative assistant to the operations VP. "What happened?"

I was in the end stall, and it was evident they thought they were alone.

Kathy's voice grew low. "I don't know exactly. I talked a little to Sandy this morning. She said that Richard was blaming Meg for the headlines in the paper, but Sandy said she thinks it was an excuse because Richard really likes that young guy who heads up corporate communications at Snowball." The admins were always as careful as the executives to use the code names of any pending acquisition or merger.

I didn't move a muscle. I wanted to hear every detail. What they said made sense. As much as I'd tried to ignore it and tell myself it wasn't true, Richard really was a good old boy. I was the only woman on his staff, and he frequently left me out of social engagements. Fact was, the boys had more fun all on their own, and there wasn't a thing I could do about it.

"That is so not fair," Christine snorted. "We have one woman executive, and they fire and replace her with a twerp. I met that guy. He had to tilt his head to look up at me, and I have to tell you he wasn't looking up to see my face. The jerk all but drooled on my shoes. What an asset he'll be."

"Yeah, well, I'm going to go talk to Joyce. Sandy said she's been crying all morning because of that darn headline. She thinks everything is her fault because she wasn't at her desk yesterday afternoon when that reporter called. She's also devastated because she thinks Meg is mad at her. You know, I'm sorry Meg got fired, but the fact is, she really was pretty abrupt with anyone who wasn't in a position to do her a favor."

"Yeah, well she was always decent to me."

"I guess she was decent to me too, but not warm or really friendly like she meant it. Know what I mean?"

"I guess I do. Somehow, I just think Meg is shy, and I don't think she always means to come off like she does. Anyway, didn't Joyce tell her what happened yesterday?"

"Nope, go figure. It's not as though it was her fault her son fell off the jungle gym at school and broke his arm."

"Joyce was only gone for forty-five minutes or so, right?"

"Uh huh, something like that. "She met her little boy at the emergency room, stayed with him until her mother showed up, and hightailed it back here. I think she was hoping Meg wouldn't notice."

I closed my eyes. Why hadn't Joyce told me? Because, I answered myself, you don't listen very well. I'd yammered on and on about Joyce being my partner, but when she really needed my support she was too afraid to ask for it.

The sound of voices dragged my thoughts back to the dock by the waterway. My butt was getting sore from sitting on the hard wooden dock for hours, and as I shifted to get more comfortable, the paper in my pocket crackled again. My fingers crept into my pocket, and I pulled the letter out.

I took a deep breath. Why not read it? I'd already heard so much bad news, what could I possibly have to lose?

Marion had written my name with a flourish in red ink on a plain white envelope. My Aunt Marion always liked to write with red ink. I smiled. Then the usual frustration squeezed away the smile, and my whole body tensed. I couldn't help it. I'd never forget what she'd done.

I ripped open the envelope and pulled out a piece of paper folded into thirds. I opened the letter, and a gust of wind caught the check inside, blowing it against the bench behind me. I grabbed it before it could fall into the water. My first inclination was to rip it to shreds, until I saw the amount.

My mouth dropped open. It really did, it dropped and hung open. Any fly could have waltzed right on in. I had no idea why my aunt would have sent me a check for $49,256. I hadn't spoken to her in more than twenty years. I was surprised she'd even been able to find me after all that time.

I closed my mouth with an audible click, meticulously folded the check, stuffed it into my pocket, and opened the letter, which was dated more than eight months ago.

October 25, 2000

Dear Meggie,

If you're reading this letter, it means that I'm gone. Sounds dramatic doesn't it? I always wanted to leave this life with a swirl and a swash. Instead, I'm wasting away with this cancer I have. One good thing I have to say is that at least I have time to get my affairs in order, but I digress.

I know you're still angry with me for the decision I made so long ago, but truly, dear, at the time I made it as much for you as for anyone else. Honestly, I did, but I spent the next twenty years regretting it. If I could have changed things, I would have.

I hired a detective a year ago. He hasn't had any luck yet, and although I was hoping I could give you some information before I died, he will keep working to find some clues to pass on to you. I have paid him through the end of next year. His name is James Reddinger, and you'll find him in the Minneapolis white pages.

What I have is yours, Meg. It doesn't amount to much, but I wanted to leave what I have to you, including the house. You know where it is, and it's sitting there waiting for you. A retreat if you will, or you can sell it. It's up to you. There may be a bit more in terms of cash once all my affairs are resolved. What you'll want to do is contact my lawyer, Gerald McPherson in Minneapolis. He's a decent lawyer. Even his name sounds like a decent lawyer's name should sound, but now, I'm really digressing.

Please forgive me Meg. I never meant to hurt you. I was afraid at the time. I apologize for that. I never had Peggy's nerve. I know if she had been in my place, she would have made a different decision.

You used to be a lot like your mother, Meg. You were such a feisty, creative little thing, and so was she. She thought anything was possible, and she wasn't afraid of anyone. Everyone loved your mother, but no one loved her more than I did. I suspect you've grown up to be quite a bit like her. I do wish we could have talked and learned to know each other as adults.

I have a request. Please don't sell the house until you visit. I've left some things for you, and I'm hoping you'll come home and remember the good times. We had them, dear. Try to remember, and please forgive me. I have always loved you.

Aunt Marion

My first thought was *no way am I like my mother*. My second was *what a kook*. Only Aunt Marion would tuck a check for almost $50,000 into a letter and mail it. What if that check had blown away in the wind when I opened it? What if I'd moved? What if it had been stolen? This kind of carelessness was classic Aunt Marion behavior.

The flash of anger died away, and I felt strange, not grief-stricken exactly. I mean, how are you supposed to feel grief for someone you've written out of your life and haven't seen in years? Yet, I remembered so many things, and the echo of that music box song drifted through my mind. Now, for some reason, I could remember the words.

Live well, love deep, and give your heart.
Your dreams are safe and true.
Shed pain, my darling, no regrets.
Your life belongs to you.

Wrenching myself back to the present, I focused on the heat of the sun, the pungent, fishy smell of the water, and the dissonant music of the seagulls in their everlasting search for food.

Restless, I stood, ignoring the tight designer shoes that lay by my side. I frowned, hearing the sound of crashing glass. I turned my head, but couldn't see anyone else nearby. Although I couldn't make out any of the words, angry voices floated toward me through the trees.

I'd parked my car back behind the trees in the parking lot. Something was going on and I decided to find out what it was. I had nothing else to do, and my butt was sore from sitting still so long.

I slung my purse over my shoulder, and grabbing my shoes with one hand, I used the other to balance my way along the wobbly deck. I crossed a narrow strip of sand and maneuvered past the playground toys so that I could peer through the woods.

The only car in the lot was mine. A Harley Davidson motorcycle leaned on its stand right next to it, a faint stream of exhaust emanating from its long silver tailpipe. A young man in his early twenties stood in an aggressive stance in the open door of my car, while a young woman cowered on the front seat. She couldn't have been more than sixteen years old, and how she kept the dirty red tube top up on her tiny frame was beyond me. Her sandy hair was pulled back into a scruffy ponytail, and even from as far away as I was I could see freckles covering all of her exposed skin.

My eyes focused on my car. The side window was smashed to bits, and as I moved forward in disbelief, I could finally distinguish the words flung back and forth between the man and the young woman.

"Damn it, Lisa. Don't you dare back out on me. You fucking drive your ass on out of here, and you do it now." He reached into the car and smacked her along the side of her head.

She gave a muffled scream, and I could see tears streaming down her face. The man turned his back, sauntered over to his Harley and swung his leg over the powerful machine.

"Hey," I yelled starting to crash through the trees. "Hey, that's my car."

Startled, the man looked up. He couldn't see me clearly because of the trees and shrubs, but he could definitely hear me coming.

"Move it, Lisa, and move it now. Someone's coming." He laid rubber out of the parking lot, leaving her to follow or not, as she chose.

I burst out of the trees to see the girl, staring at me through the windshield of my car, a look of horror on her face. I streaked toward the car to stop her, but my bare foot came down on a sharp branch protruding from the ground.

"Uhhhhhhh," I screamed in pain, stumbling forward. I jerked my foot loose and started to run again, ignoring the pain. That stick cost me big time.

The girl jerked the car into reverse and spun the wheel. My car turned on the dime it was supposed to turn on, and responding to the girl's foot on the gas, it leaped forward.

The girl turned to look at me, and I swear I could see her lips move the whole time the car was picking up speed, a lot of speed. It looked like she was saying she was sorry. She turned her head back, stomped on the gas, and looked forward to see what I myself had just noticed.

She didn't even have time to scream as the car tore out of the parking lot and was scooped up by a semi that had chosen that exact moment in time to rumble on through. The sound of ripping, shredding metal and shattering glass echoed in the twilight, and in less than a heartbeat, what had been a 2001 cream-colored Lexus was nothing more than a ball of fire. The girl inside the car was nothing more than fuel.

Chapter 17

Ben

Carly, this is really nice of you, but you didn't have to drive all the way out here to the airport to pick me up. I could just as easily have taken a cab."

Carly tossed her hair, and Ben couldn't help but see how shiny and soft it was as it swirled around her shoulders. "No problem, Boss Man. I live to serve."

Ben cleared his throat. "Well, I appreciate the gesture."

She turned a brilliant smile in his direction. "My only other option was to sit at my desk and answer the telephone, so don't be too appreciative. It may only be June, but look at this day; feel the sun. Doesn't it make you want to go to the beach and lie on a towel in your skimpiest swimming suit to soak up the rays?"

Her words were light and delivered with humor, but Ben felt uncomfortable. He couldn't exactly put his finger on what had recently changed between them, but he felt a monumental shift in their relationship somehow. Well, if nothing else, he was sure of one thing. The shift was only one-sided, and that side wasn't his.

Ben thought of the other night when he'd helped Carly get

home after she sprained her ankle, and then he thought of the note she'd given him. No way, had he done anything consciously that should have caused her to generate that note. He knew he needed to talk to her about what she'd written, but at the moment, he had one goal. He wanted to get home to Meg.

For some reason, he was twitching all over with anxiety. Something was wrong. He knew it. Meg needed him. He'd always known when she wasn't feeling well or was upset, but this feeling was different, stronger, and it kept gnawing away at him.

Ben unlocked the front door and waved good-bye to Carly as she drove away. It was only 5:30, way too early for Meg to be home. The first thing he did was drop his bags in the kitchen, reach for the telephone, and dial her office.

"Hello, this is Meg Jacobi from ESI. I'm in the office all day, so please leave your name and number, and I'll call you back as soon as I can. If you need immediate assistance, please call my assistant, Joyce Iverson, at extension 5583."

The sound of Meg's voice increased the anxiety Ben felt. He needed to talk to her, and he needed to talk to her now. He glanced at the blinking red light on the answering machine, which indicated three messages. Maybe she'd left one for him. He punched in the code.

"Meg, hi, it's me, Ben. Please pick up if you're there."

Hearing the message he'd left the night before, Ben hit forward, heard the second message he'd left the night before, and hit forward again to hear the message he'd left early that morning. His anxiety spiked. Why hadn't Meg retrieved any of his messages?

He glanced at his watch, 5:50. Sandy, Richard Jamieson's assistant, often worked late. She might still be at her desk. What was her number? Damn. It shouldn't be so hard to get access to your own wife, thought Ben. He grabbed the telephone book and looked up the general ESI number. What was Sandy's last name? He dialed, listened to the options, and finally punched in Richard Jamieson's number.

"Hello, Richard Jamieson's office. May I help you?"

"Sandy?"

"Yes, who is this please?"

"Sandy, this is Ben Jacobi. I'm trying to locate Meg. Do you know if she's still in the office?"

Dead silence. How strange. Even over the telephone line, Ben was able to sense Sandy's discomfort. He wondered what was going on.

"Gosh Ben, haven't you heard from Meg yet today?" Sandy's voice had a catch in it as she finally responded to his question.

"No, I've been out of town. What's going on, Sandy?"

He heard Sandy's gulp and the quiver in her voice. "Ben, I'm so sorry to tell you this, and I probably have no business telling you because really when it comes right down to it, Meg should be the one. To tell you, I mean." Sandy took a deep breath. "Oh, gosh, I don't know how to say this in any way that makes it easier to hear. They fired Meg today, Ben. I'm sorry. So sorry."

"What? No way. She works her butt off for ESI, and let me tell you I ought to know, since you all see a whole hell of a lot more of her than I do."

Sandy's voice continued to quiver as though she were fighting back tears.

"I know, Ben. I know, but it really happened. They've put the communication guy in charge from Project Snowball—Oh Lord, I shouldn't have mentioned that either."

"No problem. I know something's going on. I don't have the details, don't need 'em, don't want 'em. What you're telling me, is that your CEO just sold out one of his most loyal employees, someone who's worked her ass off for him ever since she was hired. I have to tell you I don't get it."

Sandy whispered, "I don't get it either, Ben. Oh, I know Meg ticked off a lot of people, but she was always nice to me, and she was good at her job. Meg was just what we needed. She worked so hard. I wish I were wrong, but I'm not. None of us understands why she was fired. It doesn't make any sense."

Ben's voice was curt. "Fine. Whatever. When, tell me when it happened."

"About 10:30 this morning. I think she was out of the building by 11:00."

"For God's sake, it's almost 6:00, and as far as I can see she hasn't been home yet. Where is she?"

The doorbell rang.

"Look, I've got to answer the door. Maybe, it's Meg, and she lost her key or something. Sandy, thanks for caring. It means a lot to me, and I know it would mean a lot to Meg, too."

Ben hung up the telephone and loped off down the hallway. He could see the figure of a tall man through the frosted glass in the front door. The smile of relief that had filled his face at the ringing of the doorbell disappeared. Ben opened the door, and as his eyes took in the uniformed police officer standing there and the solemn look on his face, Ben felt every muscle in his body lock up.

"Mr. Jacobi?"

"Yes, Officer. I'm Ben Jacobi. What's wrong?"

"I'm really sorry to have to tell you this, but your wife has been in an accident."

Ben felt all the blood drain from his face. He forced words past frozen lips. "What hospital, officer? I'll leave right away."

"Mr. Jacobi, I'll be happy to accompany you, but your wife isn't in any hospital." The police officer cleared his throat. "I'm so sorry to have to tell you, but she didn't survive the accident."

Chapter 18

Pete

Pete, come on in. It's time for dinner."

The boy didn't even look up at the sound of his father's voice. He sat still on the back porch and pretended to read.

The screen door squeaked on rusty hinges as his father pushed his way out onto the porch, but Pete kept his eyes locked on his book, refusing to look up. The boards of the old porch flexed and creaked beneath his father's feet as he walked over and joined Pete on the top step.

"Pete," his father put an arm around him and pulled him closer. "Pete, talk to me. I know you're disappointed about your mom not showing up yesterday, but it didn't have anything to do with you. She really does care about you. I know she does."

Pete grew stiff within his father's arm, and he stared even harder at the page in front of him. He said nothing. After a few minutes, his father gave him a hug and rested his cheek for a moment on Pete's head.

"Your dinner is on the table when you're ready," he said finally in a funny, rough voice before he heaved himself up with a sigh and went back into the house.

Pete set down his book, no longer interested in pretending to read the adventures of Harry Potter. It must be nice to be a sorcerer and to magically make your problems disappear. Pete thought about being a sorcerer for a moment. Maybe he was a sorcerer too, but he just didn't know it. After all, Harry Potter didn't know he had magic powers until he was eleven years old. Pete liked that thought. He liked it a lot. Maybe he was adopted just like Harry Potter. Maybe his real mother lost him somehow, and she was searching right at that very minute for him. Maybe.

Inside the house, the telephone rang, and Pete's dad answered with his easy going "Hello, Rob here." A moment later, pleasure filled his voice. "Rita, how are you?"

Pete got to his feet and moved to sit in the dusty, old wicker chair outside the window closest to the telephone. Rita was his aunt, and Pete knew she'd been trying to get his dad to let him come and live with her and his three cousins. He liked his cousins fine. For that matter, he was also fond of his Aunt Rita and Uncle Bill, but the thought of living so far away from his dad made his stomach hurt.

"Rita, you know how much I appreciate your offer. Fact is, though, I couldn't get along without Pete."

Pete's stomach settled and he felt his heart give a funny little jump. Silence for a moment as his aunt responded to his Dad.

"Peter's no trouble, Rita. Not one bit. Sometimes I wish he were a little feistier. I can't tell you how my heart breaks at the look he gets on his face each time his mother calls and offers to take him somewhere. The zoo? No, she didn't show up. Mom must have told you about that, huh?"

Pete sat very still hoping that his father would say something that would help him understand why his mother never came to see him.

"Hmmm? How long since she's come over? Well, she calls every once in a while, but she hasn't come to see him since his seventh birthday. That's almost two whole years. When she did show up that time, she wasn't quite herself, if you catch my meaning. Some days I think the best thing she ever did was to run out on us."

What? Pete was confused. His mother didn't run away. She'd told him so on the telephone. She said his dad made her go away. She'd said so more than once.

"Yeah, yeah, I know, but wouldn't it be even worse to have an alcoholic raising a child? I know I may not be the best parent, but I love him, and he's going to stay with me. That's final. Don't get me wrong, because I do appreciate how much you care about both of us, but Rita, he's already lost one parent. I'm not going to let him lose another."

His aunt must have had a lot to say because Pete's dad was quiet for a long time. When he finally did speak, he had a funny tone to his voice, almost like he was embarrassed.

"I don't leave him home alone, except for a couple of hours in the afternoon every day. I don't have the money to put him into a full-time summer program right now, but I drop him off in the morning at his friend's house, and they walk over together to the school's half-day program. When Pete gets home, he knows he can call our neighbor, Genna Johnson, if he needs anything. She keeps an eye out for him until I get home.

"He knows the rules. No friends over when I'm not home. He's a good kid, Rita. Besides, he's almost nine years old. He knows not to play with the stove, and he knows how to dial 911. Look, I'm doing the best I can. I don't always know the right things to say or do, but I do know one thing. We're a family, Pete and I. We're going to stay together, no matter what."

Pete's dad was silent for a moment. "No, Rita. I'm not going to tell my son his mother is an alcoholic. He's too young to understand. Hell, at 28, I'm too young to understand how Jessie could have ended up that way. We all experimented with alcohol in high school, but no one else in our group became an alcoholic and left their family."

Pete's dad kept talking, but Pete was no longer listening. So, that's why his mother left. She was an alcoholic. He wondered what that meant exactly. He knew it meant she drank too much, but why would drinking too much make her leave her family? Pete wondered how he could help her stop drinking. Maybe she really did still love him. She just had this alcoholic thing going on. All he had to do was find out what it meant. Then, he could talk to her and get her to stop being one so that she'd come home. They'd be a real family again.

Chapter 19

Meg

I rolled over and groaned. If I didn't know any better, I'd have thought some unknown sadist had beaten me from head to feet with a rubber hose. Speaking of feet, my left one felt like after my unknown assailant beat me with a rubber hose, he had pounded a nine-inch nail through the heel of my foot and forgot to pull it back out.

Where was I? I smelled dust and the lingering fragrance of lavender. I was laying on a soft mattress that cradled my poor aching body, and the only thing I really wanted to do was to curl up into an even tighter ball, close my eyes, and go back to sleep. A feeling of doom hovered at the edge of my consciousness, and I thought if I could avoid waking up entirely, I wouldn't have to face it.

My brain kicked over and bit by bit started to fire on every cylinder. The whole series of memories and emotions I'd been trying to suppress shot through my brain, down to my stomach, and right back up in an enormous wave of nausea. I started to retch, kicked back the covers, and stumbled out of bed, yelping in pain as my left heel met the floor. My stomach was roiling, and saliva filled my mouth. Oh Lord, I needed a bathroom, and I needed one fast.

I hobbled as quickly as I could through the door to the right of the bed and found myself in a square hallway with closed doors on three sides. Praying my memory was accurate about the door on the left, I slammed through it to discover an old-fashioned bathroom papered in yellow daisies. I was less interested in the daisies and a heck of a lot more interested in reaching the toilet before I tossed my cookies all over the floor.

I fell to my knees. I've never decided which is worse. To throw up the contents of a full stomach and at least have something to show for the pain, or to retch and retch, until finally that nasty clear fluid spurts out of your mouth—bile—and your throat burns from the bitterness of it, and your head pounds from the violence of the retching.

Since I hadn't eaten since breakfast the day before, guess which situation I found myself in that morning? Afterwards, I pulled a tiny paper Dixie cup from a dispenser above the sink, filled it with tap water, and rinsed out my mouth.

I sank down on top of the toilet seat, which was covered in a thick dark green cover that matched the stems of the daisies on the wallpaper and the rug on the floor. I'd never seen this room before in its current state, but I knew where I was. Aunt Marion's house. I'd made it to the White Plains airport the evening before, ragged panty hose, tight shoes, and all, charged a ticket, and staggered on to the airplane. When I arrived at the Minneapolis/St. Paul airport, I'd taken a cab to my Aunt Marion's house in Northeast Minneapolis. No, it was my house now. It smelled of dust, it was old-fashioned, and I'd never lived anywhere like it before, but it was mine. All mine.

So, here I was sitting on a toilet in a strange house in a strange city. I had $49,256 in my pocket, this house, my shoes, my purse, and a limp, wrinkled navy blue business suit. That was on the asset side. No dreams last night—at least none that I could remember.

Again, on the asset side. On the debit side, I'd lost everything and everybody I could count on. I have to say I was feeling pretty sorry for myself.

That's when someone knocked on my back door.

Chapter 20

Genna

Genna waited on the back porch with a smile on her face. She had no idea why she was so excited to see Peggy's daughter, but she was. Late last night, she'd heard a car pull up outside, and sliding out of bed, she'd padded downstairs in her bare feet to see who was driving into the neighborhood.

When she'd seen the taxi pull up and a woman step out, she'd known that it had to be Meg. For one thing, in Northeast, people rarely took taxis to and from places. It was more of a wait-on-the-corner-for-the-Number-4-bus kind of neighborhood. For another thing, she'd been expecting Meg to show up.

As Marion lay dying, all she could talk about was Meg and how she'd failed her. As far as Genna knew, Marion had made the only logical choice she could make all those years ago after Peggy died. The alternative would have been so hard on Meg. As always, when her thoughts strayed to Peggy, Genna got a lump in her throat.

Genna Johnson and Peggy Lofgren had been best friends since the second grade when the Lofgrens moved in next door. That first morning, Genna had seen the moving trucks coming and going, but she was recovering from the flu, and her mother would not let her leave the living room couch.

Her mother had always been very big on fully recuperating after any illness. Genna was really feeling fine, though, and after spending the previous day in bed, she was ready to bounce off the ceiling. Although she hadn't been able to get outside to meet the new neighbors, she'd carefully monitored their comings and goings from her spot on the living room couch.

She noticed the mom and dad, but they held little interest for her. She wanted to know if there were any kids her own age. She also saw a teenage girl dressed in a turquoise cashmere sweater and a swinging black skirt belted tight at the waist. No luck there, teenagers were boring, and Genna wanted someone to play with besides her pesky, five-year-old sister.

A movement in the upstairs window of the house next door caught Genna's eye, and she could see a small face peering back at her. That small face lit up in an enormous smile, and the girl in the window waved at Genna. Genna smiled and waved back. The small face disappeared, but Genna didn't care. She could hardly wait until the next day.

The next morning her mother wouldn't let her leave the house until she sat down for a glass of orange juice and a slice of toast. After breakfast, she had to stand still, or at least try to stand still, while her mother French-braided her hair and tied on red ribbons. Finally, the day was hers.

She'd gone out into the backyard to see if the other girl had come outside yet, but the yard was empty except for a man in work pants and a white undershirt. Genna hovered around trying to look as though she was actually doing something, but within a minute or so, the man sensed her presence and turned with a smile.

"Good morning. Who are you, young lady?"

"I'm Genna Johnson. I live in this house with my mama, daddy, and little sister. Do you have any little girls in your house?"

He scratched his head for a minute. "Hmmmm, let me see." He held out one hand and counted off fingers with the other. Well, there's me, that's one, but I'm not a little girl, am I?"

Genna giggled. She'd never met anyone quite like this man before. He extended his hand to shake hers and Genna felt quite grown up.

"By the way, Genna Johnson, my name is Carl Lofgren. Now, where was I? There's Mother, that's two. She's not a little girl, either, of course. Marion makes three, but she's kind of old already, if you know what I mean." He stopped talking for a minute and looked at Genna with a twinkle in his sky blue eyes. He slapped his forehead with the palm of his hand. "Oh yes, how could I forget? There's also, Peg O' My Heart."

"Peg O' My Heart?" Genna had never heard a name like that before, and she repeated the words, trying them out on her tongue.

"Yep, Peggy's my baby. Only she's not really a baby any more. By now she must be seven years old at least."

"Why, that's exactly how old I am."

"No kidding? How about you wait right here, and I'll go see if my lazy girl is out of bed yet. I bet she'd like to meet you."

He paused for a moment, and taking out a small folding knife, he cut a pink rose from the old bush he'd been examining, trimmed off the thorns, and with a small flourish presented it to Genna.

She'd felt very special and even more grown up. She smiled to herself, sniffed her rose every few minutes, and leaned against the clothes pole as she waited to meet Peg O' My Heart. She had just conjured up the image of a shy, sweet little girl with pink ribbons in her hair when Jimmy Popovich and Tommy Trompeter walked by pushing their bicycles through the alley.

"Hey Tommy, look it's Minnesota Fats."

"Yeah, I see her. How could I miss her? Hey Minnesota Fats, don't run too fast or we'll have an earthquake."

Genna's face turned red. At seven, she'd been a good head taller and overall, just plain bigger than the other kids in her class. Her mother said she'd gotten her growth early, and so, Genna figured her size was no big deal.

Tommy and Jimmy had decided between them, though, that

"Minnesota Fats" was the funniest nickname on this side of the moon, and they never failed to call her that. The two boys laughed again and started to move on. They didn't get very far though. All Genna ever remembered about her first glimpse of Peggy Lofgren was a tiny blur.

The blur shot out the back door of the Lofgren house and across the yard to fling herself on the nearest boy. He dropped his bicycle as he tried to defend himself against the small virago who was doing everything she could to punch his face.

"Don't you ever say that again, you hear me? It's mean, and I don't like mean," she panted in anger.

Jimmy Popovich hopped on his bike and sped away leaving his friend in the dirt.

"Hey, I didn't mean anything by it. We always call her Minnesota Fats," said the boy who'd been left behind as he got to his feet.

"Not any more you don't, so there." Peggy put out both hands and shoved him to the ground again. "Go home. We don't want you here."

She turned her back, a long braid flipping with her sudden movement, and she marched right over to stand beside Genna with her hands on her hips.

Tommy Trompeter lost no time leaping to his feet, jumping on his bike, and making his getaway.

Genna smiled and looked into the bluest eyes she'd ever seen. "Hi, I'm Genna Johnson. I bet you're Peg O' My Heart."

"Naw, I'm just Peggy. My daddy calls me Peg O' My Heart because he says he loves me so much. There's even a song called Peg O' My Heart, did you know that? My whole name is Margaret Eva." She made a face. "I like Peggy a lot better."

Genna made a face back in sympathy. "My whole name is Genevieve Louise Johnson. Does your Mama call you your whole name when she's mad at you? Mine does."

Peggy giggled and said in a stern voice. "Uh huh. Margaret Eva Lofgren, what are you doing? I want to see you *right this instant*. Hey

Genna Johnson, do you want to be my best friend?"

"Oh yes. I do." Never before or since, had Genna been surer of anything than she was of wanting to be friends with the tiny tornado that was Peggy Lofgren. As an adult, Genna could appreciate the humor in the situation. There she'd stood, all dolled up with ribbons in her hair. Peggy, who was at least a foot shorter, stood next to her, dressed in overalls with a long, dark red braid hanging down her back and a cowboy hat on her head.

Genna Johnson and Peggy Lofgren became best friends that day, and they never stopped being friends until Peggy's death.

Fifty-two years later, Genna spoke aloud, "Peg O' My Heart, that's what you were Peggy. You were Peg O' My Heart to all of us."

Genna looked up at the old Lofgren place. It was a shambles of what it had been. Marion moved back in 1985 after her parents died, but toward the end, she didn't have the strength to focus on details like paint and landscaping. Genna reached out absently and touched the edge of the door in front of her. In places, the paint blistered and peeled away from the old wood, and in others, it lay flat and chalky.

No question about it, the house needed some heavy-duty work. Not just the house either, she thought. The yard was a jungle. She wondered what lay beneath the overgrown tangle of weeds that had taken over the flowerbeds Carl Lofgren had so painstakingly nurtured.

Genna switched the plate of brownies she held in her right hand to her left, and knocked once more on the back door of the old house. She sensed someone was nearby, so she stood there patiently waiting. One thing she was particularly good at, she thought with humor, was being patient. According to Sylvie, she was the epitome of patience. Genna figured that was synonymous to being the epitome of boring.

As she looked through the sheer curtains on the back door window, she could see a figure approaching. The door opened, and Genna looked down to see a small woman with tousled mahogany hair and a pale face looking back at her, not a hint of interest or welcome on her face.

"Yes?"

Genna knew this woman had to be Meg. The physical resemblance to Peggy was phenomenal, but there any resemblance ended. Where Peggy had been all warmth, sunshine, and "let's get to know each other because I just know you've got to be a fascinating person," this woman was ice, stone, and something else.

At first, Genna couldn't quite pick up on what that something else was. The woman shifted her weight from one foot to the other, obviously impatient, her teeth clenched so tightly together her jaw bulged. Genna wasn't fazed. She looked into Meg's eyes and recognized a depth of loneliness and loss that made her exclaim in her usual way.

"Oh my dear, are you okay? Can I do anything to help you?" Subtlety was not one of Genna's strong points.

Meg stiffened and started to close the door in Genna's face. "No."

"Oh, there I go again. I'm sorry, dear. You're Meg, right? I was a friend of your mother's. I know it's been a long time, but I used to come over to your house quite a bit when you were young, remember?" Genna held out the plate of brownies. "Here, I've brought you a welcome-to-the-neighborhood treat."

"No, I don't remember you." Meg's face tightened, her eyes flat and empty, her words automatic and without inflection. "How unfortunate you went to all this bother. I'm diabetic, and I never eat sweets."

Meg swung the door shut in Genna's face, leaving her standing alone on the porch holding her pretty china plate loaded down with chocolate brownies.

Chapter 21

Meg

I leaned back against the door, embarrassed I'd been seen in my current condition and furious that someone had the nerve to show up at my door uninvited. Of course, I remembered my mother's best friend, but she wasn't my friend. Besides, I didn't want to be friendly to my neighbors, and God knows I didn't want them trying to be friendly with me either. It took too much time and effort to take care of such unimportant relationships.

I slid down the door to sit on the kitchen floor, realizing that all I had was time these days and no important relationships that I needed to build or strengthen.

I had no clue what to do next. I wondered how long I could hang out in this house of mine. I hadn't even been in the house since I was eighteen or nineteen years old, so I didn't even know what it was like anymore.

I'd come directly in the night before after finding the key right where Aunt Marion said it would be, and I'd gone upstairs to collapse on the first bed I found. So far that morning, I'd been a little too busy to do much more than check out the bathroom fixtures and stare at the wallpaper.

I closed my eyes, but opened them again immediately, because all I could see against the darkness of my eyelids was an orange ball of flame with my car smack in the middle of it, and in the middle of my car, I could see . . . I could see the girl, Lisa. She never had a chance. She was just a kid. A damn stupid kid, I amended, pressing my fingertips against my temples and pressing hard to ease the pain that was beginning to pound away inside my skull.

What was I going to do? I knew for sure what I was not going to do. I was not going to call Ben. He could take up with that pointy-faced Carly person. I didn't need anything from him. I'd already known our marriage was in trouble. It had just been a matter of time. That was that. I would put Ben—and the Carly person—right out of my mind. I could take care of myself.

I wondered how long I could make the $49,000 plus a little bit more last. I'd never needed to worry about money before, but I would never crawl back and ask Ben for anything. So what if I legally owned half of what we had? I was done with that part of my life, and I was not going back to any of it. Since I didn't have a job, my credit cards were not an option either. I was too smart to go into debt like that, and I intended to cut them up the first chance I got. ESI severance—I didn't want to touch a penny of that money. I was done with them.

So, getting back to the original question, how long would my money last? I didn't need to pay rent or a mortgage, so that only left taxes. The house wasn't what I was used to. Not a Jacuzzi in sight. Bare wood floors with old carpets. A kitchen that was anything but gourmet, which didn't matter because I didn't cook, one bathroom upstairs with daisy wallpaper, and three bedrooms, if the doors I'd seen were any indication of bedrooms behind them. I'd never expected to live any place like this, but the price was right.

Okay, so the living arrangements were bearable. What else did I need? I looked down at my wrinkled, dirty suit. Oh yes, I definitely needed some clothes, but I didn't have to spend the moon on them either. All I needed was enough money to buy food and essentials. I'd never been on a budget before, but I bet I could make that $49,256 last a long time if I was careful.

I wondered how much an abortion would cost.

I looked down to see that I was wringing my hands, a nervous gesture I'd never indulged in before. Strange. I stared at my hands, making a conscious effort to stop wringing them together, and I noticed that I'd never taken off my mother's wedding ring. The small golden band encircled my littlest finger like a magic talisman.

I snorted. Yes, I did. I snorted at the whimsical image. Magic? Yeah, right. Then, just like that, the words to that stupid song started spinning around in my head again . . . *your dreams are safe and true.*

I pulled the golden band off my finger and raised my hand over my head to fling it away. I know, I know, what a childish thing to do, right? At the last moment, my fingers curled protectively around it. I couldn't explain for the life of me why I hung on to it, but I did, closing my eyes for a moment. Taking a deep breath, I slipped it back on my finger.

At that moment, someone knocked on the back door again. I felt the vibration in my shoulders and head where they made contact with the door. I couldn't believe it. I was sure I hadn't had this many visitors since the day I was born and all my mother's relatives came to see the new baby. No way could I even get up to answer the door without looking as though I were rising like a phoenix from the kitchen floor.

Well, I told myself, I had every right to sit on my kitchen floor if I wanted to. I bet lots of people did for lots of reasons. The problem was, I couldn't think of a single good reason for me to be doing it at that particular moment.

Well, who said I had to explain anything? Who said I even had to answer this summons? I hadn't sent out invitations. I hadn't even moved in officially. Most important of all, I didn't want to see anyone, so, I closed my eyes and held my breath. Less than ten seconds later, someone knocked again, not once, not twice, but with a rat a tat tat, as the creative fool tried to play percussion music on my back door. Vibrations thrummed through my shoulders like a forgotten song.

Oh, the hell with it, I thought, leaping to my feet, and immediately swearing as my heel came down on the floor. Shit, that hurt. I turned with a limp and a glare that had to be visible through the curtains on the back door as I flung it open once again.

The handsome, older gentleman waiting for me on the back porch didn't acknowledge by so much as a blink that he thought it was unusual for me to have leapt up from the floor to answer the door.

He had a full head of silver hair and the most engaging twinkle in his brown eyes. The moment he saw me, he inclined his head and greeted me with a smile. He stood well over six feet tall and stooped a little. His skin was brown and wrinkled from the sun, but when he smiled, the wrinkles arranged themselves into the most charming visage. I refused to be charmed. He was invading my space. Not only didn't I want my space invaded, I didn't want company at all. His or anyone else's.

His gaze dipped to my left hand, and seeing no wedding ring, he said in the most charming voice I'd heard outside of the latest Three Musketeers Movie, "Eh, Mademoiselle, bienvenue. Welcome to the neighborhood. We are so happy you have moved in."

He bowed his head to me. For Pete's sake. What century did he grow up in?

Before I could utter one word, he pulled his hand out from behind his back with a flourish, displaying a half-opened rose, yellow with coral edges on each petal. It was beautiful, and I could smell the fragrance from where I stood.

"For you, Mademoiselle. In welcome and in honor of both your presence and your beauty."

Who was this character? All my nastiness began to well up and spill out, and to be honest, I did nothing to stop it. I too would be charming, however, while making my point in response to his bullshit.

I inclined my head—I really did. I inclined my head in the same way he had—and I looked down my nose at him. In my case, I of course had to look up, but you get the drift.

"I'm sorry, sir. We have not been introduced. Now, if you'll excuse me, I have things to do, and I don't have time to talk to strangers. Besides, I have allergies to flowers," I lied.

"I understand completely, Mademoiselle. The allergy, she would be a side effect or unrelated completely to the diabetes?"

Oh for Pete's sake, now the neighbors were sharing gossip about me, and I'd been in town less than twelve hours. No wonder I'd avoided relationships with my neighbors all my life. Who needs that kind of interference? I didn't know what to say, so I backed up two steps and closed the door in his face.

Now, at that point, I could have left things alone, but oh no, curiosity got the better of me, and I had to peek out the window to see what he was doing. Of course, even though I was being as careful as I could with my spying, he noticed me peeking, inclined his head to me and spoke as if I were still out on the porch with him.

"Ah Mademoiselle, you are right, after all. Why should you have to waste your time on an old fool like me?"

His brown eyes continued to twinkle and one corner of his mouth quirked up at me. "And so, me, I will make you a deal as they say. First, my name is Jean-Louis Regnier, and I am the neighbor on your left. Now, we are no longer strangers, you and me, eh? We have been introduced, cela suffit. Also, based on the look in your eyes, I think that you would benefit from my roses, and so, I will simply leave one for you occasionally, outside on your doorstep, you understand. That way, the allergy, she will not be affected. Au revoir, Mademoiselle."

I swear if he'd had a hat, he would have tilted it at me. He bent and laid the rose on my doorstep and ambled away, disappearing through a hole in the hedge between our two houses.

Immediately, I decided I'd find something to block that hole as soon as I could. I spun around, my back against the wall, mortified, although for the life of me I couldn't think why. He thought I needed a flower every day based on the look in my eyes. What did that mean? What was the matter with this place? Didn't anyone come to the front door like a civilized person? Didn't anyone call to make an appointment?

As though to prove me wrong, the front doorbell rang, but in my current mood, I didn't even want to see a civilized person. I swore, using words that aren't very nice to put down in print. Here, I was trying to figure out how I was going to survive, where I could go to terminate this pregnancy thing that was afflicting me, and how I was going to stretch out my $49,000 so that I could hide forever from everything and everyone I knew. I had a lot going on, and all my neighbors could do was plague me with unwanted civilities. What was wrong with them?

I stomped my way to the front door, favoring my right foot, and flung it open, revealing a young girl of about 11 years or so, standing there with a form in her hands. She looked me over without smiling. Clearly, she was not fazed by me or by my attitude. I could see it in her cool blue eyes and in the way she held her head high and alert, her long silky blond ponytail immobile, every hair in place, a blue ribbon tied in a perfect bow around the perfect ponytail.

"Yes," I said in my most frigid, unfriendly voice.

"Hi, I'm selling Girl Scout cookies. How many boxes do you want?"

Thank God. Someone I could relate to. "Are you from this neighborhood?" I asked in a brusque voice.

The girl turned and looked around, utter disdain on her face. She turned back to me. "Of course not."

"Fine. You can put me down for twelve boxes and scram."

She did her thing and scrammed in her own way, sauntering down my crooked, little walkway to the main sidewalk, making a check on her list. She continued down the sidewalk ignoring the silver BMW trailing behind, which was driven by a well-coifed matron who was also clearly not from this neighborhood.

I went back inside. Oh good, I'd purchased twelve boxes of cookies that I didn't need. Me, the diabetic. This budget thing was going to take some getting used to.

Now what?

I didn't know what to do next. I still knew nothing about my house, I had the most interfering neighbors on the face of the earth, and I had no clue where I could go to get a safe, affordable abortion.

So, I did the only thing that made sense. I climbed the stairs and sought out the bedroom with the soft bed and softer pillows. I shoved open a window to let in some fresh air, and I climbed under the covers and went right back to sleep.

Chapter 22

Meg

The next time I awoke, my headache was gone, but my foot was throbbing furiously. There goes some of my $49,000, I thought in frustration, knowing I needed to get to a doctor. I didn't move, though. I rolled over on my back and stared at the ceiling.

My mind skittered from one thing to another and as image followed thought, I suppressed each as quickly as possible.

How had I gone from executive extraordinaire with a fifteen-year marriage to pregnant, single, and unemployed? I didn't know what to do next. I'd worked ever since I could remember and every job, no matter what it had been, had taken all my energy and focus. Now, here I was with nothing to focus on and nowhere to go.

Unwanted, unbidden thoughts of Ben flashed through my mind. He'd always been the tether that kept me safe. What an odd choice of words. I scrunched my eyes shut, so tempted to roll over and go back to sleep.

A soft breeze touched my cheek, and I opened my eyes to see late afternoon sun streaming through the window in a golden path across the bedroom floor.

Outside, I could hear a symphony of birds singing their little hearts out. Funny, in Stamford, I never noticed the birds singing, or the pattern the sun made across the floor, or much of anything for that matter. I was too busy. Now, though, it was relaxing to lie in the soft bed and focus on where I was at that exact moment in time instead of on what I had to produce next, what I had to say next, or who I had to impress next.

Lord, I thought with a shock. I loved my job. I waited to feel a pang, but I felt nothing. Just emptiness, and a sense of waiting for something, but I didn't really know what. The feeling wasn't unpleasant exactly, but so foreign.

Sighing, I sat up, waiting for the rush of blood to make its way back up to my brain before I slid off the high, old four-poster bed.

On the left side of the room, a deep bay of windows complete with a window seat covered in soft green and yellow flowered cushions beckoned. I bit. Crossing over, I sank down and rested my forehead against the window to look down into my backyard.

What a mess, I thought. The grass needed to be mowed, the flower gardens needed to be weeded, and cut back or down or whatever one did to make flower gardens look good, and the shrubs separating my yard from those of my neighbors definitely needed a trim. They were pretty, though, in a ragged sort of way, sporting enormous cones of lilac blossoms that I could smell all the way up in my second story perch.

I breathed deeply, thinking maybe I could hire someone to work on the yard, but remembering my $49,000, I decided that with all the spare time I was going to have, maybe I could figure out how to take care of things myself.

Hearing voices, I turned my head to the right. In the yard next door, the woman I'd met earlier that morning, Genna Johnson, was down on her knees weeding what I could only think of as a comprehensive flower garden.

Comprehensive flower garden? For Pete's sake. I guess you could take the woman away from the corporate jargon, but it was hard to get the corporate jargon out of the woman. What I meant to say is that I'd never seen a flowerbed filled with so many varieties.

Her garden beat mine cold; that is, the garden I'd had in Stamford, and I'd hired professionals. Genna turned her head to speak with another smaller woman, and they both turned and looked at my house.

Damnation, they were talking about me. I knew it. I drew back so that they would not be able to see me in the window. I turned my head to the left, and I saw my other neighbor, Jean-Louis, clipping away at what had to be the largest rose garden I'd ever seen.

I also noticed that he seemed to be paying more attention to the two women next door than he was to his roses. Enough. I was learning far more about my neighbors than I had any desire to learn. I turned back to look into my own house.

It was old, but beautifully decorated, that is, if you like cottage, flower-sprigged stuff like the garbage they put on the covers of *Home Beautiful* magazine. I'd have to adapt, that's all. I was going to be on a strict budget. Besides, it wasn't so bad.

Sheer white curtains billowed in the breeze flowing through the window. Delicate lavender-sprigged wallpaper covered the walls halfway down, interrupted by a border and matching pattern below. It was a pretty room. I wondered who had used it before me. My Aunt Marion probably.

Large watercolor paintings of flowers, a la Georgia O'Keefe, covered the walls, accenting the wallpaper, almost as though they'd been created for this room in particular.

I slid off the window seat, favoring my sore foot, and hobbled over to look at the signature beneath the picture. Wow, I'd never realized how skilled my Aunt Marion was, but if these paintings were any indication, she'd had much more talent than I'd ever given her credit for having.

The bedroom was large and peaceful, with yellow, green, and lavender rag rugs covering the honey-colored hardwood floor that was worn to a soft luster. When I was a child, this was the master bedroom occupied by my grandmother and grandfather. My Aunt Marion had done quite a bit of updating.

Curious, I hobbled out into the large square hallway. More of my aunt's pictures decorated the walls, watercolor renderings of exotic places. I wondered if she'd traveled to those places or merely dreamed of them. I briefly peered into the bedroom directly across from the one I'd slept in. The room was smaller, the bed covered with a multi-colored quilt, each square in the shape of a different type of flower.

I moved to the next closed door, in anticipation. Now that I did not have an immediate need to throw up, I remembered it led to a stairway, and I climbed up to the large converted attic above. Afternoon light poured through the windows lining every wall.

At one time, this room had been my mother's hideaway. Marion had transformed it into a studio. A number of paintings, completed and in progress, leaned against the walls.

A door led onto a small porch that looked out over the back yard. Inside, an old green painted wicker table, chairs, and loveseat filled the room, as did a number of dried up plants and planters. I stepped outside, realizing that I could see even more of what was going on in my neighbor's yards from this position in the house. As if I wanted to. I sniffed and turned back inside.

An L-shaped desk in one corner, complete with a computer and printer, caught my eye. I was a writer after all, and for just a moment I thought about the various ways I could use this equipment, my fingers tingling and ready to create. I noticed a bright orange folder sitting smack in the middle of the desk, with my name written prominently in red on a yellow post-it note along with a notation: Detective Notes.

I remembered Marion's reference to the detective, but I couldn't believe he'd be able to find anything, not after all this time. Just for a minute, though, for the first time in so many years, my heart did a funny kind of flop, as though I was hoping that maybe I was wrong. Maybe the detective could find some information to help me.

The familiar anger welled up. Why did you have to die, Mom? Why did you have to put us in that position? Like smoke through a screen, the music box song drifted easily through my mind. *Shed pain, my darling, no regrets. Your life belongs to you.*

I closed my mind against every thought but checking out the rest of the house. I needed to focus on now, not on what might have been. It was too late for that.

I left the folder untouched and climbed as fast as I could down the stairs with my injured foot. The living room spanned the front of the house, complete with a brick fireplace and oak mantle. A generous dining room contained a mission table and china cabinet, and the kitchen was painted robin's egg blue with built-in white cabinets and an old-fashioned gas stove. I dismissed the stove with a glance. I didn't cook, so what did I care what kind of stove I had?

Well, I thought in satisfaction. The house may be old, but it's kind of unique, and it's mine.

Poking around in the kitchen, I found a copy of the yellow pages and searched for an urgent care clinic that wasn't too far away. It was 3:30. If I hurried, someone could check out my foot.

Looking down at my suit, I realized the need to stop and get something else to wear too, and maybe a comb and some makeup. I was really a mess. The bank. I'd also need to stop and set up an account at a bank so I'd have money to spend.

Motivated to do something about the mess I'd become, at least the physical mess, I grabbed my cell phone, called a cab, and was on my way within fifteen minutes. When I returned two hours later, I was $150 dollars poorer from the medical examination, $85 dollars poorer from the antibiotic—I'd never take medical insurance for granted again—and another $135 dollars poorer from the sundress, shorts, t-shirts and miscellaneous stuff I'd purchased from the local Target store. I'd never worn such clothes before, but why should I care? There was no one to see me.

I put my packages on the kitchen table, and opening the back door to let the early evening breeze into the house, I nearly tripped over the large cooler sitting on my porch. An envelope taped to the top proclaimed my name in bold writing. I sighed, wondering what I was going to have to do to get my neighbors to leave me alone.

As I reached for the envelope, a motion in the yard next door caught my eye. I turned to see a tiny woman lying on a chaise lounge openly staring at me instead of minding her own business.

It was the same woman I'd seen earlier that afternoon talking to the other one, Genna. I didn't want to have to say anything to her, so I pretended to ignore her. I wandered down the path in my backyard, sort of nonchalantly, you know, staking out my personal territory, but the whole time, I could see her quite clearly out of the corner of my eye—and I could see that she was watching me.

She was no bigger than an adolescent, and she was dressed in a long, pale peach sundress, covered with tiny flowers and bits of lace. Long spangled earrings hung from her earlobes, and a wide-brimmed straw hat trimmed with coral and yellow flowers concealed her hair.

An enormous pair of tortoise-shell sunglasses perched on her nose, covering a pair of eyes that seemed to follow me wherever I wandered through my own backyard. Granted, she was on the other side of the fence and shrubs that divided our two yards, ostensibly minding her own business, but there was no doubt about the fact that she was staring. Staring at me. I didn't like it.

Finally I turned around and stared right back at her. She didn't seem to get the message that I wanted her to mind her own business, so I glared a little bit harder. After a moment, she sent a brilliant smile my way, nodded her head—what was it about this head-nodding thing—it had to be a Minnesota habit—and returned her focus to the paperback book she held on her lap. Three more books lay tumbled on a small table at her side next to a tall glass, dripping with condensation.

I walked rapidly back up the steps and across the porch to my own back door, and I was so determined to get myself out of the woman's range of vision that I did trip over the cooler. Oh, for Pete's sake, I thought, as I snagged the note taped to the top and ripped it open.

Meg dear,

You have to eat, and since you've just arrived, you can't possibly have had time to go grocery shopping, yet. So, I did a little research into good recipes for diabetics, and I made you a hotdish.

A hotdish? What was a hotdish? I shook my head in confusion and continued reading.

One serving, which is a level cup by the way, is about 60 grams of carbohydrates, and according to my friend Dr. Bowers, most diabetics count carbohydrates these days, so you should be able to plan exactly how much you can eat.

I also made you some oatmeal cookies, but I only put in half the sugar. Dr. Bowers said you could also eat them since each has only about 25 carbohydrates. There is also a healthy green salad with onions and tomatoes, which even I know is good for you.

At the bottom of the cooler, I put in a container of green Jell-O with pears (I used the artificially sweetened Jell-O and pears in light syrup). I thought you might want a before bedtime snack, and this should do the trick for you.

Now, please don't worry about this morning. I know you were tired, and probably didn't mean to be so abrupt. Never mind, dear. We'll have plenty of time to get to know each other. Bon appetit, as our neighbor Jean-Louis Regnier would say.

Genna

I wasn't at all worried about that morning. Yes, I was tired, but that's probably why I was as restrained as I was with both she and the Jean-Louis person with the head-nodding thing. I couldn't believe Genna had gone to all this trouble.

Panting a little, I picked up the cooler and happened to glance over at the neighboring yard. That woman was watching me again. She gave me the creeps. I couldn't seem to get away from people who wanted to get into my space. Before I could look away, she tipped her dark glasses up, and I swear she winked at me. She didn't say one, single solitary word, but she definitely winked before lowering her sunglasses over her eyes and bending her head over the book she held in her lap.

I turned away so that I wouldn't have to respond, and who do you think I saw in the yard on my other side. Yes, you guessed it. Mr. or I guess that would be Monsieur Regnier. He stood stooped over clipping away at his roses, but when I turned, he nodded his head at me and sent a gentle smile my way.

Flustered with what felt like the invasion of the neighborhood pod people, I turned my head to stare straight back across the alley and noticed a small boy swinging on a gate. He didn't nod, wink, or smile, but he did stare at me, both eyes wide open, face immobile.

In desperation, I backed into the kitchen away from prying eyes. I lugged the cooler over to the sink, determined to wash whatever it contained down the garbage disposal.

Two problems with my plan. First, there was no garbage disposal. Second, when I pulled the lid off the hot dish, the warm smell of good vegetables, small round hash brown potatoes, and what appeared to be mushroom soup caused me to salivate as though I hadn't eaten in days.

Fact was, I hadn't eaten anything but a breakfast bar early the day before. Since I arrived in Minneapolis, all I'd done was sleep, sit in a clinic waiting to get my foot fixed, or shop for cheap clothes at Target. My stomach rumbled.

Oh, what the hell, I thought. If some stranger wants to feed me, why shouldn't I take advantage of it? If by some chance that stranger happens to have the same predilection for poisoning people as the two old ladies from *Arsenic and Old Lace*—so much the better. That would take care of my future without any effort on my part.

I pulled out some of Aunt Marion's china. It was old, thick, and pretty with twining blue flowers and green leaves. I filled the plate with a huge portion of hot dish—which I discovered is just a funny word for casserole—salad, and three cookies. I washed it all down with a cup of chamomile tea since I couldn't find even a pinch of coffee in any of the cupboards.

Everything tasted wonderful. I hadn't realized how hungry I was. That was my first meal in my new house. It was also the beginning of a strange, silent relationship that began to grow between me and my neighbors. A relationship, in my opinion, that grew like fungus in the dark—unwanted and pervasive—or was that invasive?

Chapter 23

Carly

I cannot even imagine how horrible it would be to have to go and identify your own wife after she's been burned to a crisp in an explosion." Toni sat slumped in a chair next to Carly's desk, her face puckered up with revulsion. "Ugh, how could Ben even know it was Meg?"

"God, that's the saddest thing I've heard in a long time."

Ann Jessup, a plump young woman with unruly, carrot red hair rioting to her shoulders, leaned against the corner of Carly's desk, twirling her hair with one finger. She turned toward Carly, her light blue eyes hungry for any details that Carly was ready to share. Since Carly very much liked being the center of attention, she was not only willing to share everything she knew, she wasn't beyond embellishing a few things along the way.

"Well, if you think about it, why would they even make him look at the body?" she said in a knowing way, trying to keep any note of satisfaction out of her voice. After all, as badly as she had wanted Meg out of the picture, it would be so uncool for her to show anything but sympathy under the circumstances.

Toni and Ann both leaned forward, intent on every word coming out of Carly's mouth.

"Think about it. There was never any doubt about who it was." Carly started ticking things off on her perfectly manicured fingers. "One, female, burned to a crisp, but definitely recognizable as female—even if she was a crispy critter so to speak."

"Well, that's a sentimental description if I ever heard one," said Toni rolling her eyes.

Carly shot a cool look her way.

"I'm only repeating the facts. That was fact number one. Fact number two: This female was in Meg's car. The semi pretty much crushed the car to bits, and the explosion burned out the insides, but the license plate was still legible. There is not a shred of doubt that it was Meg's car. Besides, Meg hasn't been seen since that explosion, so, who else could it be?"

"Gross," said Ann. She asked in a hushed voice, "Did you hear about her wedding ring?"

"Of course," snapped Carly who didn't have a clue what Ann was talking about, but as the resident expert on Ben Jacobi, no way was she going to admit that she had missed out on any of the details.

Toni sat up straight in her chair, looking around to be sure that no one was within hearing distance. She looked at Carly. "What about the ring?"

Carly waved her hand carelessly at Ann. "You tell the story."

"Okay, but it's going to break your heart," said Ann. She leaned over so that her words wouldn't carry beyond the cubicle. "I heard Jason telling Geoff about it yesterday."

Jason, the head of engineering, was Ann's boss, and Geoff was the company's chief operating officer.

"Jason said the police had Ben view the body on a video camera, but first they showed him some personal stuff they pulled off the body and out of the car."

Carly didn't make a move or show in any way that this was all news to her, but she couldn't resist the opportunity to correct Ann.

"You mean the coroner, not the police."

"Yeah, whatever."

Toni frowned. "Wait a minute. How could there be anything personal left? I thought the fire pretty much destroyed everything."

She turned to Carly again, who didn't miss a beat in picking up the threads of the conversation.

"There wasn't anything substantial left. I heard the fireball was at least eight feet tall, and that it was quite a challenge for the fire department to put out the blaze. They had to wait a long time for things to cool down so they could conduct any sort of investigation."

"Yeah," nodded Ann. "But here's the thing. I heard Jason say they had a few things in an envelope. One was a ring, and it was twisted and melted, but the stone was pretty distinctive I guess."

"Yes, it was. The ring was designed by Gabriel." Carly perked up. She was on firm ground with the ring. She noticed things like jewelry, and Meg's ring was hard to miss. She'd asked Ben about it once a long time ago, and he'd told her about it.

"The diamond has 28 facets instead of the usual 24, and it's more than a carat, which is why it practically put your eyes out every time Meg waved her hands around."

The other two women looked at Carly in surprise.

"I saw it once at a company thing, and I asked Ben about it later."

"Hey, I thought you said you'd never met Meg before."

Toni broke in with a smirk. "We all probably met her a couple of years ago at the Christmas party, but Meg wouldn't have remembered meeting us. She was way above the administrative help, right Carly?"

Carly shot her a frown. "She would have remembered me after we met a couple of weeks ago, that's for sure. I don't mean to speak ill of the dead, but Meg was a little bit full of herself."

Ann brushed off these uninteresting details and continued with her story. "Well, anyway, the ring was a deciding factor, that's for sure, and so was the car."

"What else was in the envelope?" asked Toni, waving her hands to indicate that Ann was supposed to tell them everything she knew.

Ann wrinkled her forehead. "I don't know exactly. Jason looked up and caught me listening. So, he got up and closed his door, darn it."

Toni heaved herself to her feet with a sigh. "Well, it's been nice and all that, but I've gotta get to it. If I don't get that presentation done by the end of the day, my ass is grass, as they say."

Ann straightened too. "So, like how is Ben doing, Carly? I haven't seen him at all the last two weeks."

"He's been working primarily at home, but I think he's planning to go out to Colorado for the next few weeks. I'm supposed to bring some files out to his place later today for his trip." Carly looked off into space for a minute. "Maybe I should bring some food too, you know, a casserole or something."

Toni snorted. "I think it's a bit early to start moving in on him yet, Carly. The funeral was just last week."

With a confused expression on her face, Ann looked from one to the other. "Moving in on him? What do you mean, Toni? Carly, do you have a thing for Ben Jacobi?"

Ann's voice was clear, and it carried. Furious, Carly looked around to see if anyone had heard anything.

"Just shut up, Toni, will you? Bringing a casserole to someone who is grieving is a tradition. It's simply a way to indicate that you're thinking of them. That's all."

Ann's face cleared, and with a wave of her hand, she was on her way.

"Yeah, tradition, right." Toni turned to follow Ann.

"Toni?"

She turned back to face Carly. "Yeah?"

"When I do make a move, I promise a casserole will not be part of the equation."

Toni grinned and waggled her fingers as she walked away, hips swinging suggestively.

Carly stared at her computer screen—her mind a million miles away, or to be completely accurate, exactly 9.5 miles away to where Ben had lived with Meg in an upscale part of Stamford.

She'd seen Ben exactly three times since Meg's death, and she was pretty sure he hadn't even known she was there except as an interchangeable human being who could type, schedule meetings, and answer his telephone.

Oh, he was polite, but he'd never by so much as a word or glance indicated that he remembered anything about that night a few weeks ago. He'd never said a word about the note she left him, suggesting that they get together some time for dinner. She knew, though, that she hadn't imagined the look in his eye that night. It hadn't lasted, but it had been there. She was sure of it.

Now, all she had to do was wait for a while before she made her move. She'd be sympathetic, she'd be visible, and she'd be patient. Carly had no doubt about what she wanted, and Ben Jacobi was definitely part of the package.

Chapter 24

Ben

Ben trudged up the driveway. Getting the mail had become the highlight of his day. That, and reading the newspaper from cover to cover. He read every word, Monday through Sunday, and he even worked the crossword puzzle. It kept him from thinking about all the what ifs.

For example, what if he and Meg hadn't fought that morning. What if he'd called her instead of leaving that stupid note. Or, and this was the biggest what if of all, what if he hadn't gone on that damned business trip.

Maybe he and Meg would have talked, really talked for the first time in ages, and she would never have been in that park or driven into that truck . . . and she wouldn't have . . . but there his mind refused to go.

If he lived to be 500 years old and became king of the world, he would never forget the sight of the twisted black form they'd asked him to identify at the coroner's office. That couldn't have been his Meg. It couldn't have been.

What if, what if, what if spun through his mind. So many

things he would have changed if he could have, but most of all, Ben wished he'd had the chance to tell Meg how much he loved her. There'd never been a doubt in his mind that he loved Meg, but the fact was, he hadn't even known himself how much he loved her until she was gone.

What a cliché. He thought of all the wasted times. Times he sat in front of the television alone, worked on some woodworking project in the basement alone, or went for a hike alone. All those times he could have spent with Meg. He'd thought they had all the time in the world.

His mind shied away from the fact that Meg hadn't really seemed to want to spend a lot of time with him. He should have tried harder, that's all.

Ben threw the mail on the kitchen counter, not realizing how hard he tossed it down until several envelopes slid straight across the counter and fell to the floor. Sighing, he bent to retrieve them and tossed them back onto the counter, grabbing the one on top, ripping it open, and pulling out a bill. A movement at the back door caught his eye, and he looked up startled.

A smiling Carly stood outside, a covered dish in one hand, a stack of papers in the other. He closed his eyes, letting the bill drop back down onto the counter. Company was the last thing he needed or wanted. He took a deep breath and opened his eyes again. He strode over to the door and pulled it open.

"Hello Carly. You didn't have to bring those papers over tonight. I was planning on stopping by and picking them up in the morning."

"No problem, Boss Man. Here you go."

She handed the papers to him and looked around the kitchen, gesturing gracefully with the covered dish she held in one hand.

"Hey, where can I put this? I figure you haven't probably been cooking much for yourself, so I brought you some dinner. It's just cold chicken salad and rolls. But I baked a chocolate cake and put in a big slice of that too."

"That's really thoughtful of you, Carly. Thank you. I'll enjoy it later."

Ben took the papers and dish from her and stood there waiting for her to go.

She ignored his not-so-subtle hint and wriggled her shapely butt up onto one of the counter stools. Her skirt was so short that seated as she was, he could see a whole lot more of her than he wanted to. In fact, between the very short black skirt and the very low-cut red sweater, Carly had more skin showing than she had covered. A golden unicorn horn hung from a fine gold chain around her neck. As she leaned forward, it disappeared in the cleft between her breasts. Ben moved to the other side of the counter, pointedly looking at his watch.

"Whew, it's so hot outside." She waved her hand back and forth in front of her face.

Ben shifted from one foot to the other. He didn't know what to say to get her to leave, but he really didn't feel good about having her in his house. He opened his mouth, but before he could say anything, the telephone rang.

Carly spun on her stool and reached across to pluck up the telephone from the built-in desk behind her. Irritated, Ben stood there watching her.

"Hello? Hello, who is this? Hello?" Carly turned with a puzzled smile toward Ben and clicked the telephone off, dropping it back into its cradle. "Must have been a wrong number. Oh Ben, you look so tired. If there's anything I can do to help you, anything at all, let me know. You've got to be so lonely here by yourself."

"I'm just lonely for Meg," said Ben stiffly.

Carly frowned briefly, but then she smiled.

"Well, of course you are. You were such a good husband. I have to tell you, though, Ben, I don't know how you stayed so positive all the time. Meg wasn't around much, was she? So, you must have been pretty lonely before too, weren't you?"

Ben averted his face. He said nothing. Carly looked down at the countertop, her eyes focusing on the bill he'd opened. She gasped.

Startled, Ben turned to look at her.

"Oh God, Ben, I'm so sorry. I didn't know. No wonder you're so upset."

"What are you talking about?" Ben reached for the letter, his eyes scanning the small print, the color in his face fading to a muddy gray. "Oh my God."

"You didn't know? Meg didn't tell you she was pregnant. Oh Ben, I'm really sorry."

Ben's eyes met Carly's, but even though he opened his mouth, no words came out. After a moment, Carly looked down and started tracing her forefinger on the green countertop.

"Ben, I know this isn't the right time to tell you how I feel, but I think you already know. I tried to tell you in the note I gave you the other day. I guess what I'm trying to say is that I'm sorry Meg is gone, but life goes on, you know? You're still alive, and you need someone who loves you."

She tilted her face toward Ben, eyes wide, mouth trembling a little. Oh shit, he needed this like he needed four flat tires.

Carly's eyes filled with tears. "Ben, I really care about you, and I think you care about me too. That night last month, when I fell and sprained my ankle? You drove me home and carried me inside. You were so strong and gentle, and I could tell you cared about me, but you were being a gentleman because of Meg. I know I shouldn't have sent you that note. I know I shouldn't have, but I wanted you to know how I felt. Besides everything's different now. Meg's gone. I know it's too soon to talk about us, but Ben, I just want you to know that I'll wait until you're ready. I will."

Carly's words echoed through Ben's mind. Everything is different now. Meg's gone. No. No way could he accept the fact that he'd never see Meg again. Never hold her, argue with her, or laugh with her about all the things that used to strike them both as so funny.

Ben looked at Carly. No doubt about it, she was as pretty as a rose in the morning sun, but he felt nothing when he looked at her. Absolutely nothing. An image of Meg filled his mind. Small, feisty, exasperating, passionate, and ready to do battle against anything that got in the way of what she believed. He opened his mouth to respond to Carly, but not one appropriate word came into his mind.

Seeming to take his silence for some sort of acceptance, Carly slid off the stool and moved around the counter to stand in front of him. She wound her arms around his waist and rested her head on his shoulder.

Horrified, Ben started to move away from her as a breeze drifted through the kitchen window, catching a few strands of Carly's hair and blowing them softly against his face. Her hair smelled of lemon and flowers. Meg's hair smelled the same. He closed his eyes and breathed in deeply. For just a moment, he pretended it was Meg leaning against him.

Ben straightened, pushing Carly away. "Carly, I need you to leave. Now. Please."

She backed up, her lips trembling into a soft smile. "Okay, Ben. I understand. Call me, okay?"

At that point, Ben would have promised her a lake cottage on the moon if she'd just leave. "Okay Carly, I'll call you. Take care."

He never heard her walk out the door. He never heard her drive away. All he could see was an image of Meg. All he could hear were the words they would never share about the child they would never have.

Chapter 25

Meg

A wisp of music curled up and through the window. Frank Sinatra again, singing his heart out about magic, fairy tales coming true, and laughing when your life falls apart. My mother would have loved it.

I was on the back porch leading off the studio on the third floor. Over the past few weeks, I'd replaced all the dead plants with a whole variety of green plants and bright ceramic pots that I found at Target, and so far, I hadn't killed any of them. The high, airy room at the back of my house had become my refuge, and I sat in it daily, rocking away in the old wicker rocking chair surrounded by sunlight and green, growing things. I'd intended to work on my action plan, but I caught myself humming along with Frank as the music drifted up from Jean-Louis Regnier's kitchen window.

I frowned and stopped my humming. Usually it was that darn *Live well, love deep, and give your heart* song going around and around in my head, but over the past few weeks, a whole variety of Jean-Louis's Frank Sinatra songs were mixing right in, and before I knew it, I'd find myself humming away with the oddest songs at the oddest times. It annoyed the hell out of me.

My mind drifted, as it had a tendency to do when I wasn't being especially vigilant, to thoughts of Ben. Before I could stop myself, I was in the middle of remembering the warm, humorous timbre of his voice, the way his eyes lit up with passion when we talked about anything that challenged his values, and for a moment, I swore I could smell the fragrance of his body as he lay warm and sleeping next to mine.

A forlorn little twist of a feeling curled through my stomach. Why had I thought work was so important, and why had I thrown away the time I could have spent with Ben? For a moment, I couldn't blame him for preferring Carly—just for a moment, though, because the familiar anger followed right on the tail of my melancholy.

I jerked my mind back to my current situation, trying to think of something, anything, to stifle my thoughts of Ben. The neighbors. Yeah, the neighbors were safe to think about, even though they continued to be a royal pain in the butt. My butt, to be quite specific.

I was learning far more about them, than I'd ever wanted or needed to know.

For example, I knew that Jean-Louis loved to cook. Most evenings, if I craned my neck and looked out my kitchen window, I could see him inside his own kitchen moving back and forth, as he cooked his dinner and listened to his Frank Sinatra music. I really didn't want to see him cooking his dinner, listening to Frank, or drinking his before and during dinner glasses of red wine. I wanted him to be an anonymous neighbor who minded his own business. So, unless I was feeling especially lonely, I didn't crane my neck at all.

Jean-Louis didn't seem to share my concept of an invisible good neighbor. Every single morning by the time I came downstairs, a newly cut rose—and on some days, I didn't know why, two or three waited on the back porch for me to find.

Jean-Louis left me all different colors: coral, golden yellow, lavender, white, and red, and many with striations or edgings of the other colors. At first, I'd simply ignored them, leaving them to wilt in the heat. The next day, though, another fresh rose replaced the former wilted rose, and so it went, until finally I couldn't stand to let the beautiful flowers wither from the heat, and so, I brought them in and put them in water.

Now, for the first time in my life, I always had fresh flowers on my kitchen table. I'd even started to cut big bunches of the lilacs growing in my own backyard, filling large vases with them, and putting them around the house so that I could smell their fragrance wherever I happened to be.

Okay, so I liked the flower thing. Whether I wanted to or not, I'd have to admit that Jean-Louis Regnier was affecting my life in a positive way, but only in a very small, positive way. I didn't have to talk to him or anything.

I was also learning far too much about Genna and Sylvie Johnson who shared the house on my right. They seemed to have as big an interest in me as Jean-Louis did.

I couldn't figure it out. In Stamford, I'd lived in the same house for more than five years, and I hardly knew my neighbors' names. Now, in a little more than three weeks in Minnesota, I not only knew the names of the people who lived on either side of me, I knew all the things about Jean-Louis that I've already mentioned as well as the fact that he seemed to be pretty interested in the ladies next door, or at least one of the ladies, which one I had yet to determine.

I also knew that Genna was a fantastic cook and worried not only about my eating habits, but also about those exhibited by the small boy who lived directly behind my house, across the alley.

I even knew that Sylvie had a sharp, but witty tongue, was on hiatus from something, and read anything she could get her hands on—provided it was fiction.

Genna continued to drop off food, and I ate it. Why not? I had no desire to cook, and I was getting sick and tired of an otherwise steady diet of peanut butter toast and orange juice. Besides, Genna was a fantastic cook. I was even starting to develop a taste for artificially sweetened green Jell-O with pears.

On top of my interactions with Genna and Jean-Louis, Sylvie had started to leave books for me to read. They were usually best sellers—exactly the kind of junk I loved to read, and so I did. I read every one of them and returned the books and Genna's dishes at night when they were all asleep, and there was no chance we would meet.

Of course, I left brief notes of appreciation, politely worded, but not welcoming any further contact. Both Genna and Sylvie ignored the coolness of my notes and went on with the food and books thing.

Never did any of the three, Jean-Louis, Genna, or Sylvie, try to engage me in conversation. That was good. I didn't want to know them any better than I already did.

As I rocked, I heard a young voice. I realized that the small boy who lived across the alley was crouched in his tree house talking to someone. In the past, I'd always ignored him, and he always ignored me too, bless his little heart. He was the best neighbor I had.

In spite of myself, I'd even learned more than I wanted to about the boy and his father. They appeared to live alone, the two of them. The father was so young he must have been no more than a teenager when the boy was born. Every once in a while, I'd see him out on the back porch trying to talk to the child.

Occasionally, his voice would drift across to me, and although I seldom listened or made out any of his words—I didn't want to get involved in anyone else's trouble, I had enough of my own—it was evident that he cared deeply for the boy.

It was just as evident that the boy repulsed most of his father's advances, seeming to prefer sitting by himself on the back porch or up in the tree house someone had built in a corner of the yard.

Oh well, their lives were none of my business, and why should I care?

I turned my thoughts to my own problems. For the first week, all I did was eat, sleep, and do the absolute musts like buying groceries, visiting the bank, talking to my aunt's lawyers, you know—the stuff of life.

I'd called Ben twice. The first time, that Carly person picked up. So, she'd already moved in. Nice to know he missed me. My anger grew as tall and wide as the Rocky Mountains, and I did everything I could to push any thoughts of Ben out of my mind. I called one other time so I could explain what had happened in the park that day, and I left a message. He never called me back, and so, I ate and slept some more.

At first, I ignored the orange folder sitting on the desk in the studio. I absolutely refused to get my hopes up after all these years. Finally, one night when I couldn't sleep, I picked it up and leafed through the papers inside. I found detailed reports for the past 12 months signed by that detective my aunt hired.

He'd found a contact that might have known something six months earlier, but she'd moved away, and he was tracking her as well. As I turned the pages in the folder, I thought my heart would break in two. I almost picked up the telephone and called this Reddinger character to see if he had any news.

For a few seconds, I felt a spark of hope that I hadn't felt in more years than I could remember, until I thought, it's been too long. What if he did strike gold and find the lead that would end his search—and mine. What would I say? How would I act? The memories would belong only to me, and it was far too late to begin new ones.

I put the folder down gently on top of the desk, my hand lingering on its bright orange surface. I turned my back and went about my business of sleeping and eating.

The second and third week, I made lists of my options and tried to create an action plan. I knew all about action plans. According to mine, today was the day I needed to call about the abortion. I knew that too much time was passing, and I was perilously close to missing the deadline for a first trimester abortion.

It wasn't that I had any doubt about having the abortion. It was my body after all, and I didn't want any strange creature growing inside that I'd have to spend the rest of my life worrying about. It's just that I'd been feeling so lethargic I hadn't been able to pick up the telephone. Today was the day, though. I'd written the date on my action plan.

The boy's voice intruded again on my thoughts. Irritated, I tried to shut out his voice. It didn't work.

"Information please. I need to talk to Information."

The small voice drifted across the alley, and in spite of myself, I couldn't help but listen. Sitting as high as I was on my third story back porch, I had an unrestricted view of the backyard across the alley.

Someone with a great deal of skill had built that tree house in an enormous old oak tree. It had a deck all around it, and I could see the child sitting with his legs dangling between two of the deck posts, his head leaning against the post in the middle. I looked away, but the voice kept crashing against my ears.

"Excuse me, is this the library?" A pause. "Well, could I speak to Information, please? Oh, okay, I'll wait." Another pause. "Are you Information? Oh good. Please, I have a question, and I don't know who else to ask. My question? It's well, it's . . . could you tell me what makes someone be an alcoholic? Oh, and please, could you tell me how I can help someone stop being one?"

My head turned back toward that tree house so fast, I swear my eyeballs swiveled trying to keep up.

"But I thought you were Information. No, that is, I'm sorry, but I thought if people called, you would answer their questions. Oh, well, I need to know about alcoholics. If you can't answer me, could you ask someone to call me back? My name is Pete, and my phone number is 612-555-0125." The small voice sounded proud that he could recite his telephone number. "You don't . . . but couldn't you . . ."

The boy stopped talking all of a sudden, and it was clear that the person on the other end had hung up. I glanced over to see that he'd pulled his legs back through the railing and dropped his head onto his knees. He looked so little.

I felt really strange all of a sudden. My stomach started to hurt, and I felt shaky and so twitchy I could barely sit still. I was also irritated that Pete had inserted himself, however unknowingly, into my life. I did not want to be involved in anyone else's problems. I had enough problems of my own.

I wrenched my thoughts back to my own issues. I'd identified a clinic that performed abortions. I didn't have a lot of discretionary money. I wanted a doctor who was good, not too expensive, and quick. I needed to get free of this strange invader so that I could get on with my own life.

I needed to . . . I looked up and my eyes drifted across the alley again, and just like that my thoughts skidded back to Pete and his question. My stomach started roiling, and I had an itch to do something.

For the life of me, I couldn't figure out what was going on in my head, but I was clear about one thing. I was pissed off. Couldn't they at least have listened to the kid and tried to answer his question? What was the matter with people? I jumped to my feet and walked into the house. I picked up the portable telephone where I'd left it in the studio and marched right back out to see the boy named Pete still sitting all hunched over in his tree house.

Oh shit, I thought. I don't even like kids. What am I doing? My brain was thinking one thing, but my hands were not paying any attention to my brain. They just pumped nine numbers into the telephone—why did I remember that number so clearly? Within a second, I could hear the ringing of the telephone as it lay on the deck next to the boy. His head came up, and he stretched out his hand for the telephone.

"Hello?" he said in a cautious little voice.

It was odd, like a lopsided stereo really. I could hear his voice drifting across the alley and my backyard, and I could hear it a bit louder in the ear I had pressed to the receiver. My brain tried to ask me what I was doing one more time, but before I could listen to it,

I spoke briskly into the telephone.

"Hello, is this Pete?"

I could see the small figure straighten up as he answered. "Uh huh, this is Pete. Pete Kazmarik."

"Well, hello, Pete. This is Information. You called me a bit earlier, but I was on my break and just got back. I understand you have a question. I'd be happy to try to give you an answer."

"Yes, I do. I do have a question." I could hear the excitement in the child's voice.

I closed my eyes, wondering again what I was hoping to accomplish. I didn't know the first thing about talking to children. I had no training in what to say or how to say it. Besides, what was I hoping to tell the kid about alcoholism that would help him at all?

My own experience with the alcoholic adults my mother knew had changed my life. At that moment, I could think of nothing that was appropriate to tell a little kid. Nothing except wait, eventually, you'll grow up and you can escape. Big help, huh?

So, I hung up. Just like that. I hung up on the poor kid, because I didn't know how to answer the question I knew he was going to ask.

"No, wait, don't hang up," I could hear the tears in his voice, and even across the distance that divided us, I could tell he was crying. No, that's wrong. He wasn't just crying, he was sobbing, big time, and it was my fault. It would have been better if I'd never called him back in the first place. Never given him any hope that someone would listen to his problems.

I closed my eyes tight and pressed my lips together. I lifted the telephone again and dialed.

I could see Pete snatch up the telephone. "Yes," he gulped through his tears. "Is this Information?"

I cleared my throat. "Sorry about that Pete. I accidentally disconnected the telephone."

"Oh that's okay. I don't mind." He laughed in a jerky kind of way. "Please, can you tell me what makes someone be an alcoholic?"

"Yes, I'll try," I said trying to feel my way along. "But first, can you tell me why you're asking?"

"Sure," his voice dropped to a whisper. "You see, the other day my dad was talking to my Aunt Rita? He said that my mom ran out on us a long time ago, but that's wrong. I know my mom didn't run away, because, she told me my dad made her leave. She told me that more than once. But my Dad told my Aunt Rita it was better my mom ran away. He said that having no mother at all was better than having an alcoholic raising me."

Pete started to talk fast, and I could hear the tears in his voice. "Only, the thing is? I want to see her so bad. Sometimes, she calls and says she's coming. Only she never does, and now when I think of my Mom, I can hardly remember her face, anymore. Maybe it's my fault my Mom's an alcoholic? Maybe it's my fault she doesn't love me anymore."

Well shit. How do you answer those kinds of questions? I took a deep breath, wondering what I'd gotten myself into, but knowing that I was into it and there was no getting out. So, I gave it all I had.

"Well, it sounds like you want to know if somehow you did something to make your mom an alcoholic."

Oh, good Meg, I thought, here you have a kid who's telling you gut-wrenching stuff about his alcoholic mother, and you respond like some old dried-up therapist. I rolled my eyes in disgust. Pete didn't seem to notice anything lacking in my response, though, because he tried to answer my question.

"Uh huh, and if I did do something wrong, how can I fix it so she'll love me again and come back home?"

I scrunched my eyes shut and started to talk without thinking too hard about what I was going to say before I said it.

"Well, Pete, I don't think it works that way. I wish it were that easy, but it's not. You see, alcoholics are sort of sick. They drink too much beer or wine or other alcohol. They don't mean to drink so much, but they do. The really hard part is that when they drink, they don't always act like themselves. They might run away, or they might say mean things that aren't even true. They don't mean to say those things. Do you understand?"

"I, I'm not sure," Pete responded, hesitation in his words and more tears in his voice.

"Well, Pete, they can't seem to help it. I don't know why; that's just how it is. The most important thing to remember, though, is that it is never, ever, ever, anyone else's fault that person is an alcoholic. They are the only ones who can make the decision to drink or not to drink. The other important thing for you to know is that you didn't do anything, *anything*, to make your mom an alcoholic. This is really important for you to understand. Am I making any sense to you, Pete?"

Shit, how could he understand when I didn't even understand as an adult how this alcoholic thing worked?

"Maybe," said Pete doubtfully as he tried to digest the torrent of words I'd hurled at him. "Do you mean that maybe my mom does love me, but she's sick?"

"Yes, that's exactly what I mean, Pete," I said relieved. Leave it to a kid to cut right through all the crap. Maybe kids weren't as dim as I'd always thought. "Are you her only son?"

"Uh huh, and she's my only mom."

I smiled in spite of myself. "Well, you know something, Pete?"

"No, what?"

"Here's what I think. Your mom loves you a lot. I think maybe she's sick and can't help drinking so much."

"Really?" Pete's voice was so filled with hope, that I was ashamed of myself. I was playing God. Shame on me. Of course, that didn't stop me, not one single bit.

"Yep. The more I think about it, the more I'm absolutely sure. So that's one thing you don't have to worry about anymore."

"Do you think she lied? I mean about my dad making her leave?"

"Well, let me ask you a question before I answer yours. About your dad. What is he like?"

Pete paused for a minute, obviously taking my question very

seriously. "He's tall. He has brown eyes like me, and his hair is the same color too. He's really strong, the strongest person in the whole world, I think. He works really hard, and I know he gets tired a lot, and . . . and I guess he's kind of old, maybe 28 or something like that."

Again, I smiled. I couldn't help it. Reality from a child's perspective can really make one humble, don't you think? "Does your dad tell you the truth about things?"

"Oh yeah," and I heard a smile in Pete's voice. "He's always telling me that I should never lie." He paused. "Hey, maybe you're right. Maybe my mom told a lie because she's sick like you said. Maybe it's not my fault." The relief in his voice was so thick I could have cut it into squares and served it up to company on a china plate.

"Well, Pete. In a way, I think you're lucky. It sounds like your mom has some problems, but it also sounds like she really loves you. It also sounds like you have a really good dad. How lucky can a kid get?" I was exhausted. This was hard work. "Look, I've got to go now. You have a good day, okay?"

"Wait, Information, please wait. Can I call you again sometime if I have another question?"

The damnedest words came out of my mouth before I could stop them.

"Of course you can. I work in the afternoon, about 3:00 or so. Here, let me give you another number to call." I watched as he pulled what looked like an old pen out of his pocket and wrote down the number I recited on his hand.

"Thank you, Information. Thank you." Pete hung up the telephone and wrapped both arms around himself in a hug.

"Pete, Pete, where are you? I have something to show you. Hey, Pete?"

I glanced away from Pete in time to see his dad come through the door and out into the back yard, a hint of worry in his voice. In his arms, a tiny golden fluff of a puppy wriggled, trying to get free.

"Dad, here I am," yelled Pete in response, leaping to his feet.

"Look at me." He grabbed a rope dangling from a branch above his head and slid to the ground.

The man looked surprised at the exuberance in the child's voice, and an enormous smile lit his face.

"Hey Pete, look what I've brought you."

He set the pup down, and it leapt like a rabbit here and there, rolling on his back with all four paws in the air. Then, spotting the boy as he stood with his mouth wide open, the puppy leapt over to check him out.

"He's a golden retriever puppy, and he's six weeks old."

"Oh Dad, is he ours?"

"He's yours. I think given the fact that you're almost nine years old, you need a special friend. You've got to feed him, brush him, and take care of him every day. If you do, he'll be your best friend for life."

"My best friend," said Pete, dropping to sit cross-legged in the grass and reaching out his arms to the pup gamboling about him on short, stubby legs. "I'll take good care of you, puppy, I promise."

Reaching the boy, the pup jumped into his lap, and putting his paws on Pete's chest, his tongue came out to lick any part of the child it could reach. Pete giggled, but he didn't push the puppy away.

"Oh Dad, thank you. I love him. What's his name?"

"Well, I guess that's up to you. Think you can come up with something really good?" Pete's young father sank down next to him, and then the three of them, man, boy, and puppy, rolled all over the grass together.

My heart twisted, and I couldn't stand to sit there and watch anymore. So, I got up and went inside to make a cup of tea. It wasn't until later that night, as I was getting ready for bed that I remembered I'd forgotten to call about the abortion. Tomorrow. I'd do it tomorrow.

Chapter 26

Genna

Genna, come here, you're not going to believe this." Sylvie burst through the kitchen door waving frantically and dashed back out to the porch where she'd been sitting with Jean-Louis having coffee.

Genna pressed her lips together. No way was she going to go outside and disrupt the first real conversation the two of them had had alone. It had taken her quite a bit of maneuvering to make it happen in the first place because Sylvie was harder to pin down than a lightning bug flying free in the June night sky, but that's what big sisters were for. Genna knew that if Sylvie would just hold still for a few minutes and get to know him she'd fall in love with Jean-Louis. All anyone had to do was look into his eyes and hear the warmth in his voice to know what a special person he was.

"Sylvie, you and Jean-Louis enjoy your coffee. I need to finish making these varenyky while the dough is fresh," Genna called, rolling out a batch of dough and cutting it into small perfect circles that she planned to fill with savory mashed potatoes, cheese, and onions sautéed in butter. She'd gotten the recipe from a Ukrainian friend, and it was one of Sylvie's favorites.

"Genna, get your butt out here, and hurry up or you're going to miss this," hissed Sylvie. "The varenyky can wait, and this can't. You were right, and I was wrong."

Startled, Genna turned to the sink and washed her hands. Whatever was going on, this she had to see. Sylvie rarely admitted to being wrong.

Moving out onto the back porch, she smiled at the sight of Sylvie and Jean-Louis sitting together. They made such a lovely couple. Sylvie sat curled up in the white wicker rocking chair, small bare feet tucked up beneath her. Jean-Louis, seated across the table, had his chin propped against the knuckles of his left hand, his eyes crinkled with the smile that turned his face into one you could feel good looking at all day long.

Genna realized she was staring at him, and that he was smiling right back at her. She looked away immediately, uncomfortable with the funny little curl of warmth unfolding in her belly. She blinked hard.

"The two of you look so natural sitting here together," she said finally taking a breath. "You should see how comfortable you look."

"Shhhhh, listen," Sylvie dramatically pointed one slender rose-tipped finger up toward the porch at the back of Meg's house. Meg's voice, filled with hesitation, drifted clearly down.

"Well, it sounds like you want to know if somehow you did something to make your mom an alcoholic."

"Uh huh, and if I did do something wrong, how can I fix it so she'll love me again and come back home?"

Genna hearing the small voice answer the question, opened her eyes wide in confusion. She sank down into another of the wicker chairs, carefully folding the linen dishtowel she carried and laying it aside on the arm of her chair.

Sylvie pointed with a silent flourish to the yard across the alley, and Genna, seeing the tree house in the corner of the yard and the small boy sitting high in the tree, realized that they were listening in on a telephone conversation between Meg and Peter.

Genna's lips curved into a lopsided smile. Suddenly, she felt Jean-Louis's eyes fix on her, but that bizarre warm curl made its presence known to her again, and she refused to meet his eyes. Lately, it seemed as though she felt strange whenever he looked at her. She didn't know why, but she wasn't sure she liked the feeling at all. Her personal feelings did nothing to push Sylvie and Jean-Louis together at all.

Sylvie leaned over and said in a low voice, "You were right Genna. Meg isn't the total egomaniac I thought she was. There may be more to her than meets the eye."

"Well, of course there is. She's in pain and lonely. She has her reasons I'm sure for behaving the way she does, and all she needs are some people in her life who care about her," said Genna with a spark in her eye.

She looked up to see Jean-Louis's eyes on her again. He smiled at her, one corner of his mouth curving up in his own lopsided grin. Her stomach did the funny shimmy-and-shake thing again and to cover it up, Genna folded her arms tight across her midsection.

"Oh yes, you have it exactly right, I think," said Jean-Louis, his eyes never leaving Genna's. "Our Meg just needs some friends, eh? That is the way of the world, is it not? We all need someone to care about and who will care for us as well. How else would we learn and grow ourselves?"

Sylvie, intent on the conversation going on above her head, didn't respond, but Genna, her face coloring furiously, finally met Jean-Louis's eyes, and she nodded with a grave smile.

Chapter 27

Genna

Is it three o'clock yet? Hurry up with the coffee, will you Genna? Hurry up, or we're going to miss today's call."

Sylvie was already out the door. Her long lavender skirts swished as she headed for the wicker table to get a ring-side view of both Meg and Pete as they went through their daily telephone ritual.

"Sylvie you are so bad, spying on Meg and that poor boy every day, and so are you, Jean-Louis. What's worse, I shudder at myself for going along with the both of you," said Genna as she unplugged the percolator and set it on the tray along with a freshly baked angel food cake.

She planned to leave a large piece of the cake on Meg's porch later that day with some fresh strawberries. Angel food cake was something that fit into a diabetic diet, she'd discovered.

"Jean-Louis, go ahead and join Sylvie. I'll be there in a minute. I need to put some strawberries and whipped cream in a dish for us."

"Ah, but I am becoming quite addicted to your cooking. And

so, me, I think I will wait right here for the strawberries and whipped cream so that I can be sure that you put enough of each into the bowl." Jean-Louis patted his flat stomach and made no move to join Sylvie on the porch. Instead, he moved closer to Genna and reached for the heavy tray. "Allow me, Genevieve, this tray is too heavy for you."

As always, Jean-Louis pronounced her name Jshahnavieve with a soft "j" sound rather than the harder, plainer Geneveeve that Genna had deplored her entire life. His hands brushed against her own as he grasped the tray, and Genna could feel the warmth of his skin. She looked the other way, bright color staining her cheeks. Embarrassed and self-conscious, she struggled to think of something to say.

"My name sounds so different when you say it that way." Her cheeks grew brighter still at the breathless sound of her voice. "I've always thought I had the plainest, most boring name on earth. When I was small, I believed that Sylvie and I were appropriately named. She is so pretty, and so is her name. Don't you think so?"

Jean-Louis smiled, but said nothing.

Genna rattled on. "Sylvie's name sounds like something a wood sprite would be named. And my name, when it's pronounced the English way, Geneveeve, sounds like a great big country woman's name, which when you come right down to it, does fit me, doesn't it." Genna laughed without a hint of self-deprecation whatsoever and didn't notice that Jean-Louis did not join in her laughter. "When you pronounce my name in the French way, though, it sounds almost beautiful."

"Ah, but that is because it is a beautiful name. Genevieve is a French name, and most people here in the United States do not know how to properly pronounce it. Jshahnavieve . . . listen to how beautiful your name is, Mademoiselle."

Spoken in Jean-Louis's deep voice, Genna thought that her name did seem beautiful and exotic, and for a moment, she felt beautiful and quite unlike herself, which was probably the reason she responded even more briskly than she usually did.

"Well, that's fine, but you'd better get that coffee out to the porch or Sylvie will be in here telling us to hurry it up again. The idea of it," she fussed. "Eavesdropping on the neighbors."

"Our Meg, though, we agreed she needs just a little help."

"I know. She does need someone to help her, and she's got us to watch over her, even if she doesn't know or accept it yet."

Genna kept talking as she set cream and silverware on the tray, thinking all the while about how easy it was to talk to Jean-Louis. He always seemed so interested in whatever anyone had to say, she thought, even her.

"Oh Jean-Louis, I wish you could have known Meg's mother. I owe this to Peggy. To help her daughter, I mean. I don't know all the things that Meg has been through, but I've never seen such loneliness in anyone's eyes before. She needs good food, she needs some friends, and she needs something to focus on besides herself."

"Ah yes, I agree with you completely. Me, I think that young Peter is a good thing for Meg." As he spoke, Jean-Louis's eyes never left Genna's face.

Realizing that he was holding one side of the tray, while she still had her hands on the other side, Genna gave a self-conscious little laugh. "Oh, my. Forgive me. I'm not really paying attention to what I am doing."

Jean-Louis's eyes twinkled as he hoisted the tray. "After you, eh Mademoiselle? Let's go find out what the question of the day is, shall we?"

Genna's heart skipped, and she felt as though she were sixteen years old again. "Look at us. Three old creatures, listening in on someone else's business instead of just minding our own."

"Ah, yes, but the world is so very much larger than just our three lives, eh?"

"Pssssst, hurry up, it's starting, and you're going to miss it," Sylvie whispered.

"Shall we?" Jean-Louis inclined his head, balanced the tray on one hand, and followed Genna out onto the porch.

Sylvie bounced in her chair as she poured them each a cup of coffee. "I love Information Please," she said in a low voice, referring to the name she had given the daily interchange between Meg and Pete. "I need to think of a way to package this, somehow," she added in a low voice. "There's got to be some way to do it."

"Pete? Hi, how are you today?"

Meg's voice was as clear as if she were sitting on the porch with them. Pete's voice was fainter as he responded, but it was still clear enough so that both sides of the conversation were easy to follow.

On one level, Genna felt uncomfortable eavesdropping so shamelessly. On another, as Sylvie pointed out, they were sitting on their very own back porch, more or less minding their own business. If they were able to overhear a neighbor through no extra work or machination on their parts, well why not?

Greetings over, Pete was ready to launch into his question.

"I have a really important question today," he said simply.

"Go for it," responded Meg. "I'll try to have a really important answer."

"Okay. If you're ready, here's my question. A lot of people believe in God, right?"

"Uh, yes, that's true. A lot of people do believe in God."

Genna could hear a startled note in Meg's voice. Good, she thought to herself, gray eyes gleaming. We all need to be startled out of our comfort zone sometimes. She suspected that Meg had always worked hard to create a safe, predictable world that hummed along just the way she wanted it to. Genna also suspected that something had recently destroyed Meg's carefully controlled world, and she hadn't yet found her balance.

Take her conversations with Pete as an example. He had a way of asking questions that didn't necessarily fit into Meg's neat and tidy world, and it was clear from the tone of her voice that she didn't always have a ready answer.

Still, Genna thought to herself, she had to give Meg credit. She always worked hard to provide an answer, one that a child could understand. That's when Genna could hear an echo of Peggy Lofgren's warmth and vitality in her daughter's otherwise cool, unemotional voice. Jean-Louis caught her eye, smiling at her in a conspiratorial sort of way.

The tingle she always felt when Jean-Louis was around did its thing, but she was not only getting comfortable with the feeling, she was beginning to like it.

Pete continued. "I don't just mean a lot of people, you know, like thousands, though. I mean a lot, like all over the world. You know, millions and millions and kazillions of people believe in God, right?"

This time Meg didn't hesitate at all. "Well, yes, that's true, Pete. In different cultures and places, people have different names for God, but you're right, around the world an awful lot of people do believe in their God."

"Okay, so here's my question." Pete's voice was excited, and maybe a little bit scared. "Last night I was laying in my bed staring out the window? The sky was so dark, except for some sprinkly stars, you know, and the moon wasn't around anywhere. So, I got to thinking, just thinking—I'm not saying I believe this or anything—but I got to thinking, what if . . . what if everyone is wrong. About there being a God, I mean."

Silence. The seconds ticked by. Sylvie leaned back in her customary rocking chair, sapphire eyes dancing as she fixed them unwaveringly on the porch above them. Jean-Louis's gaze was also fixed on the porch next door, his crooked smile in place as he waited for Meg's answer.

Genna found herself staring at Jean-Louis again, and after a moment he turned his head toward her, his eyes meeting hers, and she felt that jolt of something along with some new feelings as well. Recognition? Friendship? Genna blinked. She blinked again. Unsettled, she took a sip of coffee, turning away from the strange look in Jean-Louis's eyes and focused on the porch.

"Information? Please, are you there?"

They could hear Meg clear her throat. "Yes, I'm here, Pete. It's just that you asked such an important question, and I'm trying to think of a good answer. You are very good at asking hard questions, you know."

The child chuckled. "Well, I think you're pretty good at giving answers. So, what do you think? What if everyone is wrong?"

"Okay. Here's the deal. This probably isn't written down in any book anywhere or anything, so I can't look it up and tell you these are the facts, okay?"

"I don't mind," said Pete in a breezy voice.

"Here's what I think. When you come right down to it, how could so many people in so many parts of the world all be wrong about the same thing? I guess I think that God is such a big thing to think about, and we're only small, small people with tiny, little brains. Do you understand what I'm trying to say?"

Meg's voice sounded a little desperate, Genna thought fondly, confident that Meg was doing a fine job in answering the child's question.

"I think so," said Pete slowly. "It's kind of like the X-Files, right? Mulder doesn't always know the answers, but he always keeps looking for the truth even though sometimes really weird things happen and Scully has to help him figure things out."

"Uh, right," said Meg, confusion evident in her voice. Another silence.

"Information, are you still there?"

"Yes, Pete, I'm still here. Let's try the answer to your question this way. Have you ever looked up at the sky, or smelled all the green smells of summer—you know, like freshly cut grass and flowers, or maybe you just felt so good you wanted to run until you're out of energy?"

"I think so. When my Mom didn't come to see me, a couple of weeks ago? I felt so bad. I went to bed, and when I couldn't sleep, I kept staring up at the sky and the stars and the moon, and after a while, I didn't feel so alone anymore. Is that what you mean?"

"Yeah, that's exactly what I mean. I guess the way I look at it is that there is so much going on in the universe, and I can't possibly understand it all. Sometimes it feels like there's someone, watching over me, though. That's when I just *know* there has to be something much greater than any one of us in this world. And, I know that it's okay if I don't have a picture of what that something or somebody looks like. It's enough to know that I'm never alone. It makes me feel safe and loved."

Pete laughed out loud. "Thank you. I like that answer. Oh, oh, my puppy's trying to climb down out of the tree house by himself. I gotta go. I'll talk to you tomorrow, okay?"

"Yes, definitely okay. You take care of yourself, Pete."

"I will. Goodbye."

Sylvie let out a deep breath. "I love hearing the question of the day, don't you?"

"Well, I have to admit, Pete is a good thinker. I couldn't come up with half the questions he does."

"Ah, me? I believe the questions are the easy part. It's the answers our Meg comes up with that enchant me," said Jean-Louis.

"Well," said Sylvie, a satisfied look on her face. "I need to find some way to get Meg's gift promoted. What do you think? A column maybe? A telephone line? Think, Genna, think. You're the one with all the local contacts."

"Yes, I am, and right now we need to leave Meg alone. She's healing from something, and even though I don't know what it is, I do know that she needs time and distance from her problems," said Genna her voice serene. "You leave her alone for now, Sylvie. Promise?"

Sylvie crossed her arms over her chest and looked at Jean-Louis for support.

He raised his hands palms up in a gesture of surrender. "Don't look at me, Mademoiselle. I think Genevieve is right. Let's give Meg some time."

Genna colored again at the sound of her name on Jean-Louis's lips. Sylvie looked from one to the other, and one of her brilliant smiles broke out across her face.

"Well, we'll see. I promise not to bother her, at least for a while."

Chapter 28

Meg

My first thought upon waking was that today was the day. Every muscle in my body tensed for a moment beneath the warm covers, until I took a deep breath and forced myself to relax. No way was I going to back out of this abortion because I was afraid of a little pain. I grimaced, and laughed an ugly, bitter little bark.

I wasn't just afraid. I was terrified and confused, but I hadn't been able to unravel how I felt about anything going on in my life these past few weeks. Why should this one issue be any different?

I'd been able to get a referral from the clinic that helped me with my foot. I'd already gone in for the counseling session and examination. The doctor explained that I was right on the edge of my first trimester and if I was sure about moving forward, I needed to schedule the abortion without delay. Today was the day.

I rolled over so that I could see the clock. 7:00 a.m. I had an hour and a half to get myself up, ready, and to the clinic. The sun was shining through the window. So, no sign of clouds or rain today, the day that I was going to snuff out a life. Snuff out a life—how horrible—it made me sound like a murderer. Only I wasn't.

My body belonged to me, didn't it? What I was having the most trouble with was the gap between my philosophical beliefs and my emotions. I didn't want the pregnancy to continue, and God knows I didn't want a child. I'd never wanted a child. Ever.

On the other hand, I'd had a lot of time to think over the past few weeks. I'd had one recurring emotion that on my good days made me squirm, and on my bad days justified my decision a hundred-fold. The emotion? Grief. Grief that Ben didn't even know about this child. After all, it was his child, too.

I would justify my decision to abort by telling myself that I'd always been completely open and honest with Ben about never wanting children. The problem was that although he said he understood, I knew he had never stopped hoping that I would change my mind. He would have been so excited about this pregnancy.

As I said, on the days I didn't want to take out a contract on Ben to break both his kneecaps and pull out all the Carly person's hair, I felt a strange sense of grief that I could not understand. I was convinced the grief was for Ben, the lying, cheating son-of-a-bitch. Then, I'd find myself reaching for my stomach with a gentle hand to see if I could feel the tiny life that was inside.

Of course, I never did feel anything because it was too early. The only signs I was even pregnant were the awful nausea that rousted me from bed in the morning and the unexpected tenderness in my breasts.

I'd avoided going to the library to read up on my condition, so I guess I didn't really know what to expect anyway. Why bother with any research? The pregnancy was short-term only. I closed my eyes waiting for the familiar nausea to hit me, surprised that I hadn't already made my usual dash to the bathroom.

Nothing. Odd in a black humor sort of way that the very day I was going to end this little creature's life, he was starting to behave. He or she? I wondered which it was.

I groaned. I didn't need all these strange thoughts going through my head.

I'd had the oddest dream, all jumbled up and inhabited by people I didn't know, except for one. Pete was in my dream. I liked Pete. I liked him a lot. I'd really started to look forward to my 3:00 calls. Pete never failed to entertain me, not to mention challenging the bejeebers out of me with his questions. In the dream, he kept asking me if the baby had done something to make me mad and if that was why I was going to kill it. I shuddered. The dream had seemed so real.

I thought about his question from the day before. What if we all believed in God, and we were all wrong. What he was really asking, of course, was if God existed. I thought about my theological beliefs for a moment. How could a supposedly good God let bad things happen to good people? I shook my head. Leave it to Pete to get me to examine my own feelings about God. I'd never articulated them out loud before, but all of a sudden I was feeling relaxed and at peace, for the first time in weeks.

Suddenly thoughts of the abortion curdled through me like spoiled milk. I was going to kill a baby. No, I was going to kill my baby. Although, it wasn't officially a baby yet, right? Officially, it was just a fetus. I ignored the haunting thought that after today, it wouldn't even be that.

Sighing, but determined, I rolled out of bed to get ready for whatever the day would bring.

I was in the kitchen with my usual peanut butter toast, coffee, and orange juice when the telephone rang. I took a swallow of juice and reached for the telephone.

"Hello?"

"Information, please are you there?"

"Yes, Pete, it's me." He choked, his voice filled with tears, and my heart started hammering. "What's wrong, Pete? Talk to me."

"I need help. Joey, he's hurt, and I don't know what to do. Help me, please, help me. He's going to die, and it will be my fault."

Pete was sobbing so hard I could barely make out his words. I was already out on the back porch, and I could see the puppy rolling and thrashing on the grass in the yard across the alley. I wondered if someone had thrown poisoned food over the fence.

"Hang on Pete. I'll be right there." I didn't stop to think. I didn't hesitate. I dropped my peanut butter toast and ran.

Pete didn't seem to be surprised at all that Information turned out be his backyard neighbor. He opened the gate and pointed at Joey, tears streaming down his face, his shoulders shaking.

"I just gave him a bone. Dogs like bones, right? What happened? I don't know what to do. Please, please don't let him die."

The child's face was full of anguish and fear, and his fear shot through my body in a surge of adrenalin that was unlike anything I'd ever felt before. Pete didn't need any more trouble in his life. I was going to help him no matter what.

I reached the puppy, and I could see that he was thrashing and whimpering as he pawed furiously at his muzzle. What's going on, I thought, and knelt in the grass. I grabbed the small creature, pulling him closer until I could see exactly what the trouble was.

Pete had given him a round bone, the type that sits in the center of a round steak filled with marrow. Evidently, the puppy had enthusiastically attacked the bone, and somehow as he gnawed and played with it, the bone had flipped over his lower jaw, and locked in place. A wave of relief poured through me.

"He's okay, Pete. Joey is feeling uncomfortable, but this isn't going to kill him. Not by a long shot."

Pete squatted down, dragging his sleeve across his eyes and nose, sniffing hard. He reached a gentle hand toward the puppy. "It's okay, Joey. Information knows everything. She can help you."

When I heard the faith and confidence in Pete's voice, my heart flipped over with a rush of feelings I'd never had before. It's true that I didn't personally know any children. How could I since I'd avoided them like the plague?

Somewhere along the line, though, Pete had become important to me. I didn't even know when it happened. Was it during that first call when he asked me about his mother? Maybe it was when he asked me to help find a name for his pup, and we decided to call him Joey, because Pete said he looked like a baby kangaroo when he jumped up all the time. Or, maybe it was just last night when he asked me about God.

My right arm left the puppy and wrapped itself around the child. I never even saw it move, it was just suddenly there around Pete hugging him tight.

"Don't worry, Honey. Joey's not really hurt, the bone is just caught around his jaw, see? We'll get it off."

Pete gulped, and I could feel his body calm. I turned back to the puppy. The little imp had done a fine job in jamming that bone tight against his jaw and behind his lower canine teeth. To compound the problem, his jaw had swelled around the bone so that I couldn't dislodge it without really hurting him. Pete and I were not going to get that bone off Joey without some help. As I picked him up, I heard the gate squeak open behind me, and I turned to see who was there.

My neighbors, Jean-Louis and Genna moved into the yard. Sylvie followed right behind them. For once, I didn't resent their intrusion.

"Perhaps, we can help," said Jean-Louis holding out his hands for the puppy.

Without hesitation, I handed Joey to him and sighed with relief. "Oh please. You can see how the bone is clamped tight around his jaw. We're going to need to cut it loose, and we can't do it without some extra hands. Thank you. Thank you so much for coming to help us."

Genna moved forward and reached a large gentle hand toward the puppy. "What do you think, Jean-Louis, a small saw? I have one we can use, and if we wrap this scamp up tight in a towel, and Pete helps to hold him, I think we can cut the bone off without hurting him at all."

I backed away. Pete and the puppy were in good hands. I turned to go home, but before I could take a step, Pete reached for my hand.

"Please don't go. I need you."

That's all he said, and yet those three little words tethered me to that place in the universe as surely as the strongest steel cable. I need you. For a moment, every cell in my body rebelled against Pete's words. I didn't want anyone to need me. Ever.

Then, like fog in a strong breeze, the bad feelings just blew away. How long had it been since anyone needed me, really needed me? I don't mean needed me to do a job, but just plain needed my company. Another thought followed swiftly. When had I ever let anyone need me? Yet another thought bit through me. Why would anyone have wanted my company? All I ever talked about was work.

My thoughts turned to Ben. Was that why he'd turned to someone else? Was he just lonely? I pushed the thought away, not forever, but for later when I was alone. Now, Pete needed me. We had a job to do and a puppy to fix.

"En avant, mes amis," said Jean-Louis, leading the way. "This young puppy is in a great deal of discomfort."

Without another word, we all turned and trooped our way over to Genna's house. As we entered her kitchen, I looked around, enveloped by bright light, the smell of good home cooking, and pretty touches like the blue and green place mat centered on the pine kitchen table. On top of the mat, pewter candlesticks with yellow tapers flanked a green glass vase filled with what had to be Jean-Louis's flame-colored roses.

Genna took over. She disappeared into the back of the house, returning shortly with a large yellow towel. She handed the towel to Jean-Louis who firmly swaddled the struggling pup in its terrycloth folds.

Genna rummaged around in a drawer beneath one of her counters until she found a small u-shaped saw with a thin blade. She sat down and reached for the pup. Jean-Louis handed him over, taking the saw from her hand, and gently pushing Pete into place so that the child could rest a small comforting hand on the puppy's side.

"Ah now, Genevieve," he said sending the loveliest smile in her direction and kneeling by her side, "are you ready?"

"Absolutely," she said bending her silver head over the writhing pup. "Gently now, gently. Pete, be careful you don't get into Jean-Louis's way, Honey, okay? We don't want him to slip and accidentally cut Joey—or you—with the saw."

The child nodded, never taking his eyes off the puppy.

It was over in a few minutes, the bone cut free, the puppy unwrapped and handed wriggling with all his might over to Pete. Jean-Louis sat back on his heels next to Genna and looked up into her face.

Loneliness bit me like a poison spider. Ben. All thoughts but one disappeared from my mind. Oh no, my appointment. I looked at my watch to see that I was thirty minutes late. Where had the time gone? What was I going to do now?

"What's wrong, Meg? Are you late for something? I wouldn't worry if I were you. You can explain what happened," said Sylvie, her eagle eyes locked on my face.

I frowned. Nothing was private with these neighbors of mine, but no way did I intend to share any information about my appointment.

Sylvie kept talking in her breezy way. "After all, when you come right down to it, what could have been more important than rescuing a puppy in distress? So, just ask yourself what I do when something goes wrong. I just ask myself, 'Well, Sylvie, did any babies die?' Because no babies ever do die, of course, and so I always figure that whatever it is I did, it can't be all that bad."

"Sylvie, not now," said Genna watching me.

I could feel the blood draining away from my head to somewhere south of my ankles, and I knew I had to be turning white. Without warning, I started to laugh. Once I started, I couldn't stop.

Yes, I wanted to tell Sylvie, you figured it out. Because I missed my appointment, no babies will die. I laughed harder and harder.

Every time I started to calm down, a bubble of laughter would spiral up from my stomach and I'd take off again, certain my neighbors thought I was crazy.

I looked around at the four faces in front of me, searching for signs of disgust or scorn. Instead, I saw only concern.

Pete moved close and took my hand again. "It's okay. Joey's okay now. You did it Information, you saved him." The child completely disregarded the real help he'd gotten from Jean-Louis and Genna and stared at me with admiration in his eyes.

Genna moved over and put her arm around me. "That's okay, dear. You just let it all out. You've needed to for a while, you know. We're here for you, Meg. You don't have to pretend any longer."

Sylvie nodded vigorously.

"Oh Meg, I'm sorry I was so flippant. I didn't mean anything by what I said. I never do, my big mouth is just a bad habit. Don't be sad, okay?"

I was shocked. How did they know how I'd been feeling? I didn't even know how I was feeling. I gasped and tried to stop laughing, but that set me off again. I was embarrassed, but that didn't stop me. After all, people didn't show their emotions like this. God knows, I never did. I'd suppressed my emotions for so long, that the laughter, even if it was hysterical, felt good.

Genna guided me over to the kitchen table and pushed me into a chair. She turned to the others. "Why don't you go out on the porch, and I'll bring out some coffee and Danish in a few minutes. Pete, why don't you take Joey out into the backyard and throw a stick for him. I bet he's a good retriever. Oh look, there's your friend, Ricky. I bet he's come to collect for your latch-key program. Why don't you go tell him you're going to spend the day with us? Your dad won't mind. I'll explain things to him later."

The kitchen was empty except for the two of us. Genna put an apron on over her dress.

"Oh gosh, you were dressed up to go somewhere, weren't you?" I gasped between gales of laughter.

"Never mind. I head up the Northeast Minneapolis Meals on Wheels Program, and for once they can get along without me. It was only a committee meeting."

I was overwhelmed. By emotions, by people, by lack of air. I needed to get out of there.

"Really, I have to go. Thanks for helping. You were the one that Pete needed, not me."

"Oh my dear, that's not true," said Genna looking concerned. "You're his friend. I've heard how you talk to him on the telephone sometimes, and if you only knew how he has improved over the past few weeks. He used to be so lonely. You've become very important to him you know."

No. No, I didn't want to be important to anyone. I wanted to be left alone. My neighbors were driving me crazy. Why didn't they all just mind their own business? Maybe if I left right away, I could still get into the clinic.

I jumped to my feet, and as I stood, red fire pierced the right side of my lower stomach, and a trickle of warmth began to drip from between my legs. I doubled up, gasping in pain, not understanding what was happening. I looked up and saw Genna's kind, soft face quickly turn in my direction, and I followed her eyes down to where my feet met the floor. A small but steady stream of bloody fluid pooled around one foot.

"Mesdames, may I help with the coffee . . . ," Jean-Louis took one look at me and before I could move, he stepped forward and lifted me in his arms. "Genevieve?"

Genna whipped off her apron, grabbed her purse, and moved quickly towards the door. "Follow me. I'll drive."

Chapter 29

Ben

It is so good to have you back, Boss Man." Carly's smile lit up her entire face as Ben walked into the office.

Ben's smile was stiff. He didn't really know how to respond. Getting through each day was like struggling through a sea of hip-high Jell-O. And, the nights. The nights were the worst. He would fall asleep, and he would dream. The dreams were so real, that he swore he could smell and feel the warmth of Meg's body in his arms only to awaken and realize she was gone. That's when he would understand that the loss he felt was only the beginning of the rest of his life.

Ben took a breath and tried once again to smile at Carly. Meg's death wasn't her fault, and she had done everything she could to help him through the last few weeks.

"Thanks Carly. I appreciate all you've done, really, but . . ."

She cut him off before he could continue. "No, no thanks are necessary. We're a team you and I, remember?" She pouted for a minute. "I have to say, though, that I think it was really rotten for Gary to send you out to Colorado for three weeks in the middle of your grieving."

"I didn't mind. It was good to get away from the house. No matter what you say, though, I do want to thank you for picking up my mail and paying my bills while I was gone."

"Oh, speaking of your bills, here are the receipts and a record of totals paid."

Carly bent over and if Ben had been more observant, or interested, he might have noticed the excellent view down her blouse, which she obligingly provided him as she dug through her bottom desk drawer.

He also might have noticed, in spite of the care she took to hide her movements, that before she stood upright, she slid a Visa bill out of the file she was digging through and let it fall to the bottom of her drawer. A bill, had he had the chance to examine it, which included an airplane ticket to Minneapolis charged the night Meg supposedly died in a car accident.

Carly shoved the desk drawer shut with one foot and smiled at Ben.

"Here you go, Boss Man. Everything all neat and tidy."

Chapter 30

Meg

Life can be filled with so much irony that sometimes it takes my breath away. These were the facts of my life. Facts numbered one to three. I scheduled an abortion to end my pregnancy. I didn't want to be pregnant. I didn't want a child. Not then. Not ever. Fact number four. Before I could even make it to the appointment, I had a miscarriage. Okay, that happens. It happens to a lot of people, not just me. Besides, nature—or was it God?—simply took care of what I wanted to do myself anyway, right?

It was fact number five that threw me for a loop, though. Because the instant I believed I'd lost the baby, I knew I wanted that baby more than God wanted his people to be good.

I lay writhing in pain in Genna's car and later in the emergency room, and all I could think was, "Please God, don't let this baby die. Please, just let this baby live, and I promise I'll be good. I promise."

The bizarre things we promise when we are afraid of losing something precious. The thing that confused me the most, though, was that I hadn't thought my pregnancy was precious—not at all.

So, why all of a sudden was I so upset?

I also wanted Ben, and I was too sick to care that I wanted him. I was scared. I was lonely, and I wanted my best friend by my side so badly I thought I would choke from the wanting of it.

I lay on a narrow emergency room hospital bed, while the ER nurse checked my vitals, the IV team poked and poked until they found a vein that would accept the IV catheter, and the doctor came in to check things out.

The pain kept coming and going. About fifteen minutes into all the flurry, before the doctor could do much more than ask me one or two questions, another of the stabbing red fire pains took over. I convulsed and felt something warm slip out between my legs.

I closed my eyes, my body relaxed as the pain diminished, and I thought it's over. My baby is dead. The ER doc figured out pretty fast what was going on and tried to clear the room. Genna refused to leave my side, but Jean-Louis patted my shoulder in a clumsy way and told me he'd be in the waiting room just a call away in case I needed anything.

The doctor pulled up the heavy sheet that covered me and poked around between my legs. I didn't move. After a moment, he lifted a small wet, transparent gray-blue mass with what was clearly a tiny fetus inside, put it into a kidney-shaped plastic dish, and handed the dish to a nurse.

"Mrs. Jacobi, I'm going to take you down for an ultrasound. I'd like to see exactly what is going on in that body of yours."

"What's the point of an ultrasound now," I whispered, turning my face to the wall. "It's pretty obvious what happened isn't it?"

He patted me on the shoulder. "Bear with me. I'd like to check things out, okay?"

Someone, wheeled me down the halls and into an examining room where the doctor and a nurse waited. They hoisted my gown, squirted cold, clear gel on my belly and started moving this little mouse-like thing around in the goo while they stared at a monitor.

Genna didn't budge a muscle away from my side. I couldn't figure her out, but I have to say for once I was glad for her company. I reached up with one hand, and Genna took it in one of hers. The contact kept me centered.

I can't say the medical team wasn't efficient. They were. I can't say they didn't seem to know their stuff. They did. But, they didn't talk to me as they manipulated that stupid little mouse-like thing. They spoke to each other in technical terms that I wasn't in the mood to try and decipher.

I wanted them to acknowledge me as an individual, a person who was unique among all the other people who passed through their hospital every day. I felt like a lump of flesh with no distinguishing characteristics from all other lumps of flesh while the doctor played with his mouse gizmo. He focused on the monitor as though it were the Rosetta Stone. Finally, he spoke.

"You definitely had a miscarriage, but it wasn't absolute."

The nurse nodded as though she completely understood. I had no clue what either of them understood. I'd had a miscarriage, or I hadn't, right? Seemed pretty simple to me.

Genna was watching every expression on my face, and she spoke right up.

"I'm afraid you're going to have to be a little more explicit. The two of us aren't seeing whatever it is you're seeing on that monitor, I'm afraid."

"Look." The doctor gestured at the screen. I followed his pointing finger, but all I saw were a bunch of whorls of white on black. Seeing my confusion, he finally explained matters in language that even I could understand.

"Mrs. Jacobi, I'm sorry to have to tell you what I suspect you already know, but the news isn't as bleak as you might think."

Well, I thought. Now everything is as clear as mud.

The doctor kept talking. "You did have a miscarriage, but you were carrying twins, fraternal twins, each in its own package, so to speak. I believe the other fetus is still viable. I'm going to keep you here for a few hours and observe things, but I think you can go home later today. You're going to want to be on bed rest for at least the next thirty days, but your own doctor can give you specific details. I want you to see your doctor tomorrow if at all possible. You do have someone at home who can help you, right?"

My face felt numb. The irony of all ironies had caught up with me, and I didn't have any words at the forefront of my brain. I heard someone push the door open, and I realized that Jean-Louis had stepped into the room and was standing at Genna's side.

Genna squeezed my hand; she'd barely let go of it since we'd gotten to the hospital.

"Yes. Meg has all the help she'll need. Just tell us what to do."

Genna's voice was confident, and Jean-Louis nodded in agreement.

Part II

July-September 2001

Chapter 31

Meg

I am going to lose my mind if I don't get up out of this bed. I can't stand lying here anymore."

I kicked my feet with a whump under the warm covers, hearing the petulance in my voice and not caring enough to change my tone. I was so tired of this bed-rest thing.

"Too bad, so sad," sang Sylvie with altogether too much cheer as she plunked a lunch tray down over my lap. "You, my darling Meg, have no choice. The doctor said it was bed rest for the next month or else."

"Yeah, yeah, yeah, or else what? I'll lose the baby? Been there. Done that."

I was on a roll, and my mouth was going a mile a minute. One of the nice things I'd learned about Sylvie was that it didn't faze her if I said exactly what was on my mind.

I tried to be more careful with Genna and Jean-Louis. They didn't deserve my sarcasm. Neither did Sylvie for that matter, but since it didn't bother her, I let myself go when she was around. It was such a relief.

"Who says I want this baby? Huh?"

I hadn't been out of my bed, except to go the bathroom, for more than seven days. I'd had no privacy even in the bathroom, though, because someone was always lurking about outside to make sure I didn't need anything. My neighbors had taken over my life on a carefully rotated basis.

On one level, I was so grateful I couldn't even begin to put my thanks into words. On another level, I wished they'd all leave me alone.

Sylvie ignored my bad mood. "Well, maybe you do want this baby—and maybe you don't. Maybe you don't even know yourself what you want."

Sylvie pulled a chair over to the side of my bed and plunked down in an elegant slouch.

Another thing about Sylvie. She seemed to have the knack of stating almost verbatim what was in my mind. I found it frustrating, unsettling, and kind of comforting in a bizarre sort of way. How's that for being inconsistent?

The others all thought that I'd been devastated by the miscarriage, and I was ecstatic to find I was still pregnant with another viable fetus growing inside me. Viable. I shuddered. Viable was the medical term. Not mine.

As far as what was I really feeling? At any moment, I could swing between hope, terror, dismay, and joy. Sylvie was right, I didn't have a clue how I really felt, and when I was with her, I didn't have to pretend.

I wasn't just confused about the baby, though. Ben was on my mind almost constantly. I felt his absence as much as I'd feel the loss of my arms.

So many times over the past week, I'd picked up the telephone to call Ben. Once, I even let it ring through so that I could hear his voice on the answering machine. Until I remembered the Carly person, and how she'd answered the one time I'd had the courage to call. So, I hung up.

I also remembered how mean and unreasonable I'd been to Ben for the past—oh, fifteen years, and so the other reason I hung up was because if he'd answered, I wouldn't have known what to say.

"Well, I know one thing, my head hurts, and I don't want to think anymore," I growled, turning to the lunch tray on my lap.

I'd never eaten so well in my life, and I figured I had to be gaining a ton. Genna and Jean-Louis were the primary cooks, and today, I could see Jean-Louis's touch in the neat triangle of quiche Lorraine and the elegant little spinach salad, sprinkled with strawberries, green onions, crunchy green pea pods, and balsamic dressing. A small fruit tart was the pièce de résistance, and the aroma of rich dark coffee almost made me drool in my spinach.

Slightly mollified, I muttered what might have served as a clumsy apology.

"I also know that I am totally confused about why all of you are helping me like this. Especially Genna. She acts as though we're related. I know I saw her sometimes while I was growing up, but I didn't really know her—and she definitely didn't know me."

"You would have known her much better, but she spent most of her time during your childhood in Europe, working as the executive assistant for some corporate muckety-muck. At any rate, don't ever doubt for a minute that we all have our own reasons for helping you. Some time we can talk about those reasons if you'd like," said Sylvie in her breezy way. "Besides as far as Genna is concerned, you are family because you belonged to Peggy. She loved Peggy as much as she loves me—and believe me I hold no jealousy about that. I loved Peg too. Everyone loved her. We all called her Peg O' My Heart, you know."

I hadn't known. What's more, I didn't want to know. I ignored Sylvie's implicit invitation to learn more about my mother. She paused only a few seconds, and when I continued to look about the room in feigned disinterest, she continued her monologue.

"As I was saying, you belonged to Peggy, therefore, you are part of Genna's family and part of what she cares about more than anything on earth."

I continued to ignore the reference to my mother. I might have had to lie helpless in bed while all my neighbors took on Meg-duty with a familiarity and casual comfort that astounded me, but I didn't have to think about my mother.

"That is too bizarre. Genna doesn't really know me."

"Don't be too sure about that," said Sylvie in a clipped, flip way. She laughed letting her voice take on a droning tone. "You can't escape. You belong to us."

I laughed in spite of myself. I couldn't help it. Sylvie was so funny, and I was so bored.

"Sylvie, if I don't find something to do, I'm going to implode. One day you're going to show up and find nothing left of me in this bed. I am bored out of my freaking mind."

Sylvie sat up straight in her chair, her small figure vibrating with intensity.

I drew back slightly on my pillows. Weird. Now, what was going on? I didn't have to wait long to find out what was on her mind, though, because in true Sylvie-style, she spilled her guts.

"Bingo. I told the others that you were ready," she said triumphantly.

A wave of annoyance washed over me. "Well that's fine. How about cluing me in if I'm so ready."

Sylvie raised her nose imperiously and looked down it at me, which should have been ridiculous given how tiny both she and her nose were, but Sylvie sat there radiating confidence, power, and control. I don't know how she did it. For the first time, I wondered what she did when she wasn't spending the summer with Genna. Maybe I'd even ask her someday. Maybe.

"Your Information Please column, of course."

"Huh, you lost me somewhere between the words information, please, and column."

"Well, you're a writer, aren't you?"

"I can write just fine if that's what you're asking."

"Oh, for Pete's sake, Meg, why don't you get down off your high horse? Over the years, you've headed up corporate communications at several companies if I'm not mistaken. That means if you're worth your salt at all, you can write, correct?"

"How do you know anything about what I did?" I asked, avoiding her question while I jabbed at a leaf of spinach.

"Well kid, I have to tell you. None of us lives in a vacuum—even when we try. Your Aunt Marion used to talk about you all the time."

"But she didn't know what I did for a living. I hadn't spoken to her for more than twenty years. No way could she have even known where I worked, let alone what I did for a living." I speared a strawberry next, and if it had been alive before I speared it, it was definitely dead afterward.

Sylvie sniffed and looked at the polish on her nails. "You think? Well, you're wrong. You might not have given one hot damn about your only living family member, but she gave a good hot damn about you. She always knew where you lived and what you were doing. She wanted to make sure that if you ever needed anything, you'd have it pronto. Didn't know that, did you?"

Her words stung, but I wouldn't have let her know that for the world. "You changed the subject. What is an Information Please column, and why should I want to write it?"

"Thought you were bored."

"I'm listening, if you'd like to just get on with it," I said with as much dignity as anyone can have when she is sitting on her butt in bed with a tray on her lap.

"Well, here's the deal. I think you're really good at answering young Pete's questions about kings, and cabbages, and sealing wax," sang Sylvie with a lilt in her voice. "Aha," she said with a wide smile at the look of irritation crossing my face. "You didn't know that we could hear every word of every conversation, did you?"

"For God's sake, is nothing private in this neighborhood? Don't any of you have lives or integrity when it comes to listening in on private conversations?" I said through gritted teeth. I started stabbing at the fruit tart, mutilating the artistic array of strawberries, blackberries, pineapple, and kiwi.

"Oh get over it, Sweetie," said Sylvie with a wave of her hand and another cheery smile. "That's just it. We do have lives, and you're part of them. I can't tell you how much we all look forward to the question of the day. Genna didn't think we should listen in, but I convinced both she and Jean-Louis that we weren't really eavesdropping because we were just sitting on our own porch minding our own business. It's not our fault you talk so loud."

"I do not talk loud. Genna was right. You were eavesdropping. I can't believe you guys."

Sylvie ignored me and kept speaking. "Meg, you are really, really, really good at this Q&A process. You don't condescend, you're interested, and your answers are creative and sensitive. My own personal favorite was around Pete's God question. You really handled that very well."

I mustered every bit of sarcasm I could and loaded it dripping into my voice. "Thank you so very, very much."

Sylvie beamed. "You're welcome. Well, here's the deal. If I'd been home, I'd have gotten with my own contacts, but I don't have the same number of connections here in Minneapolis."

Now, I did want to know what she did for a living, but no way was I going to ask. No way.

"Anyway, I had Jean-Louis and Genna call around to all their local contacts, and wouldn't you know it, Jean-Louis is acquainted with the executive editor of the Minneapolis *StarTribune*. So, I wrote the proposal, Jean-Louis pitched it, and voilà, as he would say. You can start whenever you want for a trial period. They love the concept, and if it takes off, you'll have an ongoing job with them."

"Wait a minute, let me get this straight. You pitched a proposal with my name on it?"

"Well, of course I did. You weren't in any shape to do it."
Sylvie raised dark perfectly shaped eyebrows over eyes brimming
with laughter. "I also provided the writing samples. I just wrote up
the questions you'd already answered, so really the work belongs to
you, anyway, in case you're worried."

"Worry is the last thing on my mind," I said in exasperation.
"Did it ever occur to you that I might not want you butting in on
my business?"

"Well, shucks no, Ma'am," drawled Sylvie with a glint in those
brilliant eyes and not one trace of shame or regret. "I just figured
that given how hard all of us are working to help you out, you
might be grateful for an interesting job that has all sorts of
opportunities. Especially, since you are, now let me get this exactly
right, 'bored out of your freaking mind.' Feel free to correct me if I
got it wrong."

I picked up a fork and started attacking the quiche. I would
never have admitted it to Sylvie, but I was intrigued. A column.
Never in a million years would I have thought of writing a
newspaper column, but I could do it. I knew I could do it. My
heart started to pound a funny little tap dance in my chest.

"So, what exactly is this column you've got me all signed up to
write about?" I pretended a lack of interest.

Sylvie smirked—she really did. She smirked. "I knew you'd be
interested. I knew it."

I slammed my lips together and did not let one single nasty
word escape. I was proud of myself—even though I was sure the
creative combination of words passing through my mind would
have had Sylvie's mouth hanging open in admiration.

"Okay, here's the deal. The readers of the column will be
parents. The purpose of the column is to respond to their worries
or concerns about parenting in general and more specifically to
help them answer the difficult questions their children ask. You
know, like 'is there a God,' 'why are their more stars in the sky at
cousin Johnny's farm in Des Moines than there are at ours here in

Minneapolis,' 'where do babies come from,' and so on. Pretty much anything goes.

"Your job is to do the research, which you can do from your very own bed using the Internet. When you're ready, all you have to do is write up the column in a scintillatingly fascinating way, providing places or resources that parents can go to for more information."

"Oh, that's all, huh?" I was interested. Really interested

"Yep, the concept is brilliant, really," chuckled Sylvie following my line of thought and without a hint of modesty. "One of my better concepts. To begin with, it's going to be a weekly column, in the Saturday paper. If it's successful, who knows?"

Sylvie waved her arms in the air to demonstrate the breadth of possibilities. "Think of it. This sort of job won't take up all your time, you can work from home, and once the baby comes, you'll still be good to go."

"When do I start?" I sighed deeply so that she wouldn't know how excited I was about this new opportunity. Sylvie would never know that my heart had passed from a little tap dance to a full-blown river dance as a host of ideas spun through my head.

"If you're ready, you can start tomorrow." Sylvie laughed. "Genna is going to flat out kill me for bringing this up to you right now, but gosh darn it, I think you're ready."

Chapter 32

Carly

Hey girl, ready for a cuppa java?"

Toni came barreling around the corner without warning, holding a dollar bill high in one hand, a big smile on her angular face.

Carly flushed bright red. She grabbed a lime green folder from a stack on the corner of her desk and slapped it down over a newspaper article she had been studying.

"I'm kind of busy, Toni. I'll catch up with you later, okay?"

"But we always go for coffee around this time." Toni crossed her arms beneath her chest, focusing on Carly's face. "Hey, what's up? Are you okay? You look kinda funny this morning."

"I'm fine. Nothing's up." Carly's flush started creeping down her neck, becoming visible in the deep V of her sweater. She reached for the tiny gold heart suspended around her throat and nervously slid it back and forth on its chain. "You go on. I'll snag a cup later."

Toni's keen glance swept over Carly's face and down to the file folder. She was obviously waiting for Carly to say something more.

"Oh, what the heck. Come on, let's go. There's nothing going on here that can't wait a few minutes." She scooped up the file folder and the article with it and shoved them both into her top desk drawer.

Toni plunked herself down in the chair by Carly's desk.

"Uh, uh, girlfriend. Coffee can wait. I want to know what's going on. Come on, tell me. It's something to do with Ben, isn't it? Let's see what's under that green folder you just hid in your top drawer." Tony rubbed her right forefinger and thumb together. "Let's see what's under that greeeeeen folder. Oh God, I sound like a game show host." She giggled. "C'mon Carly, give."

Carly stared at her friend, hesitating, debating the wisdom of spilling her guts, until finally she leaned forward with an enormous sigh. "Okay, I'm dying to tell someone, but you've got to swear you'll keep your mouth shut no matter what. So swear, okay?"

With absolutely no hesitation, Toni held up her right hand. "I swear. Now give."

"Okay, but before I show you this article I found, I have to tell you something else. A few weeks ago, you know when Ben went off to Colorado to work for a while?"

"Yeah. I remember. You were twitchier than a little kid walking barefoot on hot, pointy rocks waiting for him to come back."

"Whatever." Carly tossed her hair over one shoulder with a grimace. "Before he left, Ben asked me if I'd get his mail and pay his bills. No big deal."

"Did he give you keys to his house?"

"Of course he did. He trusts me completely."

Toni honed in on the gold heart. "So, he trusts you completely. Should he? Like, uh, where'd ya get the pendant?"

Carly flushed bright red again. "None of your business. For the record, though, yes, he can trust me. He can trust me to help him get over that wife of his and move on to a relationship that will make him feel a whole lot better than he has been feeling" Carly realized her voice was rising, and she quickly lowered it. "Darn it all, Toni, you got me off track."

"Yeah, well, I also got my answer about where you got that heart, didn't I? It used to belong to Meg, and you stole it. If Ben sees you wearing that he's gonna know where you got it."

"I don't think so. Besides, it wasn't Meg's anyway. I found it in an old box of junk jewelry she left sitting out on their kitchen counter. This little heart is old. It must have belonged to someone else, and if Meg isn't going to wear it, why shouldn't I, given my relationship with Ben?"

"I'm not even gonna comment on your relationship with Ben bullshit," muttered Toni under her breath.

Carly's eyes flashed. "What did you say?"

"Oh, you heard me just fine. Carly, you're gonna do what you're gonna do, and you're right, it's none of my business. So, why don't you tell me what's in the green folder before we both die of old age just sitting around here, huh?"

"Well, here's the deal. I was paying Ben's bills one night, going through each of them to be sure nothing looked out of line, and I found this one airline charge on his Visa that was peculiar."

"What did you find? A trip for two to Venice? Oh, no, no, wait, I've got an even better one. A trip for two to Paris, the city for lovers, and you think he's gonna ask you to go with him for a romance-filled weekend." Toni snorted with laughter.

Carly frowned. "You know, you're supposed to be my friend, so, knock it off, okay? The charge was for a trip to Minneapolis, and it was on one of Meg's cards."

"Yeah, so what?"

"Here's the so what. The ticket was for the evening she supposedly died in that car crash."

Toni looked disappointed. "That's all? So, what're ya thinkin'? That's she's alive or something? No way. Meg probably bought that ticket earlier in the day."

"Yeah, well that's what I thought, too. I did wonder though, if there was any way she could still be alive. I talked myself out of it, though, like you did just now. Besides, that's not the only thing that happened."

Carly hesitated, looking at the items on her desk, her nails, and back at the items on her desk.

"So, come on already. What happened?"

Carly flushed, reluctant to divulge her actions. When she'd been taking care of Ben's house, it had seemed natural to go through his mail, and why wouldn't she have checked his answering machine as well, right? It was one thing to have made the decision, but it was another to tell someone what she had done.

"When Ben was gone I, uh, also checked on his messages. You know, to be sure that he didn't miss anything important."

"Yeah? So, big deal. You always check his messages." Toni narrowed her eyes. "What am I missing here, Carly. You look like you got caught with your hand in Ben's cookie jar."

"I checked his messages at home, okay? One day, I found this message from someone, I guess it had to be Meg, because she was telling Ben not to worry about her. She said she was fine, and that if the police needed to talk with her about what happened to the car that day, they could find her at her aunt's place in Minneapolis. She didn't leave a telephone number or anything."

"Oh, my God, this is so great. I can't believe Meg is still alive. Whatta ya suppose really happened? Ben must be so hap . . ." Toni stopped, her eyes focusing in on Carly's face again. "Wait a minute. You never told Ben, did you?"

"No." Carly tossed her head. "I'm not going to tell him. I can't stop her from calling again, but he didn't need to hear that message. It was cold if you ask me. You don't get it, do you, Toni? She walked off and left Ben. Just like that."

"Yeah, but you've gotta tell him . . ." Toni's voice rose.

"Shhhhh, something else happened. Yesterday, this article showed up in the mail addressed to Ben." Carly's voice dropped to a hush. She reached into her top desk drawer and pulled out the article.

Toni reached for it with greedy hands. She stared at the one-inch by one-inch photo that topped the Minneapolis *StarTribune* column, her eyes growing larger by the second. "Oh my God, it's her. It's Meg, isn't it? It looks exactly like the woman in the picture Ben has on his desk."

"Yeah, it's Meg alright. Now, are you starting to understand? She walked away, leaving Ben to grieve for her, and she started a brand-new life without him. I can't believe what a bitch she is, can you? She doesn't deserve him."

Toni didn't answer for a minute as she scanned the article. She looked up. "Ben hasn't seen this either, has he?"

"No way. I have to figure out first how to break all of this to him."

"Uh, wait a minute, and clue me in on something, here." The sarcasm was clear in Toni's voice as she waved one hand in the air, watching the expression on Carly's face. "This was addressed to Ben, right, not to you, to Ben. Just like the telephone message was for Ben, not you.

"Carly, what gives you the right to decide 'how to break' anything to him? Did you ever think that maybe it's not your job to be butting in on their lives?"

Toni closed her eyes and tilted her head toward the ceiling. "My God, I can't believe Meg is still alive. Ben's gonna be so happy. You have got to show this to him the minute he walks in the door, okay?"

Carly shook her head. "No, I can't, not yet. You don't understand, Toni."

"I understand more than you think, and what I think is that you are way outta line in keeping any of this from Ben." Toni was scanning the article, her eyes zipping back and forth over the lines of type.

"Say, this is really good. Did you read it? I like the way Meg answered this question."

She started reading out loud. "Mary Keenan from Plymouth asks, 'I'm pregnant with my second child. My first is a little girl who is two years old. Here's my problem. I've heard of how powerful maternal love can be, but I never expected it would be as strong as it is. I could literally rip someone apart if he threatened my Lacey, but what if I don't feel the same way about my second baby? What if I don't love this second child as much as I love Lacey? I'm so worried about that, and I don't know what to do.'"

As Carly started to interrupt, Toni held up a hand.

"Wait, this is really, really good. Let me finish. Here's Meg's answer. 'I understand how you might worry about your feelings toward your second child. After all, you haven't even met your new baby yet, and right now, all of your focus is on Lacey. Let me share a metaphor with you that a very good friend once shared with me about love. She said that love is like a candle flame. If you light one candle from another's flame, you don't take any light away from the first candle. In fact, you can light another candle, and another, and another without taking one bit of light away from that first candle. In the end, all you get is more light—never less.

"'My guess is you will love your new baby just as much as your first, Mary, though perhaps in different ways, because your new baby will be as unique as Lacey. In the end, you'll just have so much love floating around in your house, you won't know what to do about it. Mary, I wish you all the luck in the world with your babies. Meg Jacobi.'

"Wow. I like this."

"Big deal, so she sounds good on paper. That doesn't make her a good person, and it definitely doesn't make her a good wife."

Toni took a breath and skewered her friend with a glare.

"Carly, you're my friend, but I gotta say, you are so outta line on this. You're interfering in the lives of two people, and I don't care what your motivation is. You are flat-out wrong."

Toni adjusted the multiple gold chains hanging around her neck with long, nervous fingers.

"Ben has the right to know that Meg is alive. It's up to them to decide what to do about their relationship. Not you." She spoke in a loud voice, her face flushed bright pink.

"Shhhhh, someone's going to hear you," hissed Carly.

She snatched the article back from Toni and shoved it into her top drawer.

"Toni, you've got to promise to let me tell Ben in my own way. You're my best friend, and I need your support. This is my whole future, we're talking about here."

"Yeah, Carly. I'm your friend, and that's exactly why I'm still tellin' you how outta line you are. Ben deserves to know that Meg is still alive. It's up to them to decide if they want to be together."

Toni stood to leave, but Carly grabbed her arm. "Wait, Toni, I'll tell him, I promise, but not yet. I need some more time with him first."

"Why? So you can seduce another woman's husband." Toni spit out each word. "Carly, I've gotta tell you, if I ever found out another woman was going after my Roger, I'd rip her face off and shove it where the sun don't shine, if you catch my drift."

"Yeah, yeah right. I'm sure you would, and you'd be justified because you love Roger. You didn't fake your death, waltz off to another city, and start up a glamorous new job while your husband is grieving about you.

"Please, please, please, don't screw this up for me, Toni. I just need a chance to spend some time with Ben, so that he will love me back. Come on," Carly wheedled. "You promised you wouldn't tell anyone."

Toni stood and looked at her friend for a moment as though she'd never seen her before. Her face expressionless, she waved her hand through the air as though she were batting away a dozen pesky flies. "Whatever. It's none of my business any way you look at it. You do whatever you have to do."

She walked away. Carly let out her breath, and reached into the drawer to pull out the newspaper column. No way was she going to take a chance that Ben saw that article until she was ready.

She smoothed the newsprint out with her hands, and started to reread Meg's response. She didn't think the writing was all that good. She frowned and shook her head in disgust. Toni was supposed to be her friend. What was the matter with her . . .

"Hey Carly, what's up? You look like you just bit into a sour apple." Ben stopped next to her chair.

"Oh my God, Ben, you scared me to death," gasped Carly turning as gray as the newsprint in front of her.

"What's the matter? Did Dear Abby say something you don't agree with?" Ben craned his neck to see what she was reading.

Carly swept the article off her desk and crumpled it in one fist. "Uh, no, I mean, the stupid things people do, sometimes. You wouldn't believe it."

She tossed the newsprint into her wastebasket and turned to give Ben one of most brilliant smiles. "Got a busy day, Boss Man?"

"I do. Better get started, don't you think?" Ben turned a curious eye towards the crumpled up article and strolled into his office.

Carly snatched the article out of the basket, smoothed it out, and stuck it back in the lime green folder inside her desk.

Chapter 33

Meg

I lay and stared at the ceiling. I was alone because it wasn't mealtime, and my neighbors were off tending to their own lives. I should have been content. At least they weren't hovering over me.

In my usual contrary way, instead of being content or pleased, I was feeling left out. I was so tired of lying around.

I'd been writing my column for the past three weeks, sitting up in bed and using Sylvie's laptop. It was a good one too, loaded with memory and the latest software.

Who would have thought that Sylvie would have a laptop? I was wondering more and more about just what it was that Sylvie did when she wasn't visiting Genna for the summer. Someday I'd ask her.

I loved writing the column, but I was still stuck in bed, and no matter how much I'd liked my bedroom when I first moved in, I was getting sick and tired of lavender, green, and yellow.

Oh well. Next week, I had another doctor's appointment, and if things were going well, I could stop with the bed-rest thing.

I turned on my side, the usual drowsiness beginning to seep through me. As much as I railed against it, I must have needed all this rest because I found myself napping intermittently throughout each day.

I closed my eyes for a moment, before opening them to gaze out my windows. The sun was shining. Earlier that morning when he stopped over, Rob Kazmarik had opened the windows wide so that I could hear the birds singing and feel the breeze blowing through the summer day and into my room.

Even Rob had become part of the neighborhood Meg patrol. He was a nice man. He came less than the others did, which made sense, because he was a single parent with a job to do. Even so, I was beginning to look forward to the small chats we had about raising children. As young as he was, he knew a lot. If anyone ever doubted his commitment to his son, they had only to watch the love in his eyes when he talked about Pete.

Sometimes Pete came with Rob to visit, but even if he did, Pete also came every single afternoon at about 3:00, and I looked forward to seeing both he and his scamp of a pup.

Joey would leap onto the end of my bed, and settle in while Pete and I talked. I didn't mind a bit. I'd never had a dog before, and I discovered that I loved the feel of Joey's warm, squirming body next to mine.

A brisk little breeze whirled through my window, bringing with it the smell of roses and the faint notes of a song that was wafting out of Jean-Louis's kitchen. It wasn't Frank Sinatra this time, it was some woman, and she was singing that *Live well, love deep* song my mother had loved so much.

I was annoyed enough to want to get up and close the window, but I was too lethargic to move. I pulled the covers up around my ears, but I could still hear the music echoing away in my head, even as I began to drift off to sleep.

I'm sure that's why I dreamed what I did. Since I'd moved into my house, the dreams had stopped—until that afternoon.

"Don't let me go, Meggie. I'm gonna fall," screamed Jenny as she reached out to clutch my shirt. She looked so little standing on the rooftop in her rose-sprigged flannel nightgown with my bed sheet tied in a big knot under her arms.

I checked the knot one last time to be sure it would hold. I prayed it would hold. The shingles of the roof were cold and gritty against my bare feet, and the wind slammed against us with the ferocity and chill of a North Sea gale. My teeth chattered in rhythm right along with Jenny's.

Inside my bedroom, I heard a crash that signaled Ron Buckman's successful entry. Jenny and I had run out of time.

"I won't let you fall, Jenny, I promise. I'll take care of you always."

I lifted her over the roof and let out the sheet bit by bit until she was safely on the ground. Ron Buckman crashed his way to the window, and I dropped to the roof, turned and pushed myself over the edge to hang by my hands and fall to the ground.

I snatched Jenny up into my arms, and I ran. At the edge of the lawn, I looked back to see Ron standing in my window pointing the gun out towards us, but before I could move, he turned the gun, pointed it at his own head, and he pulled the trigger.

I whirled so Jenny couldn't see the way Ron had fallen out of the window and onto the roof, tightening my arms around her small body.

"We're safe, Jenny, we're safe. I'll take care of you always. I promise."

I turned to go, but standing in front of me were two adults who had materialized out of nowhere, a man and a woman who had eyes for nothing but Jenny.

The man was dressed in a business suit and red tie, and the woman was wearing a coordinated rose-colored skirt and sweater set with pearls around her throat. I cuddled Jenny closer, and she wound her arms around my neck and hung on tight.

"Give her to me," said the man. "You're too young to take care of her."

"Yes, give her to us. We'll take care of her now. She'll be our little girl."

The woman reached for Jenny, the yearning for a child clear on her face, and I turned away from her. Coming up behind me were three police officers, and they pulled out their guns and pointed them at me.

"Give them the child. You're too young to take care of her."

I turned the other way and tried to run, but Jenny was so heavy, and my feet were rooted somehow into the ground so I couldn't move.

The man walked up to me. "I'll take her now." He pried Jenny away from me and pulled her screaming from my arms into his own.

"Meggie, don't leave me. Meggie, I'm scared."

The wind whipped Jenny's words away. The police officers disappeared like smoke in a steam bath, and the man and woman walked away with Jenny. She reached for me, tears streaming down her face.

All I could do was stand there and watch her go.

"Meg, wake up, it's only a dream. Wake up, dear."

I could feel gentle hands shaking my shoulder, and I opened my eyes to see Genna's worried face looking down at me.

My own face was wet with tears and my arms were empty. The worst was the burden of guilt that seemed to be pressing me down into the mattress, suffocating me.

I didn't pause to weigh my words. For the first time in twenty-one years, I didn't try to hide my feelings.

"Genna, I broke my promise. I didn't take care of Jenny. I tried, but I couldn't stop them from taking her away."

Tears kept trickling down my face, and I couldn't stop them. It was as though after all these years, my eyes had sprung a leak.

Genna pulled a chair over to the side of the bed, and she reached out to take both of my hands in hers.

"Meg, you were barely more than a child yourself. You couldn't have taken care of Jenny. She was a baby, and you had your whole life in front of you."

"Oh Genna, Marion could have taken her, but she refused, no matter how hard I begged. That night, when the police showed up, they took us down to Child Protection Services. When Marion showed up, she said she could take me, but that Jenny would be too much for her. They put her into a foster home, until those people adopted her. They wouldn't let me . . . they wouldn't let me . . ." I was sobbing so hard, my words clumped together like mud.

"Meg, let it out. You've pushed your feelings away for so long that you don't even know how to feel anymore. It's okay to cry. It was okay then, and it's even more okay now."

Genna squeezed my hands, and I hung on tight, bawling like a baby.

"Tell me what happened, Meg. I only heard Marion's version. Tell me yours." Genna pressed some tissues into my hands.

I blew my nose and swiped at the tears, but they just kept trickling down my face no matter how hard I tried to stop crying.

"Genna, I only had six months more of high school. I could have gotten a job after school to help pay for things. I wanted to adopt her, but no one would listen to me. They said I was too young. I tried. I wrote up a plan with a budget and everything."

I gulped and blew my nose again. "I must have looked so pathetic. Seventeen years old and trying to convince a bunch of adults that I was mature enough to take care of a child. They said that I could still see Jenny whenever I wanted to, but even that was a lie."

"Tell me what happened, Meg."

I took a deep breath, and the words started pouring out of my mouth. I'd never told anyone the whole story. Not even Ben.

"When it finally happened, I thought things would be okay at first. They seemed like such nice people. Their names were Ken and Kathy Ann Richardson. The man was an executive at some company or another, and he seemed to make a lot of money. The woman stayed at home and took care of Jenny. They had no other children, and they seemed to love her so much. The man was like Ward Cleaver, you know from *Leave It to Beaver*, the television show. The woman was like June—even down to wearing this stupid string of pearls with everything she owned."

Shaking my head at the memories, I just kept talking.

"Jenny used to come running when I came to visit. I'd open my arms, and she'd jump right into them. She would always say, 'I missed you, Meggie, and so did Maudie.' She always had this little rag doll in a pink gingham dress clutched in her arms that she called Maudie. I gave it to her when she was a baby, and she took it everywhere." I gulped and blew my nose so that I could breathe better.

"Jenny was always so happy to see me, but when it was time for me to go, she would cry and beg me to stay. I think the woman resented how much Jenny wanted to be with me.

"After a while, I didn't feel very welcome when I came to visit. I was too young to realize that she was probably insecure in her role as a new parent. I'm sure I was arrogant about the fact that Jenny and I were blood relatives, while she was only Jenny's adoptive parent.

"One day, Kathy Ann told me to go home. She said that I wasn't good for Jenny because I made her so sad. Jenny didn't help because she started screaming. She kept saying that she wanted to go home to her real Mama, that she wanted to live with Meggie and the boys. I remember promising her that I'd always be there for her, no matter what anyone said. Right in front of Kathy Ann. Pretty stupid challenge coming from a teenager, wouldn't you say?"

"Anyway, in the end, Kathy Ann proved clearly enough that she had the legal right to Jenny, not me. A week later I showed up to see Jenny on her fourth birthday. I'd brought her a little blue gingham rag doll so that Maudie would have a brother, only when I got there, all I saw was a For Sale sign, and they were gone. No one would tell me where. No one. I never saw her again." A hoarse laugh fell out of my mouth. "All Marion had to do was back me up. I needed her help."

"Oh Meg," Genna looked at me, the sorrow on her face reflecting the sorrow I could feel on my own. "I'm sorry. I'm so sorry. I came home for the funeral, but I was working in Europe at that time, so I never knew what was going on with you until much later. By the time I moved back, you'd already graduated and moved out East.

"I do know that Marion never liked change of any kind. I think at the time, all she could think about was that she was on the verge of gaining some recognition as an artist. She didn't want anything to get in her way.

"I also know that afterwards, when it was too late, she was sorry that she hadn't tried harder to keep Jenny—or at least to help you keep her."

I sniffed hard. "After I left for college, I never saw her again. Mama's insurance paid for my college, and I didn't need Marion or anyone. I still don't. I can take care of myself."

"Sometimes I don't know how you made it through, Meg."

I thought of Ben, and I thought about how I lost him—not because of the Carly person, but because of my own actions. I said nothing about Ben to Genna, though, because I had no words to say that would matter. That part of my life was over, and all I could think about was how I would feel its loss until I took my last breath. Genna didn't seem to notice my withdrawal from our conversation.

"You're a very strong person, Meg. You're very much like your mother, you know."

Well that statement brought me back with an automatic response.

"No, I'm not. I'm not anything like my mother. She was a dreamer. If it weren't for her, none of this would have happened. She never planned for anything, she just spent all her time helping strangers, and look what happened.

"Because of her, we lost our whole family. How can you say she was a strong person? She was careless, and thoughtless, and accepted whatever came along."

"Is that what you think?"

Genna sat back in her chair, pulling her hands loose from mine. She looked at me.

"Your mother was the most special person I've known in my life. She cared about everyone and everything, and she didn't just care in a theoretical way from the comfort of a chair in front of a fire. She did something about what she believed in, and she worked her butt off."

Genna smiled, but the smile wasn't for me. She was remembering things I'd never heard before.

"Do you know that the day your mother found out your father had been killed, she'd just been to see the doctor? She'd just found out she was pregnant with you. She loved your father so much, Meg, but instead of giving up when she found out that she was a widow with a baby on the way, she went down and enrolled at the University of Minnesota.

"She had to move back home so that she could afford to go to school, but your grandparents helped her as much as they could, even remodeling the attic so that she'd have her own space to live with you.

"When you were born, she strapped you into a pack on her back, and kept on going until she could graduate with a degree that would support you. Don't think it was easy for her, because it wasn't. When you got to be too old to sit with her through classes, your mother switched to night classes, and Sylvie and I helped take care of you. That's why we have had such an interest in you, you know, Meg. We've loved you since you were a tiny thing."

"But why did she always have to help everyone in sight? Why couldn't she have focused on her own family?" The anger in my voice surprised even me.

"You tell me the answer to that one. Until the accident, how did you feel about your mother's work?"

I turned my head away. I'd never allowed myself to think much about my mother, let alone her work.

All of a sudden, memories started sparking through my mind, memories and feelings I'd forgotten all about. I remembered all the people who sent my mother little thank-you gifts in the form of cookies, or bars, or some handmade object. I remembered how wherever we went, people seemed to love my mother, and she'd seemed to love them right back—no holds barred, no expectation of any return.

Oh, and I'd forgotten about the Thanksgiving dinners she organized for the homeless. We all helped serve. It felt so good to sit with this enormous group of people who didn't really have a family and help to create a temporary family filled with warmth, laughter, and good food. My mother organized those dinners, but that wasn't all. She was ready to take on any cause.

We never had much money, but I don't remember ever needing anything important either. We had enough, and my mother was always willing to share what we had

I'd been proud of my mother and all the things she'd accomplished. When did that change? Why? A sense of shame started creeping through me, and I could feel the blood gathering warm beneath the skin on my face.

"Your mother also helped me when I needed it so very badly." Genna's words broke into my thoughts. "You know, she was my best friend from the time we were seven years old. We were like Mutt and Jeff.

"You're probably too young to remember that cartoon strip, but it was about two friends, one tiny and one enormous. I was the enormous one, and your mother was this tiny tornado. Peg O' My Heart, that's what we called her, you know. It was your grandfather's pet name for her, but the rest of us thought of her that way too."

"Peg O' My Heart," I said slowly, savoring each word. "I remember a little gold heart she wore all the time. My father gave her that heart."

"Yes, he did." Genna hesitated. "Meg, I want to share something with you.

Her words came out slow and rusty, as though she had tucked away the thoughts behind them so far and deep that she had to work hard to pull them back out into the light.

"When I was in college, I met this boy. I'd never dated much, you know. I really wasn't the sort that boys went for. I was too fat and terribly shy in those days."

I opened my mouth to argue with her, but she didn't notice. She kept talking, and I decided not to interrupt the flow of her thoughts.

"Well, this boy told me he loved me, we got involved, and I got into trouble as we said in those days. When I told him I was pregnant, he walked away and never looked back. It's one of the oldest stories in history. I felt so stupid, falling for him, and I was terrified to tell anyone what happened."

"Oh Genna, that can happen to anyone. What a jerk he was, and you are not fat. I think you're beautiful."

With an unconscious gesture, she brushed away my words about her appearance like crumbs from a kitchen counter.

"Yes, I suppose he was a jerk. So was I to believe him. Anyway, one day—I must have been about three months along, or so—I felt the most awful pain in my stomach. I thought I was going to die. I started to bleed, just like you did the other day.

"Your mother was with me, and when I begged her not to tell anyone, she ignored me and ran next door and got her father— your grandfather. I wish he hadn't died when you were such a little thing so that you could have known him better. Carl Lofgren was one of the most wonderful men in the world. Well, between the two of them, they got me to a doctor that your grandfather knew. It was lucky they did, and it was lucky that your mother took things into her own hands, because I was hemorrhaging so badly, that the doctor said I would have died if I'd been left on my own.

"Of course, I lost the baby. Your mother took me home to her apartment, and she took care of me until I could go home again. No one ever knew. You see, in my family we didn't talk about such things—and of course, 'things' never, ever happened to us. There was no way I could have told my parents what happened. I've suspected that maybe Sylvie had an inkling, but she's never asked, and I've never told."

Genna looked down at the tissue she'd shredded.

"Oh Genna, I'm so sorry you had to go through that. Now you're helping me. Because of my mother."

She shook her head and reached for my hands again. "No, Meg, never think that. We don't love you because of your mother. We all love you for who you are, not for where you came from."

My throat got all tight, and I didn't know what to say. I wasn't used to having that kind of conversation, you know, the kind that makes you all weepy? I'd always kept my thoughts to myself, rarely sharing them even with Ben. Before I could think of anything to say, Genna spoke up again.

"You know that Marion hired a detective to track Jenny down, don't you? Finding Jenny became a kind of quest for her toward the end. I think she wanted to make things right with you."

"Yes, but it's been so long, I don't think we'll ever find her. Besides, I don't even know what I'd say to her. I just keep hoping that she's had a good life, a safe life with people who love her. I couldn't bear it if she was all alone."

Another tear trickled down my cheek, and I rubbed the back of my hand against my face, scrubbing it away. "I think of her that way sometimes. All alone with no one to belong to."

"But isn't that what you've been trying to do, Meg, sequester yourself so that no one can get at you? So no one can make you feel?" Genna asked the words simply, with no judgment.

I stared at her in shock. That's not what I'd been doing. Was it? Ben was the one who turned away, not me. Although, if I were to be completely honest, I'd kept myself so busy that no one could have had much of a relationship with me, even if he wanted to. I gulped, not wanting to face the thoughts that were growing in my mind.

"I had Ben," I whispered softly, looking at Genna through new tears, "but I ran away and left him. I left him a long time ago, really. We just kept sharing the same space. He must have been so lonely, but I was too busy and too important to care. And now, he's found somebody else, and I can't even be angry with him."

Chapter 34

Carly

I did it, I finally did it," thought Carly in triumph as she did a quick, hip-wiggle dance around her kitchen, mouth stretched wide in a silly grin.

She'd wracked her brains for almost two weeks about how to get Ben alone so that she could carry out her plan. She'd hinted a few times that maybe they could have dinner. Given his level of response, she might as well have been a cocker spaniel with a submissive urination problem for all the interest he showed in getting together with her.

Carly kept thinking that given enough time, Ben would forget all about Meg and turn to her. Then the icing on that cake dripped all over when Meg called and left the voice message. Of course, she'd deleted it. Carly thought she had everything under control until she found the bill with the airplane charge on it and that blasted column with Meg's picture on it.

Meg was turning up all over the place. Carly knew it was just a matter of time before Meg's continuing existence on the planet came to Ben's attention.

Her argument with Toni hadn't helped, and her sense of urgency grew as she racked her brains about how to approach Ben.

Finally, she decided that she'd just tell Ben in her own words how Meg had chosen to disappear and start a new life without him. She thought she could spin the story in a way that didn't give him all the details, but that would cause him to be so angry at being dumped that he never wanted to hear from Meg again.

Carly, of course, would be nearby to pick up all his pieces. All she had to do was set the stage, write the script, and deliver it with meaning. First, she'd needed to figure out how to get Ben alone. Hence, The Plan.

Carly hadn't worked with Ben Jacobi for the past three years without learning a few things about him. He loved to help people out. It was his Achilles heel really, and one that Carly would work to rectify once they finally did get together. In the meantime, she could use Ben's weakness to her advantage.

In the end, getting Ben alone had been a piece of cake. She'd waited until he was working at his desk one afternoon. She'd been sure to turn toward his door and speak loudly enough so that he could hear every word. Ben would never know that she'd dialed her own answering machine.

"What do you mean it will cost me $850 to get my car fixed? That's not even highway robbery—it's freeway robbery. Yes, I understand that labor is expensive, but you have to understand that everyone doesn't have that kind of money to throw around."

Out of the corner of her eye, she noticed that Ben had wandered over to stand in his doorway, and that he was listening to every word she uttered. She heightened the note of desperation in her voice.

"Is there any way you could do the work for less? I don't have that much to spend right now. Oh, well sure, I understand." She plunked the telephone down in its cradle and dropped her head in her hands to show how overwhelmed she was—all for Ben's benefit. She'd been sure he'd bite. He did.

"Carly? Are you okay? Is your car acting up or something?"

"Oh Ben, it's going to cost me a fortune to get my car fixed. Do you believe it? How can people afford to pay so much?"

Ben came out of his office and perched on the edge of her desk. Carly loved it when he sat close to her like that. It was all she could do to stop herself from grabbing him around the waist and hanging on for dear life.

"So, what's wrong with your car?"

"Oh, it's the brakes. I need to rotate something or another and change the brake pads—I'm not very good with mechanical things. It's going to cost, well, you already heard all that. Besides, it's not your problem. I'll figure out how to take care of it." She frowned and lowered her head to her hands again. "Somehow."

Even though her delivery of the message was calculated, for a second she was worried that she'd overacted, but, nope, good old Ben fell right into her trap. Within two seconds, he offered to fix her car. He said he liked working on cars and that he owed her for all the help she'd been giving him, paying his bills and so on. He'd gone on to say that *she* was really doing *him* a favor.

Carly kept her triumph to herself, and simply asked him if Saturday would work out. Ben said he'd be there around 3:30.

Now, she had a dinner in the oven that was guaranteed to knock his socks off—and everything else above his ankles, too, with a little bit of luck.

Carly sashayed through her kitchen with an enormous smile. She pushed open the door to her garage, holding it ajar with one hip while she leaned out to see how Ben was coming along with her car.

"How's it going?"

"Your timing is perfect. I'm done, and in a few minutes I'll be out of your hair," Ben's voice was muffled, and all she could see were a pair of long legs sticking out from beneath her car.

"No way, José. I don't let the men I know come over, work on my car, and then go home hungry. When you're finished, come on in and you can wash up."

The body beneath the car grew still. Carly stood waiting for some sort of response from Ben, but for several seconds, he said nothing. He wriggled out from under the car.

"Carly, that is so thoughtful of you, but I can't stay. I've got to be somewhere."

Carly kept smiling, her voice light and teasing. "Oh you do, do you? And just where do you have to be, Boss Man?"

"Uh, I've, ah got some chores that I need to get done at home." Ben's face turned red as he tried to come up with an excuse for why he couldn't stay and have dinner. Carly thought he was even cuter when he tried to fib to her. She decided to cut him a little slack.

"Well, you have to eat, right? I also hate to tell you this, but unless things work differently at your house than they do at mine, the chores will still be waiting when you get home."

Ben cleared his throat, but he met her eyes with a steady gaze. "Carly, I don't think it's a good idea for me to stay for dinner. I'm just not ready to see anyone."

Carly laughed, tilting her head back and letting the sound flow from her throat like music. She knew how pretty she was, and she knew that most men responded to her flirting with little hesitation. She didn't care about most men, though. She cared about Ben.

She snuck a look at him and was pleased to see that he looked puzzled by her response. She decided to hit the nail on the head and to confront Ben about what she knew to be his key concern.

"Hey, no pressure, but here's the deal. You need to eat, and frankly, I can't accept your help with my car unless you let me feed you. So, we're in a Catch-22 situation here unless you give in. I promise I won't try to leap your bones—at least until after I serve dessert." Her words were light and calculated to make Ben feel as though he were out of line.

Ben's face turned even redder, if possible, and he looked away. He opened his mouth to say something. After stammering incoherently for about two seconds, he closed it and cleared his throat. He looked at her helplessly, as though his vocal chords were frozen solid.

Good, she thought. He needs a little shaking up. He also needs to start thinking of me as someone other than the administrative assistant who answers his telephone and pays his bills.

Now, she'd load on a little guilt, and she bet he'd cave like a sand castle in a rainstorm. She changed her tone, becoming serious and a little nervous. She hadn't starred in all those plays in high school without learning at least one or two good acting techniques.

"God, Ben, I'm so sorry. I'm being really presumptuous to assume you're free for dinner? I apologize."

She let her voice quiver, but just a little bit. It never paid to overact. She smiled, her eyes locked on his, not failing to notice the guilty expression creeping across his face.

"Hey, I know. How about I carve a few slices off the roast, and wrap up some of the vegetables and potatoes and send them home with you. That way, you'll still get your dinner, but you won't have to stay here with me."

She let her voice trail away with a forlorn little note and looked down at the floor as though she was about to cry. She started to count to ten, betting that he'd back down before she hit five.

She didn't even get to four before Ben blurted out a clumsy, "Oh gosh, Carly, I didn't mean to make it sound like that. I'm sorry, really I am."

Ben shoved greasy fingers through his hair, heedless of the mess he was making. "Look, I'm a filthy mess, and I don't think I'd be good company . . ."

Carly jumped right in before he could say any more. "Hey, no problem. Let's do this. I promise I won't tease you anymore. You can clean up in my bathroom, have a quick dinner, and still get home in time to do those chores, okay?"

She saw Ben hesitating, and before he could say no, she fired her last shot. "If you leave, what am I going to do with all this food?"

Ben looked down at the floor for a moment, clearly uncomfortable. He looked at Carly. "Okay. You've been so much help, and I do appreciate all the work you did on dinner. It smells wonderful."

Carly laughed gaily and taking him by the hand, she pulled him down the hall and pushed him into the bathroom. "Okay, scrub off all that grease. Dinner will be ready before you know it."

Chapter 35

Ben

Ben slowly closed the bathroom door and stood there staring at himself in the mirror. Big mistake. Big mistake. You are making such a big mistake. Like the lyrics of a rock song, the same message kept beating through his mind.

He definitely looked out of place in Carly's bathroom. Although it was small, it was immaculate and beautifully decorated. A flowered border bisected the walls, painted a creamy coral on the bottom and a pale eggshell on top. A light flowery scent filled the air, emanating from a small ceramic dish on the counter. Tiny soaps shaped like seashells filled the dish.

Ben looked at himself in the mirror. Greasy black streaks covered him from the tips of his fingers to his elbows. Grease also stained the front of his shirt and one side of his face as well. On top of all that, he'd raked some heavy-duty streaks through the front of his hair with his fingers when he'd been trying to get out of staying for dinner.

Ben looked at the tiny soaps and the dainty lace trimmed hand towels hanging from the rack. He looked at himself again in the mirror. He pulled off his shirt, but made no move to desecrate soap or towels.

A brisk knock on the door caused him to jump a foot.

"Ben? Here's a bar of real soap and a towel that might wrap around more than your wrist. I also brought you an old nightshirt of mine. It's extra-large, so it ought to fit you well enough for dinner with a friend."

Laughter was clear in Carly's voice, and Ben turned with relief to open the door. He looked down into her laughing face, and the loneliness in his gut twisted like a kite in strong wind. Sable brown eyes gazed up at him, and standing so close to her in the small bathroom, Ben could smell the fragrance of Carly's hair.

What am I doing here? This is wrong. This feels so wrong.

Carly shoved the towel at him along with a big bar of soap. "Feel free to use the shower. You're never going to get all that grease off otherwise. Hurry up, your drink awaits you, and you're just poking along in here."

Carly reached into the shower, turned the water to hot, gave him a dazzling smile and backed out of the room, leaving him alone.

Ben turned toward the shower with a sigh of relief, his hand going to the snap on his jeans. He hesitated before quietly locking the bathroom door. He shucked his clothes and stepped under the steamy spray of the shower.

Ten minutes later, a bit more relaxed and without a single smear of grease on his body, Ben entered the kitchen to find Carly bustling about.

"Hey, you look pretty good without all that grease smeared across your face."

Carly leaned down to slide a large aluminum pan out of her tiny oven to check on the roast.

"You know, you've been working way too hard, Ben. I've looked at some of the times you've sent emails to different people, and I see 1:00 a.m., 2:30 a.m. You're working around the clock, and that isn't good for anyone."

Ben couldn't think of an answer, and so he remained silent as Carly carefully checked the thermometer and slid the pan back into the oven. A savory aroma curled through the kitchen, and Ben's mouth watered. It had been a long time since he'd had a home-cooked meal. He'd been existing on take out, and after a while, everything started to taste the same, full of fat, salt, or sugar. No wonder he was getting soft around the middle.

He realized that Carly had been talking for the past few minutes, and he hadn't heard a word she said. He tried to focus.

"Everybody at work has missed you, Ben. It must have been hard to be all alone in Colorado all those weeks. You know, away from everyone you know?"

Ben grunted in embarrassment. "I didn't mind. It was good to be away. The house feels, oh I know this sounds trite, but it feels empty. Like a movie set really, where the audience is waiting for the actors to show up—only they never do."

Carly shivered. "You are so good with words, but that image makes me lonely."

Good with words, Ben thought. His words trailed his thoughts. "No, I'm not. That's Meg, not me. I'm good with numbers and analyzing facts and figures, but I'm terrible with words."

"Well, I think you express yourself very well."

Ben started to relax. Carly's attitude was upbeat, friendly, and familiar. She seemed to have forgotten the conversation they'd had in his kitchen right after Meg died. He sighed. It was good to be with another adult. All he'd done for the past two months was get up, go to work, eat, sleep, and start all over again.

"Okay, here's the deal. Dinner will be ready in about thirty minutes, and in the meantime, here's what I want you to do."

Carly moved over to her cupboard and pulled out some gin.

"I'm going to make you the best martini you've ever had, and we're going to go sit down and relax in the living room. You can tell me what Sam Rivera and all the guys in Colorado are up to."

"I don't drink much, Carly."

"Don't be a stick in the mud, Boss Man," said Carly not pausing as she poured alcohol into a crystal shaker, added ice, and shook vigorously.

"Have you ever even had a martini?" she challenged him as she poured a stream of sparkling liquid into one of the two chilled glasses she pulled from her refrigerator. Opening a bottle of mammoth green olives, she plunked three into each glass and handed one to him.

"No, I've had the usual, Jack Daniels and water, wine with dinner, you know. Alcohol has never been my thing."

"Another indication that you are unique among the men I know. Now, unless you want to hurt my feelings, at least try it, won't you? I've planned an extremely elegant dinner complete with drinks and dessert. Your job, should you choose to accept it," she droned with humor, trying to sound like the Mission Impossible operative in charge, "is to simply eat, drink, and tell me how much you admire my ability to cook, okay?"

Carly put a gentle hand against Ben's back urging him to move over to a leather recliner.

He sank down into the chair with a sigh and took a tiny sip of his drink. The alcohol washed over his tongue with a smooth bite and a tang of pine needles burst in his mouth. He took another small sip.

"I like it," he said in surprise sinking back into his chair. "Good job."

"Well, I don't mean to say I told you so, but I told you so," said Carly, dropping onto the matching couch that sat at right angles to his chair. She tucked her feet up beneath her.

It felt so good to lean back and suspend all emotion. Ben looked around the tiny living space. Carly had set the table with china, a creamy lace tablecloth, and crystal goblets. Tall ivory candles served as a centerpiece, while a number of pillar candles in a variety of sconces flickered warm, amber light throughout the living room.

Ben turned his eyes toward Carly. He'd never seen her in her home before, and he was surprised to see her personal persona so different from the one she exhibited at work.

In the office, she was all crisp, friendly efficiency, and she tended to dress in preppy slacks topped by soft pastel sweaters or open necked shirts and blazers. She looked different tonight. She wore a teal silk shell and soft untailored slacks that clung to the shape of her body. Around her neck, she wore a tiny gold heart.

For a moment, Ben's stream of consciousness came to an abrupt halt. Hadn't he seen a heart just like that recently? For the life of him he couldn't figure out where. Whatever. The lovely deep hue of the teal set off the deep brown of her eyes. Long swirls of dark brown hair hung to just below her shoulders.

For the first time since he'd known her, he wondered who Carly really was, what she thought, how she lived. He'd always taken her for granted. She was a good admin, he needed a good admin, and that was about as far as he'd ever thought. That is, until she sent him that note.

For a moment, his sense of unease returned, but her soft voice, the soothing warmth of the apartment, the comfort of sitting back, letting go, and anticipating what smelled like a fantastic dinner all conspired to make him settle deeper into the leather chair. He took an enormous sip of his martini and smiled at Carly.

"So, what do you do when you're not at work?"

She tilted her head back, a trill of laughter escaping her throat. Ben's eyes never left her face as he waited for her answer.

"Well that's a pretty big question. I eat, I sleep, I read. I don't know. I'm not all that interesting, really."

"Well, I'm sure that's not true."

"I guess mostly I'm looking for someone to build a life with, someone who loves me and who I love back. To have children." She laughed. "I sound like the American dream cliché, don't I? I'd like 2.5 children, a loving husband, a house in the suburbs complete with a lovely garden, and a big goofy dog. It may be a cliché, but that's what I want."

"I don't think you sound like a cliché. Well, maybe just with the 2.5 kids part," Ben grinned, and his eyes lost focus as his thoughts turned inward. "I wanted those things too. Now, with Meg gone, oh, I don't know. I feel like I should have died with her."

"Oh Ben, no. Don't ever say that. You can still have the family, even the dog," Carly leaned toward him smiling a sad little smile. "It will take some time to get over Meg, that's all."

"Well that's not ever going to happen," he said in a matter-of-fact voice, pulling an olive out of his empty martini glass and raising it to his lips.

"No, no, no. Put it back. You have to wait."

Startled, he dropped the olive back into his glass and looked at her. "What am I waiting for?"

"The perfect moment to eat them, of course."

Carly leaned over and wrapped slender fingers around the cocktail shaker resting on a silver tray on the oak coffee table. She reached over, took his wrist to steady his hand, and started to refill Ben's empty glass. His skin tingled where she touched him.

"Carly, stop, I don't need any more." Ben held up his hand, but Carly ignored him and kept on pouring.

"Yes, you do. You have to soak those olives at least twenty minutes before you eat them. In the meantime, you can sip away at a new martini."

Ben looked at her in surprise. "How do you know all this stuff?"

"I used to date a bartender. I learned how to make and ingest almost any alcoholic beverage that's in style."

"Style? Drinks are in or out of style?"

"Of course they are. Martinis were really in style back—oh I don't know for sure—but back in the forties, fifties, or maybe it was the early sixties. I'm not very good with the history of alcoholic beverages. I do know they're popular now, though, because wherever you go these days, restaurants have a whole column in their menus devoted to martinis. There are cosmopolitan martinis, gin martinis, vodka martinis, lavender martinis, even dirty martinis, and I've just scratched the surface."

Ben laughed. "A dirty martini? What on earth is that?"

Carly jumped to her feet. "Here, let me show you. You said you like olives, right?"

"Yes, I love them." Ben was starting to have fun for the first time in long time.

"Okay, I'm going to make you a dirty martini. Stay right there until I get back." Carly danced into her kitchen and started clinking things together.

Ben settled into the chair. He was so tired, and the alcohol was more than doing its share to relax him.

"Here, try this." Carly handed him a new martini and stood, waiting for his reaction.

Ben took a sip, "Hey, this is good. What did you do?"

"I added some olive juice, that's all. Go ahead and enjoy it. The roast's done, and I'll get things out on the table."

Ben struggled to his feet. "What can I do to help?"

Forty-five minutes later, Ben was back in the living room with a glass of brandy in his hand. After three martinis, a couple of glasses of wine, the roast, mashed potatoes and gravy, corn, fresh rolls, and salad, he was stuffed—and he definitely didn't need any more alcohol.

Carly insisted, though, and he was feeling so comfortable and relaxed that it seemed easier to acquiesce. Next she brought out dessert plates filled with chocolate cake.

"Oh Carly, I don't think I can eat another bite."

"Okay, you don't have to eat it all, but try one bite. This is the best chocolate cake. You're gonna love it."

After dinner, Ben had ended up on the couch, somehow, and Carly nestled in the corner next to him, pulling her feet up beneath her. It was a small couch, and he could smell her perfume every time she moved. A sense of unease crept through him, but Carly didn't seem to notice.

She leaned over so that she could pick up the fork from his plate where it rested on the coffee table, her breast brushing the side of his arm. Ben took a gulp of his drink, and shifted his body closer to his side of the couch.

Carly cut off a bite of the cake and turning, she rested one hand on Ben's shoulder while she held the fork in front of his mouth.

"Come on, try one bite okay? It's really good."

Carly's face was less than twelve inches from Ben's. She gazed into his eyes. He opened his mouth, and she slid the bite of dessert between his lips. He chewed and swallowed past an enormous lump in his throat. The chocolate coated his tongue with sticky sweetness.

"Well? What do you think?" Carly put the fork back down on the plate and reached for Ben's mouth with the hand that wasn't curled around his shoulder. "Here, let me get these crumbs." She leaned even closer and brushed her thumb against the corner of Ben's mouth.

He closed his eyes, his lips tingling, his senses reeling. Carly nestled even closer, her breasts pushing against Ben's chest, causing his heart to thump.

He raised his hands to grasp her shoulders and push her back, but before he could move, she said his name, once, softly. He opened his eyes to find her staring at his mouth. She leaned forward and brushed her lips against his once, twice, and then again.

Ben froze, wanting to push her away, but also wanting to fill his arms with her warmth. God, he was so lonely.

When he didn't move away, Carly pressed even closer, wrapping her arms around Ben's neck and kissing him again, more deeply, running her tongue along his upper lip.

Ben's lips opened slightly, responding. He lurched to his feet.

"I can't. I'm sorry, Carly. You are so beautiful and desirable, but I can't do this." His voice was raw and wretched.

"Why, because I'm not Meg?"

"Yes. No. Yes, I mean, she has only been gone for such a short time. I've never loved anyone else."

"Well, maybe it's time you did love someone else, Ben. You think Meg was such a saint." Carly rose to her feet and moved closer.

"No, I don't think Meg was a saint," said Ben eagerly, trying to explain, "but she was my best friend. I love her, and I can't even begin to think about being with anyone else. Not yet. Not right now."

Carly reached for him, but he backed up.

"I've got to go. I'm really sorry." Ben's face was all crinkled up in embarrassment, but the resolve in his eyes was clear.

Carly's face twisted, her eyes going from soft and bright to hard and glaring. It was clear to Ben that she was fighting for control, but when she spoke anger and frustration spilled out with every word.

"Ben, I didn't want to just spring this on you. I was trying to find a good way to tell you about what your wife has been up to all this time you've been mourning her."

"I'm not sure I'm following you, Carly." The tone of Ben's voice echoed his confusion. He stood and looked down at her. Waiting.

"Damn," said Carly savagely. "It wasn't supposed to work out this way. Ben, you've got to start seeing Meg for what she really is. A liar and a cheat."

Carly stalked over to the tiny coat closet at the end of the hall. Reaching inside, she pulled out her large black carryall, jabbed her hand around inside for a few seconds, and snatched out the green folder that held Meg's newspaper column. She stalked back to where Ben stood watching her, his mouth hanging open, a question in his eyes.

"Here," she slapped the folder against his chest and backed up two steps, facing him, waiting, bright red spots staining her cheeks.

The folder slid through Ben's fingers as he tried to catch it, and the newspaper clipping flew out and spiraled down to rest face up on the floor.

Ben froze, his eyes riveted to the image of his wife on newsprint. "Where did you get this?" His voice was hoarse.

He reached for the small scrap of newspaper, his eyes lasering in on the small photograph of Meg nestled in the midst of a series of questions and answers.

It couldn't be Meg, and yet even though the photograph was grainy and small, he recognized her face in an instant. Massive relief coursed through him, causing his knees to tremble. He dropped into a chair, hands shaking as his eyes devoured the print on the page before him.

"Ben, Ben, are you okay? Oh God, I didn't know how to break this to you. Ben, talk to me."

Ben looked up in confusion at Carly's voice. He'd forgotten where he was. All he could think about was Meg. All he wanted to do was find her. His eyes snapped up to meet Carly's, blazing with the need to know anything that would help him understand what was going on.

"Where did you get this article? When did you get it?"

"It, uh, came one day, in the mail," she started to stammer under his scrutiny. The color in her face came and went as she struggled to respond to the harshness in his voice.

"You opened my mail, didn't you? As usual, right? That's okay, but instead of giving it to me with all the rest of my mail as usual, you kept it from me. Why? I want to know why? And what was all this supposed to be?" He waved his hands at the kitchen, the table still covered with the good china, the remains of the roast sitting on top of the stove.

She reached for him, but Ben took two steps back.

"Ben, please, it's not like that. I just didn't want you to be hurt when you found out what Meg did."

"That's just it. I don't know what she did. I thought she was dead. I thought she was dead," he repeated. The anguish in his voice rang out loud and clear. "How long have you had this? Tell me, I need to know."

"About three weeks," Carly whispered.

"You've known that Meg was alive for three weeks, and you didn't tell me?" Ben's voice rose along with his anger.

Carly avoided his eyes, and his suspicions grew.

"What else have you kept from me? There's more isn't there?"

His eyes slid down Carly's face to focus on the tiny heart on the fine gold chain she was wearing around her throat. He stared at it for a moment, awareness growing.

"After Meg was gone, I found a heart exactly like that in a box of jewelry she'd left by the couch in the living room." His eyes traveled back up to Carly's face, noting the quick color that came and went, noting the guilty expression that she couldn't hide as he stared at her.

"I found it laying on the counter when I picked up your mail. I put it on so that it wouldn't get lost." Carly reached up to unclasp the pendant and she dropped it into the hand Ben automatically stretched out. He slid it into his pocket as though it were the most precious object he owned.

"Hard to see how it could have gotten lost, Carly. That jewelry box seems pretty safe and stable to me. Did it crawl out and lose itself on the counter?" Ben's voice was clipped, his eyes fierce. "What the hell were you thinking? You went into my house, and you stole my wife's jewelry? You found out she was still alive and didn't tell me? What were you thinking? What else have you kept from me? Tell me. Now."

Carly gulped, backing away from Ben, and letting the tears spill from her eyes. Ben stared at her. In spite of her tears, she still looked like a summer rose, but her beauty left him cold. All he wanted from her were answers.

"Ben, I've loved you since the first day I met you. These past three years, I've seen how miserable you are. Meg was never there for you, not ever, but I would be. We could have such a wonderful life together. We could, I know we could."

Ben stared at her for less than two seconds. He turned away and was all the way to the front door before Carly could catch up with him.

"Ben, wait. What are you going to do?"

"I'm going to go find my wife, and I'm going to bring her home." Ben paused. "And, Carly? Don't bother going into work on Monday.

Chapter 36

Meg

A toast, a toast to our Meg. Bed rest is officially over."

Jean-Louis raised his glass of merlot high and all the others followed suit. I blushed. Genna smiled her beautiful smile at me, Sylvie winked and tilted her glass in my direction, Rob Kazmarik said 'hear, hear,' and Pete wriggled with excitement and immediately took a big gulp of ginger ale from his own stemmed glass. Jean-Louis? He nodded his head at me, of course, the twinkle apparent in his eyes as always.

A lump the size of Texas lodged in my throat. I'd never known people like this before.

"I don't know how to thank all you guys. Baby Esmeralda and I are both so grateful for all your help these past few weeks. We wouldn't have made it through without you." I patted the small bulge that was beginning to show and raised my own glass of white grape juice.

All of us sipped from our glasses, big smiles on every face. Pete took another big gulp of his ginger ale and suddenly frowned.

"Esmeralda, no way. Come on, Meggie, tell us you're kidding, okay? No way can you give our baby such a geeky name." Pete's expression was half, you're-pulling-my-leg-aren't you and maybe-you-mean-it-and-I've-gotta-talk-you-out-of it.

I decided to pull his leg a little further, enjoying everyone else's expressions.

"Well, yeah, Pete. Didn't you know that Esmeralda was my absolute favorite name, that is, except for Frederica?"

"Yuck!" Pete had no trouble expressing his opinion.

"Hey, watch out, you're going to hurt her feelings," said Sylvie jumping into the spirit of things.

Genna smiled at all of us, and Jean-Louis smiled at Genna.

"But Pete, those are great names, unless I have a boy that is. I was kind of thinking maybe Horatio, or Humphrey, or mayyyyyybe Hubert for a boy."

"Hmmmm, how's that for a little bit of alliteration," murmured Sylvie out of one side of her mouth.

Pete giggled, and Rob reached over and ruffled the boy's hair.

"Now I know you're kidding. If you named our baby any of those geeky names, everyone would pick on him in school, and no way would you let that happen, right?"

"You're right, no way would I let that happen, Pete."

"So, have you picked out any names?" asked Rob Kazmarik in his quiet way, his eyes sharp and lively.

I'd become so fond of Rob during the short time I'd known him. I counted him as my friend.

With a sense of surprise, I realized that I counted every face in the room as my friend. I realized something else too. I'd never really had any friends as an adult—except for Ben.

The familiar longing popped to the forefront of my heart, or brain, or wherever it is that longing pops into. I'd picked up the telephone to call him so many times, but it always came down to one thing. I didn't know what to say, and I was afraid he wouldn't want to talk to me. I shut out my feelings and turned to face Rob.

"I don't have any names really. The field is wide open for suggestions."

"I know, how about Ignatius," sang out Sylvie, "or . . ."

"Maurice," interrupted Jean-Louis with another twinkle. "I've always liked the name Maurice—especially for a girl."

Sylvie tossed a piece of popcorn at Jean-Louis' head, but he caught it mid-air and popped it into his mouth with a flourish.

"I'm kind of partial to Maybelle," said Genna with a straight face.

"No, no I know, I know, how about," and having gotten our attention, Pete couldn't think of a single name. "How about . . ."

We all waited patiently, knowing that he was trying to come up with something as ridiculous as the rest of us.

"Frodo Baggins," he yelled in triumph, referring to the main character in his favorite book, *The Lord of the Rings*. When he sat with me during my bed rest, I swear we read that darn book from cover to cover. "That's it. Let's name our baby Frodo Baggins."

At some point along the way, the child who was never supposed to be not only became a viable fetus, it became our baby, jointly claimed by the entire neighborhood. I found that I didn't mind one single bit.

"Okay, okay. Enough with the names. I have a toast."

Everyone looked at me, expectation on each face.

"To all of you. To Genna, who fed me in spite of my nastiness when she showed up at my door with that beautiful plate of brownies that made me drool. To Jean-Louis, who never failed to bring me a rose to cheer me up every single morning—even though I said I was allergic to them. To Pete, who made me think and who is my very good friend and the genesis of my new job."

Pete's grin couldn't have been any wider.

"To Rob, who sat with me and traded stories about raising up babies, and to Sylvie, who sat by my side and allowed me to freely abuse her with my wicked tongue whenever she came to visit. May she go back to work tomorrow rested and ready to come visit us on weekends as soon as possible."

Everyone clapped and sipped.

Sylvie grinned, eyes sparkling. I knew all about what Sylvie did now as a professor of literature back in Chicago. I knew quite a bit about all of them. I knew that Jean-Louis had met and married his high school sweetheart, Leonie. I knew that they'd immigrated to the United States in 1985 after General Electric acquired Jean-Louis's company and offered him a local job. I knew that Leonie died of breast cancer ten years ago.

I knew more about Rob's wife, and I understood more about why she'd left when Pete was five years old. I also knew about Rob's aspirations to become a writer, and I was helping him with the night classes he was taking at the local university.

I knew how Genna . . . but there I paused for a few moments, realizing something I'd never realized before. I knew that Genna was a fantastic cook. I knew that she helped anyone who even remotely appeared to need it. I knew that she'd loved my mother. However, until the other day, I hadn't known anything about her, and I still didn't know very much. Not really. Not about how she felt, her fears, her hopes.

I knew that Genna took care of all of us, but who really took care of Genna? My eyes rested on her face, watching as she and Jean-Louis spoke quietly together.

In that odd way that happens when someone is looking at us, Genna seemed to feel my eyes upon her, and she turned at once to smile at me. My own lips curved in response, and a little jolt went through me as I realized that I'd grown to love her over the past couple of months. I'd grown to love all of the people in that room.

I cleared my throat because some gunk seemed to be clogging up the works. I had one more thing to say.

"Seriously, I couldn't have gotten through these past few weeks without you guys. I owe you all big time."

"No, you don't, Meg. Someday, you'll give it all back to someone else who needs help. That's all." Genna made life sound so simple. She made it sound so good. She smiled at me again, and

I felt so wonderful I couldn't even think of any words to describe the warmth filling my heart. Or, would that be my brain? Whatever.

"Hey, it's time for one last Pictionary match before I have to go back to Chicago. I get Pete on my team. He draws faster and better than anyone." Sylvie's face was pink, her eyes sparkling.

Playing Pictionary on Sunday nights had become a ritual over the past few weeks. At first, I think the idea was a collective "what-can-we-do-to-keep-Meg-from-losing-her-mind plan" while I was stuck on my back in bed. Now, we were hooked. Every one of us.

That first Sunday night, everyone had shown up as I was finishing my dinner. All of them crowded into my bedroom toting game, flipchart, and markers. I have to admit, I was less than gracious to have what I thought of as the whole neighborhood in my bedroom.

"Oh get over it, Meg," Sylvie had laughed at me. "We're here to provide you with fun and intellectual stimulation so that you don't fade away into a trembling, inert mass of boredom."

Pete had noticed immediately that I was less than pleased. "Meggie, we brought you a party. Don't you want us here? We thought you'd like to play a game. You know, so you won't be so bored. Do you want us to go home so you can be alone?"

Well, what could I do at that point, but grit my teeth and tell Pete that of course I wanted to play a game. Funny thing? I realized somewhere between Jean-Louis's drawing of a lopsided circle that was divided into sections to represent the zodiac, and Rob's hilarious attempts to get us to say milky way by drawing a pretty sad bunch of tiny stars over and over again, that I'd never had so much fun in my life before.

Now, each Sunday, Genna brought a flip chart, borrowed from one of her committees, Pete brought his set of those bright-colored fruit-smelling markers, someone brought a decadent, calorie-laden dessert, and we spent a couple of hilarious hours playing picture charades and laughing like crazy.

"Okay, okay," I laughed now, "but first, let me make some more popcorn to sustain us through the ordeal. We'll save the chocolate cake until later. Hang on, I'll be right back."

"I'll help fill the bowl," responded Jean-Louis, getting to his feet. "You know, to be sure that you put enough into it for all of us, eh?"

Everyone laughed because as much as he ate, Jean-Louis never put on one single ounce of fat.

I tossed a bag of popcorn into the microwave oven and turned to see Jean-Louis leaning against the counter, a forlorn look in his eyes.

"Jean-Louis, what's wrong? How can I help?"

My eyes grew wide as I realized that I hadn't offered to help anyone in the near past, no make that ever in the past. I'd pretty much focused on me to the exclusion of everyone else.

A small, warm glow began to grow in the middle of my chest. It felt good to want to help someone.

"Well, here is my problem." Jean-Louis stopped and scratched his head. "But me, I don't know how to find the right words."

"Let me help you. I have much less compunction about speaking my mind than this epitome of gentlemanliness standing in front of us," said Sylvie briskly as she breezed into the kitchen. "Here's the deal, Meg. Genna has it in her darling head that I need a partner, and she's decided that Jean-Louis is the ideal man for me because he's strong, handsome, and oh so incredibly intelligent."

Jean-Louis frowned. "You make me sound like the hero on the cover of one of those disgusting romances you read."

"Oh, don't be so humble. You're a great find for someone who's interested. But I already have a partner back in Chicago who I need to introduce to Genna only I don't know how to explain Terri . . ."

For the first time since I met her, Sylvie was without words. Realization dawning, I tried to help her out. "Would that partner be a woman?"

She turned in her quick way and hugged me. "Yes. I need to try to explain to Genna. It's the only secret I've ever kept from her, but she's always been so, oh I don't know, straight-laced, and I don't know how she'll take it."

"My Genevieve is not straight-laced. You are just a coward about this particular subject." Jean-Louis sniffed.

"Oh, yes, I know. Your Jshanevieve, she is perfect, eh?" said Sylvie in a fair imitation of Jean-Louis's accent, kissing the tips of her fingers, and expressing absolutely no malice.

Jean-Louis's face reddened. He said nothing, gritting his teeth.

Sylvie grinned.

"Wait a minute," I said. "Let me catch up here just a bit. Obviously, you two have had this discussion before. I have to admit that when I first met you, I thought a relationship was brewing between you two . . ."

"No, way," said Sylvie grimacing.

"Good God, no," said Jean-Louis with a comical look of horror on his face.

"It's okay. It's okay. My initial impression certainly didn't last very long, honest," I laughed. "It was crystal clear that you had eyes for no one but Genna, Jean-Louis. So, what's the problem? Haven't you told her how you feel?"

Jean-Louis groaned. "How am I to do that, Mademoiselle? I ask you this question very humbly, you understand, because I am at my wit's end. Whenever I try to have a personal conversation, Genevieve bustles right back into her kitchen to make me a cup of coffee or to slice a cake. Or, she calls this one," he turned to look with exasperation and a fair amount of affection as well in Sylvie's direction, "and she tries to leave us alone so we can bond, eh?"

"Well, take her out for dinner or something so that she can't bustle back into the kitchen. Besides, 'this one' will be back in Chicago as of tomorrow. Wait, I've got a better idea. Ask Genna to dinner, and make it all romantic with your Frank Sinatra records in the background. Make something French with lots and lots of calories. I'll help you." I closed my mouth, once again astonished at my offer. Astonished and pleased. Hey, maybe I wasn't such a jerk after all.

"Excellent idea," said Sylvie, patting her pockets. "While the two of you hatch your plans, I'm going to duck out for a quick break."

She disappeared through the back door like a wisp of smoke, leaving Jean-Louis and me alone to, uh, "hatch" our plans.

Chapter 37

Ben

Ben drove straight home after Carly's revelation, booked a seat on the first flight out the next day, and spent the rest of the night trying to understand why Meg had chosen to disappear.

From the newspaper clipping, he knew that Meg was in the Minneapolis/St. Paul area, and so he planned to track her down through her Aunt Marion.

When he arrived in Minneapolis the next day, he strode off the airplane and dug Marion's name and address out of the local telephone book. On his way to rent a car, he stopped in the middle of the aisle, people streaming by on all sides. He realized he didn't have a clue what to say if Meg opened the door.

The sky was indigo with evening, a few hours later when Ben finally walked up Marion's sidewalk. He heard peals of laughter floating out the open front window. Leaning forward, he caught a glimpse of his wife inside the small, brightly lit room, and his heart started to pound. He walked around the house to peer in a side window.

He was disgusted with himself. Instead of coming directly to find Meg from the airport, he'd chickened out and checked into a hotel, had dinner, and watched the news. Now, instead of marching up and knocking on the front door, he was playing Peeping Tom and skulking around. If the neighborhood police drove by, they would cart him away in a heartbeat.

Ben started to head back toward the front door and stopped. He didn't know what to say, especially in front of all these people.

He looked through the window again at the hilarity going on inside. Although he couldn't hear what was going on, he didn't need to hear the words to recognize warmth and camaraderie when he saw it.

What was going on?

As he watched the group inside, his emotions bounced from relief to confusion, to something else that he hadn't quite identified. That something else was causing an ocean of adrenalin to play tag-you're-it from one nerve to another throughout his entire body.

He barely recognized Meg. The changes weren't just physical, although her appearance was far from the polished professional he knew. If someone had taken a picture of the scene inside and presented it to him, he would have had a hard time believing the small woman with the big smile and the mischief in her eyes was his missing wife.

Meg wore a pale yellow dress that pouched out a little in front, and she looked softer and prettier somehow. Her face was a little rounder, her cheeks pink with laughter. He'd never seen Meg laugh as she did in response to something a young boy had just said.

Who were these people? Ben wondered how Meg had become so familiar with them in such a short space of time. She never socialized.

He dismissed the others almost immediately, his eyes following every move his wife made as she stood and left the room. Several moments passed, but Meg didn't return. Ben started to pace in a tight, little circle.

"Have you decided whether you're coming in or not? It sure took you long enough to decide to come at all. I sent that column to you three weeks ago, and I've been expecting you any day."

Ben turned to see an undersized woman sauntering toward him from the back of the house. The glowing ember of her cigarette glittered like a beacon in the dark.

"Who are you?"

"I'm Sylvie Johnson, a friend of Meg's. You, I assume are Ben, her husband. She never speaks of you."

"That's supposed to make me feel bad?" Ben clenched his teeth. He'd finally recognized the final emotion coursing through his body. It was anger.

"Don't know how it makes you feel. Don't especially care either. Why did you let Meg go away all alone in her condition? Didn't you care?"

Ben opened his mouth, closed it, opened it and for the first time in his life, words spewed out, without conscious thought and planning.

"Didn't I care? I don't know who you are, Sylvie Johnson, or whatever your name is, but I've got to tell you, you don't know jack shit about Meg or me or about anything else.

"If you think I let Meg leave on her own; in fact, if you think I could ever in my life get Meg to do *anything* she didn't want to do, you are flat-out wrong, and you don't know her at all."

Ben paused, but only to take a breath.

"She disappeared on me. Did she tell you that? She just flat out disappeared and let me believe she was dead. So, what do you think about that, Sylvie Johnson? Huh?

"I know we had problems to work out, but she walked away from me, taking our baby with her. She didn't even tell me she was pregnant. Oh, and I guess since Meg never speaks of me, you also didn't know that I have wanted a child with her more than anything in this entire world. Except, she refused to have children—ever. All she did was work."

Sylvie took a hit off her cigarette and paused to pick a bit of tobacco off her tongue.

"Well, clearly, I asked you the wrong question. The right one would be more along the lines of why did she choose to leave you? I know Meg can be a bit prickly. . ."

"Prickly? Is that what you call it? Prickly?"

Ben's voice was an octave higher, and his words came out in brief, sharp staccato bursts.

"Prickly is not what I call it. I call it thoughtless. I call it selfish and egomaniacal. You know what I'm starting to think? Huh? Well, I'll tell you. I think Meg's never cared a bit about anyone in her life since she lost Jenny. But you know something? I can't fix that for her. I never could. No one can. No one. It's done. I'm done. And now, I'm outta here."

Ben turned on his heel and in less than a minute, he was in the rental car at the curb. He cranked the ignition and threw the car into gear.

The last thing he saw as he drove away was Sylvie standing where he'd left her, cigarette smoldering at her side, red tip glowing, until she dropped it to the sidewalk, stubbed it out with her left foot, and wandered back around the house, apparently deep in thought.

Chapter 38

Meg

I booted up my computer, preparing for my morning's work. Overall, I was feeling pretty satisfied with myself. My column had been so successful during its first month that now I was writing a daily column.

As I waited for my computer to go through its wake-up routine, I smiled remembering all the fun we'd had the previous night. My heart gave a funny little jump. For the first time since I could remember, I had friends, time to think, and I was learning how to play, not just work around the clock. Most important of all, I *belonged* somewhere.

I loved my little house and the way it wrapped safely around me. I loved not having to prove anything to anybody. I'd even stopped worrying about making more and more money all the time so that I could buy more and more things I really didn't need.

I paused, my hands poised over the keyboard. I'd also been thinking more and more about this baby of mine. Yes, my baby, not a viable fetus. I rested my hand lightly on my stomach. I felt a tiny flutter inside.

Oh my God, I thought, *the baby moved.*

The flutter brushed again ever so softly. I felt a stronger kick, a roll, and another tiny kick. No doubt about it, my baby was real. I wanted to run and tell Genna, or Jean-Louis. No, I wanted to tell Ben.

The smile slipped off my face and fell to the floor somewhere between my feet. God, I missed Ben, and I wanted him back.

I sat up straight and reached for the telephone. No time like the present, right? I dialed our number in Stamford, my stomach knotted and tense.

I had no idea what I was going to say. I just knew that I needed to connect with Ben. I counted two rings, three rings, four, and my stomach tensed with each ring until I knew he wasn't home.

The answering machine picked up, and I listened to the timbre of his voice as it came to me through the telephone wire. My heart twisted at the sound.

"Hello, this is Ben Jacobi. Leave a message, and I'll call you back."

That was it. I hung up and called again. I called three more times, just to listen to his voice. He sounded curt, not at all the way he usually sounded.

For the first time, I wondered if I'd hurt him when I left. I couldn't believe I'd never had this thought before, but even if he was having an affair, I knew he cared about me. My hand lingered on the telephone until I pulled it away and tried to redirect my thoughts to my work.

In the past, no competition would have existed between my concern about Ben and my need to complete a task. I'd changed, though.

I don't know when it happened. Maybe when I lost one of my babies and Genna and Jean-Louis stood by my side and held my hand. Maybe when I first met Pete and tried to help him understand that even though his mother was an alcoholic, she loved him in the best way she could. Maybe it even started that first day when Genna showed up with the brownies, and Jean-Louis brought me a rose. I didn't know. I really didn't.

I just knew I'd never focus on work again to the exclusion of everything else in my life. I loved writing my column, but I also liked taking time off to have coffee with Jean-Louis, Sylvie, and Genna. I liked taking time to listen to Pete and to watch Joey's funny antics.

I also didn't think any more about being important, because I finally understood what Ben had been saying all along. I already was somebody important. Somebody with tons of faults and maybe, I hoped, even some good qualities too.

I reached for the telephone again, and dialed my old home number. No answer. I sighed and turned to my computer.

This morning I had five new emails. I seemed to get between five and seven emails every day for the column. Mostly mothers and fathers sent them, asking about a particular challenge they were facing. Sometimes, they sent a funny story, which my editor also loved to print.

Thank goodness, I had complete access to the Internet, because I was certainly no expert on this stuff.

My editor said it didn't matter that I wasn't an expert because the information was all there ready for me to dig up. She said the only thing that mattered was that I had the knack of putting it all together into columns that people loved—she really said that.

I couldn't get over the fact that instead of writing about stuff that made people feel bad, you know, like being laid off and losing all your income and so on, that I was helping to make people feel good. What a hoot. I *loved* this new work of mine.

I scanned the email titles on my screen. *I'm afraid I'm going to have to have my son's wife toilet train him, because I'm not having any luck.* That one showed promise. *How long do chicken pox last?* I didn't have a clue, but that was what Dr. Spock's reference books were all about. *What's your philosophy on infant inoculation?* I'd have to check out a few websites—this was a hot topic—even I knew that. *What are the night terrors—I think my four-year old may be having them?* Night terrors? I'd never heard of them, but that was what I loved about my new job. I was learning about all kinds of new things. I'd have to do some research on the night terrors, too. *What do you tell people when your wife disappears?*

What? I opened the last email, my eyes zipping down the copy.

Dear Information Please,

I don't know what happened or what I did wrong, but one day, I got home from work expecting to see my wife as usual, and she never showed up. She just took off without saying a word to me. No note. No telephone message. Nothing.

It took me a long time to track her down, and when I finally did, I learned that she never even speaks of me. What should I do? Why would someone move away and refuse to explain? Please help me understand. Because at this point, I don't have a clue what I did wrong.

Lost and Alone

My head was reeling. For a moment, I wondered if the email could be from Ben. My hopes soared and plunged again as I read the name at the top of the email.

Who was I kidding? No way could it have been from Ben. He didn't even know where I was. Second, the writer of this email never even got a message from his wife, and I'd left a voice mail for Ben.

Besides, this guy sounded as though he were in agony over his wife's desertion, while Ben was fooling around before I even left.

I sighed. With all my heart, I wished the email could have been from Ben. What would I have said if it had been? I didn't have a clue how to respond to this poor guy. I was a wife who ran away, and if Ben asked me why, I wouldn't even know where to begin to explain all the feelings, the doubts, the fears. So, who was I to give someone advice about what to do when someone's wife ran away?

I got up and started to pace around my attic office. I was feeling agitated in a way that had become foreign to me over the past few months. I moved out onto the porch, my eyes searching for Pete, or Jean-Louis, or Genna, but no one was out, and besides what would I say?

I walked back to my desk and sat down, trying to compose myself and write an acceptable answer. Although we didn't print my response to every question, my policy was to answer every email that came in. I didn't know where to begin with this one.

Dear Lost and Alone,

Were you and your wife having problems before she ran away?

I thought of my own situation and about how confused I felt. I continued writing, my fingers tapping out my thoughts.

Maybe something was going on that you didn't know about. Maybe it was something you said or did. Maybe it was a combination of a whole series of factors. I don't think people ever really mean to hurt someone they love. I think, though, that someone could become so overwhelmed that they thought their only option was to run away and start over.

Can you talk to your wife? Can you ask her what happened? It sounds as though you know where she is. I wish I had a magic answer, but I don't. I hope you find each other. Take care of yourself in the meantime.

Meg Jacobi

I read over what I'd written, and I thought it pretty much sucked. Even so, before I could hesitate, I hit send.

I started to go through my other emails, but my thoughts kept returning to Ben. I tried to call our number, but still no answer. I looked at the clock, which read 7:50 a.m. He would have already left for work by now, and somehow I couldn't bring myself to leave a message with Carly. I just couldn't. I'd have to wait until that evening to try to reach him.

I pushed my chair away from the desk. I could not work. I decided to walk over and see if Genna had time for a cup of coffee.

When I knocked on her door, Genna took one look at me and pulled me into her warm, fragrant kitchen. She nudged me toward the table and immediately turned to dump out the coffee in her old-fashioned percolator, fill it with fresh grounds and water, and set it to perk.

"Oh Genna, I've made such a mess of my life, and I don't even know how to begin fixing it."

She turned to look at me. "Would you like to hear my philosophy of life?"

I grinned, feeling better somehow. "Sure. God knows, it's got to be better than mine."

"Okay, here it is. My philosophy is that nothing's irrevocable but death."

"Huh?"

"You haven't made a mess of your life, Meg. You've tried out a few things, and now you can try out some other things. Nothing's irrevocable. If you don't like your life, change it."

"I don't know if I can. I don't know if Ben will even talk to me." My voice was small.

Genna poured me a cup of coffee in one of her special rose china cups, handed me a slice of her butter pecan coffee cake, and came to sit down next to me.

"Aren't you going to have any?"

I took a bite of the coffee cake and closed my eyes, reveling in the flavors of cinnamon, cloves, nutmeg, and buttery crust rolling around in my mouth. Genna's coffee cake sure beat the soggy breakfast bars I used to eat. When Genna didn't say anything, I opened my eyes and looked at her.

"Are you okay?"

For the first time since I'd met her, Genna didn't meet my eyes.

"Genna, what's wrong." I'd never seen her upset about anything before.

A puzzled look crossed Genna's face, and she frowned. "Jean-Louis asked me to dinner at his house. Alone." She said the words in a flat tone.

"And, this is a problem because . . . ?"

"Because," she said a look of pain on her face, "I think he's decided since he can't have Sylvie that he'll settle for hanging out with me."

I choked on a crumb of coffee cake, trying not to laugh, but when I looked at her face, I realized that she really believed what she was saying.

"Oh Genna, you have got things so wrong. Jean-Louis never wanted to have a relationship with Sylvie—at least other than the one he has. I think in spite of the fact that they bicker back and forth, they really do care about each other."

"Well, that's what I kept hoping. Only it's not going to happen."

Genna looked over at me, and finally I could see a smile in her eyes. "Sylvie left me a note explaining her relationship with Terri. Can you believe that? She was too nervous to tell me she is a lesbian and has a partner she loves. As if I would have been anything but positive about any relationship that worked for her."

I smiled. "Okay, so now we all know that Sylvie has a significant other, and it isn't going to be Jean-Louis. It was never going to be Jean-Louis, Genna. He's never been interested in anyone but you. How could you not know that?"

Genna started picking at the fringe of the placemat. "I don't think so. I think he's lonely, and I'm easy to talk to, that's all. Oh, don't think I feel sorry for myself, because I don't, but I have no illusions about what I look like at my age."

I opened my mouth to argue with her, but before I could get one word out, Jean-Louis stepped into the room. Genna and I both looked up, startled. We hadn't heard him at the back door, but now, he closed it behind him and came into the kitchen.

"Genevieve, I will tell you what you look like to me."

Genna's face turned the loveliest shade of rose, and she turned her head away.

Jean-Louis looked nervous, but it was clear to me from the look on his face that he was going to say his piece this time no matter what Genna tried to do.

He walked over to where she sat, and he pulled her to her feet, urging her across the kitchen to where a mirror trimmed in oak hung on the wall.

He stood behind her, his eyes meeting hers in the mirror. Genna didn't look away, but the color in her face deepened. She looked so vulnerable I wanted to hug her and tell her everything was going to be okay.

I needn't have worried, though, because Jean-Louis knew what he was doing. I wondered what had taken him so long to do it.

He raised his hand and tucked a silver curl behind Genna's ear.

"When I look at you, Genevieve, I see a face that is as soft and lovely as one of my roses. I see someone who cares about everyone around her. I see someone I want to be with when the sun comes up in the morning and when the stars shine down at night."

His hands moved from her shoulders, down her arms, and to her hands. He took a hand in each of his and crossed them in front of her, pulling her body back against his own and rested his chin on top of her head.

"I love you, but you have to stand still and listen to me sometimes and not go off to make the coffee or to cut the cake, eh? That is, at least, not every time I look at you."

Genna smiled at Jean-Louis, leaning back against his chest looking more peaceful and beautiful than I'd ever seen her look before.

"Hey," I said softly, not wanting to break the mood. "I'll just be going home, now."

I don't think they even heard me leave. I smiled all the way home.

With new resolve, I ran straight upstairs and sat down in front of my computer. I grabbed the telephone, and before I could think of all the reasons I didn't want to call Ben at work, I dialed. I didn't know what I'd say to Carly. I didn't know if she'd even put my call through, but it was time. It was way more than time that I spoke to my husband. I tightened my hand on the receiver and waited through three rings.

"This is GSC, Ben Jacobi's telephone. Can I help you?"

It didn't sound like Carly. "Is Ben in, please?"

"No, I'm sorry. Ben is out of town this week. Can I help you with something? If you prefer, I'd be happy to leave him a message. I'm sure he'll be calling in soon. He always does."

"No, that's okay, thanks." I hung up the telephone, feeling lower than a speck of dirt on a cellar floor. I'd never wanted anything so badly before in my life as I wanted to talk to Ben.

Frustrated and out of sorts, I punched the computer keyboard. My email list came up, and I could see that I already had a response from Lost and Alone.

Oh good, I thought. *I can't even keep my own life straight, and I'm trying to help someone else? Sheesh!*

I opened the email.

Dear Information Please,

What could have possibly been going on with my wife that she couldn't have told me about? You said maybe she found something out. What could have been so bad that she couldn't share it with me? I want to understand. Please help me.

Lost and Alone

Oh, what the hell. This one will never go in the paper anyway. Maybe I'd just tell this stranger how it had been with me. I had nothing to lose. I'd already lost the most important thing in my life, and I didn't know how to get him back.

I poised my fingers over the keyboard, and started to click away like mad:

Dear Lost and Alone,

A whole variety of things might have been going on with your wife. Maybe she lost her job. Maybe she found out she was pregnant. Maybe she found out something about your relationship. Then, maybe her whole life seemed like it was too much to bear, and the only way she could handle things was to run away. Only now, she doesn't know the way back. If you know where she is, I'd urge you to contact her. What have you got to lose?

Meg Jacobi

I took a deep breath, and hit send. My stomach rumbled, and I thought about going downstairs for a peanut butter sandwich, but before I could move, my computer dinged.

I glanced at the monitor. Lost and Alone must have been sitting at his computer, because he'd already sent back an answer.

Dear Information Please,

What could she have found out about our relationship? Nothing was going on. If she'd found out she was pregnant, I would have been out-of-my-mind happy. She would have known that. And, a job! Oh please. You can get a job anywhere.

I'm afraid if I try to contact her, she'll close me out and refuse to talk to me. I'm afraid to risk it, that's all.

Lost and Alone

Before I could stop to evaluate what I wanted to say, my fingers did their greased lightning thing, and I pounded out the first words that came into my head.

Dear Lost and Alone,

Maybe she found out you were interested in someone else. It happens. I should know. Maybe she didn't know that she could get another job, and maybe she was afraid to be pregnant. Maybe all those fears bunched up into a need to escape, and so she did.

Go talk to her. Tell her you didn't mean to have an affair with someone else. Tell her you still love her even if she is a workaholic. Reassure her that your baby is going to grow up healthy, and safe and nothing bad will ever happen to it—even though she will know that the two of you will really only ever have limited control over what happens in your lives.

Just tell her that together you will figure things out as they happen. If you can tell her all those things, maybe she'll come back to you. Maybe she even wants to come back already, but she doesn't know how to begin.

Meg Jacobi

I was so agitated that I ignored my cardinal rule: I didn't reread what I'd written. I hit send and stopped moving, aghast at what I'd done.

I wasn't behaving professionally at all. My response had been personal and way out of line—it was all about me, my life, my fears. No indication existed that this guy's wife was experiencing any of the things I'd experienced myself. I knew better than to mix my own personal problems with those of my readers.

Oh Lord, I needed to take a break and not respond to anyone else until I could get myself under control. If what I'd just written ever came out, my career as a columnist would be over before it even started.

Chapter 39

Ben

Ben pushed his chair back from the hotel desk, his eyes wide with shock.

Tell her you didn't mean to have an affair with someone else.

Could Meg possibly have thought he had something going on with another woman? Carly was the only woman who'd ever come on to him, and he'd never responded to her.

He felt a stab of guilt, remembering his brief response to Carly the other night, but he shook his head. Nothing happened that night either. Carly was the last person he'd ever choose.

Carly was a piece of work, though. He wondered if she could have said anything to Meg to make her think they were having an affair?

Ben's heart turned over. He was one of the few people who understood Meg's vulnerabilities. Meg came off all tough and ready to handle anything that came her way, but he knew her better than that. She would have been terrified about being pregnant and to lose her job at the same time? She lived for that job.

Those two things together would have been more than she could bear. What if Meg thought he was being unfaithful to her on top of everything else.

Unwilling to lose their connection, as tenuous as it was, he quickly tapped out another message.

Dear Information Please,

Why would my wife think something was going on between me and another woman? That was never even a possibility. Besides, wouldn't she have asked? We were best friends. How could she ever believe that I would be interested in someone else? How could she have known me all this time and believe that I'd ever cheat on her? I love my wife. More than life, more than anything. I want her back.

Lost and Alone

Ben hit send, hoping that Meg was still online and that she would respond to him. He drummed his fingers on the table, until finally he stood and began to pace around the hotel room.

He'd been on his way back to the airport the night before, when he'd made an abrupt turn and headed back to his hotel. No way was he leaving town until he and Meg talked.

He'd sat up all night trying to figure out what he would say to her and how he would say it. He was terrified that she wouldn't give him the time of day, let alone sit down and have a civilized conversation. It was nearly dawn when he'd thought of setting up a fake email account and emailing her under the guise of her column.

The computer dinged, and he was back in the chair reaching for the keyboard before he'd even made a conscious decision to move.

Dear Lost and Alone,

Your wife is so lucky. Maybe she doesn't know what's in your head or your heart. It's such a funny thing really, isn't it, how we can live with someone for so long, and still forget how to talk to that person? How can we get so lost and become so lonely in a world that is filled with others who feel exactly the same way? Maybe if you just stop worrying about how she will respond and go talk with her, you will find that she is missing you as much as you are missing her.

As I said before, what do you have to lose? You have everything to gain. I hope you will go to her, and I hope she will listen to you. Good luck to both of you.

Meg Jacobi

Ben switched off his computer. He grabbed the car keys and was out the door before his computer stopped humming.

Chapter 40

Meg

I pushed my chair back from the computer. No new emails. I sighed, wondering if I'd ever find out what happened to Lost and Alone.

I'd spent the afternoon in Jean-Louis's kitchen, chopping and sifting as I helped him make a series of complicated recipes. Gosh, that man knew how to cook. He was determined that everything about his dinner was going to be perfect for Genna.

I'd helped him make everything from the stuffed mushroom appetizer to the beef bourguignon to the crème brûlée. Jean-Louis even taught me how to use the hand-held chef's butane torch to caramelize the sugar that topped the brûlée. In spite of myself, I was learning to cook. I was even beginning to like it.

I wandered out onto my porch and looked down into Jean-Louis's kitchen. Frank Sinatra was singing again about fairy tales coming true if you're young at heart. I could see Genna and Jean-Louis standing near the stove, sipping glasses of red wine.

Genna looked up at Jean-Louis, who was laughing at something she'd just said. He leaned forward, cupping her face in one large hand. They just stood there in Jean-Louis's kitchen smiling at each other. I turned away, not wanting to intrude on their privacy, loneliness knifing through me.

Hearing the doorbell, I hurried downstairs, thankful for any diversion.

A man's silhouette, backlit by moonlight, filled the half-window of my oak front door. I knew that silhouette as well as my own. Ben. I gulped. All day, I'd wanted to talk to him, and I'd ached with the wanting. Now, here he was and every word I knew dried to dust on my tongue.

I pulled the inner door open, and I stood there gazing at him through the screen door. I was terrified I'd say the wrong thing.

"Meg, can I come in?" He stood there, waiting for me to respond. He held a cardboard Special Delivery packet in his hand.

Still, I could think of nothing to say. Any words I could process seemed too small for what I was feeling. I clicked back the lock, and opened the door. I stood aside as Ben entered my house and re-entered my life.

As he moved past me, I could smell the cool September night on his shirt and the warmth of his skin. I could smell Ben, my best friend, my mate.

"Here, this Special Delivery letter was stuck between your doors."

I took the packet from his hand and turned away to set it on the mantle. My heart was hammering away, my mouth was dry, and I could feel warmth trickling down my cheeks. Ben came closer, and his eyes met mine in the mirror over the fireplace.

"Oh Meggie, you're crying. In all the years we've been married, I've never seen you cry," he said with a note of wonder in his voice.

Turning me to face him, he lifted his hand and caught some of my tears with his forefinger. He looked into my eyes, and suddenly his hands were around my face, both thumbs softly catching the tears as they fell, rubbing them away. As soon as he rubbed one away, though, another replaced it, and the dam that began breaking the day I told Genna about losing Jenny finally burst all the way.

A small sob escaped before I could stop it.

"It's okay, Meggie. It's okay."

Ben pulled me into his arms and rocked me back and forth while I leaked all down the front of his shirt and huddled against his warmth.

After a while, I straightened, my hands sliding up Ben's back, and I found myself hanging on tight. Ben cupped the back of my head in one hand and wrapped his other arm around my waist pulling the length of my body against his.

In the past, we'd always laughed at how well our bodies fit together. That night, we both noticed the small bulge that pushed us apart at the same moment.

"Oh Meg, it's the baby," Ben laughed, his voice unsteady.

He loosened his grip so that he could slide his hand between us and explore the roundness of my abdomen, his fingers gentle and searching. He stepped back.

"Let me look at you. Oh God, Meg, I've missed you so much. I've been sitting outside for hours waiting for you to come home, but when you did, I was too scared to knock on the door."

I opened my mouth to speak and then closed it. Still, I had no words. All I knew was that I didn't care what had happened in the past. I wasn't afraid of anything—except that Ben might turn around and walk right back out the door if I said the wrong thing.

So, I just stood there and looked back at him.

Ben pulled me back into the circle of his arms, drawing me toward the couch. Blue and amber flames roared in the fireplace, welcome heat pushing back the chill of the evening.

As we sank down onto the couch, I stiffened for a moment as I thought of Carly, and then I relaxed against Ben's familiar warmth and shape.

"Meggie, please don't shut me out. I need you." Ben tipped my face up towards his and lowered his own so that he could press his mouth against the side of my head. I closed my eyes, tingling from the hair follicles on the top of my head to the tips of my toes.

"Ben, I've missed you, too." The words were small, but they reflected all the loss, the loneliness, and the pain of the past three months. "Please don't leave me. Don't leave me." My voice broke.

"Well, that isn't going to happen. I'm never going to let you go again." He smoothed my hair back from my face. "But how could you let me think you were dead? Meg, how could you? No, no, I'm sorry. Never mind. We're here now, and that's all that matters."

I grew still in his arms.

"Dead? No, you couldn't have thought that, Ben. I called and left you a message, explaining what had happened and how to get hold of me. Only you never called."

"But I never got a message."

Now, Ben's body tensed against mine. "Carly. It had to be Carly who erased that message. Damn it, she had no right."

"Ben, we need to talk about Carly. If you want to start over, I understand. Really, I do. In spite of what I said a minute ago, if you need to leave, I'll understand." My voice broke in spite of my resolve.

"But Meg . . ."

"No, please, I need to say this to you."

I closed my eyes and felt his head nod against mine.

"I know that I haven't been there for you. I haven't been there for anybody but myself over the years. I'm trying so hard to understand why, and I think I'm making a lot of progress. More than anything, I'd like to have another chance with you, but if you want to be with Carly, I'll let you go without a fight. I promise."

Ben snorted, and my eyes flew open.

"You'll let me go without a fight? That's supposed to make me feel, what? Good? I don't think so. Meg, do you have any idea how much I love you? It's like a plague."

My eyes widened.

"Oh God, no, I didn't mean it like that." Ben pressed his lips together and looked to the side. "Not a plague," he muttered. "Not a plague, but a sort of storm. Yeah, a storm."

A gurgle of laughter escaped my lips. I clapped one hand against my mouth, trying to hold it in.

"Oh Meg," said Ben with the most ridiculous look of embarrassment on his face. "You know I'm not good with words. What I'm trying to say . . ."

"But Ben, what about Carly?"

"There is no Carly," he bellowed, his eyes dark with frustration. "There never was any Carly. I don't know where or how you got the idea that she had any place in my life, but I've gotta tell you, it's all a fantasy, somebody's fantasy. But it's not mine, and I'm the one who gets to choose."

"But she said . . ."

"Wait a minute, when did you ever talk to her?"

Ben's face filled with fury, but I knew the anger was not directed toward me. My heart leapt, and I started laughing in relief.

"Meg, tell me, did Carly contact you? Quit laughing, Meg, I need to know."

So, I told him. We sat on that couch in front of the fire, and we talked like we'd never talked before. Ben shared more of his thoughts, feelings, and dreams than he'd ever done in the past.

Me? I was so proud of myself, because I shut up and let him talk. I listened. For the first time in our relationship, I listened with every fiber of my being to this man who had loved, listened, and supported me for all of my adult life.

A log in the fireplace fell with a hiss and a rather spectacular shower of sparks.

Ben laughed and looked at his watch. "Oh my God, Meg. It's after one o'clock in the morning. Do you remember the first time we met? We talked all night, and I wondered where all the time had gone."

I leaned my head against his shoulder. I laughed too, and with the laughter, all the sorrow and worry dissipated. I was home.

"Oh Meg."

For a moment, I closed my eyes, feeling the warmth of Ben's lips moving against my brow. I leaned back so that I could see his face. The room was dark except for the dying fire. Warm red light and dusky shadows played tag against every surface, highlighting the planes and curves that I knew so well.

My hand moved without conscious thought to cup the side of Ben's face. I could feel the roughness of evening whisker growth, and my fingers curled and stroked.

Ben closed his eyes, leaning into my touch. His tongue came out to wet his lips. His hands started to caress my face, my throat, and came to rest on my shoulders. He reached over and pulled the curtains closed. His hands were shaking.

"Meg, I want to touch all of you."

In answer, I began to unbutton his shirt, slipping my hands inside and splaying my fingers against the springing hair that covered his chest. I leaned forward, my nose rubbing gently against his skin, breathing in his scent.

Ben groaned, and with that sound, any restraint he'd been exercising disappeared. He pushed my cardigan aside and dropped it to the floor. My dress followed, and I lay in his arms nearly naked in the warmth from the fireplace my belly protruding between us. I stood and tried to cover myself, unsure about this new body of mine,

"No, Meggie, don't. Do you have any idea how beautiful you are?" Ben's voice was husky, his hands unsteady as he also stood, reaching behind me to release the clasp of my bra. He fumbled around for a bit. "Damn it. Some things never change. Help me out here, Meggie, will you?"

I laughed again. The laughter felt so good, and all self-consciousness melted away. With one quick twist and squeeze, I released the catch, slinging the bra across the room.

Ben stood still for a moment. He swallowed, placed both of his hands on my shoulders, and leaned down to kiss my forehead, my chin, my throat.

I closed my eyes, knowing that the tingling in the back of my eyes and tongue were only a prelude to the tingling I could expect.

I reached for Ben, but he pushed me back.

"Not yet, Meggie. Let me look at you."

I caught a glimpse of shadows leaping against the wall and turned my head slightly so that I could see as well as feel every move that Ben was making.

My shadow looked small next to his, the top of my head just reaching his shoulders. My hair had grown over the past three months, and shadow curls rioted around my shadow head.

My breasts thrust out fuller and larger than before, while a small—but very noticeable mound created an interesting shadow of its own.

As I watched the shadow people, I could see the man's hands slide from the woman's shoulders to her breasts and down to stroke her stomach.

A jolt of pleasure exploded low in my abdomen, and I reached for him again, forgetting all about the shadow people. Ben gently pushed my hands away, his own moving back up to cup first one breast and then the other.

I groaned deep in my throat tilting my head back. I reached for Ben to pull him closer, but he took my hands in his and looked down into my eyes.

"I'm afraid I'll hurt you, Meg."

"No, you won't. The only way you're going to hurt me is if we stop what we've started. Come here."

"Meggie?"

"Hmmm?"

"Do you have a bed in this house of yours?"

"I do."

"Let's go try it out, shall we?"

Chapter 41

Meg

I *dreamed. I dreamed that I was lying in a hospital bed and that I'd just given* *birth. Ben was there, and so were Genna, Jean-Louis, and Sylvie. I knew that* *Pete and Rob were nearby as well, because I could hear Pete's exuberant* *questions and Rob's quiet answers. I held our baby in my arms, and I felt safe.*

"Hey, I brought you coffee."

The dream drifted away with Ben's voice, but all the peace remained. I sighed, stretched, and opened one eye. Ben stood next to the bed, balancing a tray and smiling at me. I opened both eyes and smiled back.

"You shouldn't be drinking too much coffee, right? I would have made you breakfast, Meggie, but do you know that all you have in your refrigerator is some old orange juice? Your cupboards are even worse. All you have is some bread and peanut butter. Oh yeah, and you have some dog biscuits. Why do you have dog biscuits?"

"Oh, those are for Pete's dog, Joey."

"Huh? Who's Pete?" Ben shook his head. "Never mind. We can talk about all that later. You have to eat better now for the baby, Meg. We're going to have to find out all about the right nutrition, vitamins, and all that stuff. I'm sort of at a loss here, you know, because I've never had a baby before."

I laughed. Downstairs, someone knocked on the back door.

"Well, who on earth could that be?" said Ben with more than a hint of irritation. "It's only 7:30."

I took a sip of the coffee and tilted my head, listening. "Oh, that's Jean-Louis."

Ben looked at me. "You can tell it's Jean-Louis because . . . ?"

"His knock is more musical than Genna's and less impatient than Sylvie's—besides, Sylvie went home to Chicago the other day. I know it isn't Rob, because he always calls me first and asks if I have time to talk. And Pete? He never knocks. He just yells out my name until I open the door."

I was so busy sliding out of bed, that I barely registered the stunned look on Ben's face.

"Ben, will you go down and let Jean-Louis in? Please give him a cup of coffee while I'm getting dressed, okay? I'll hurry."

"Well, I suppose I can do that, but I'm starving. I was sort of hoping we could go out for breakfast, not entertain guests. So, if you can hurry this guy on his way, I'd appreciate it."

I smiled at his grumpy tone. After all, I'd had several months to get used to my neighbors' comings and goings, and Ben hadn't even met them yet.

I pulled on a pair of maternity jeans and a moss green, oversized v-necked jersey. On my way out of the bedroom, a flash of gold caught my eye. I stopped to fasten the tiny golden pendant around my throat. Mama's heart as Jenny used to call it. Ben had given it back to me the night before.

By the time I got down to the kitchen, Ben was sitting at the table sipping his coffee, while Jean-Louis prowled around, ignoring the cup of coffee steaming on the other side of the table. When he saw me, he let out an enormous sigh.

"Meg, mon ami, I need your help."

"Of course, what can I do?"

Jean-Louis waggled his eyebrows in Ben's direction. He smiled and said nothing. I knew that he was waiting for me to make the appropriate introductions and ask my husband to leave the room so that I could provide a private consultation.

"Uh, right."

I looked at Ben, amusement in my eyes, as I tried to figure out how to tactfully ask him to scram. I needn't have worried though, because Ben could take a hint and was already on his feet.

"Jean-Louis, you've met my husband, Ben?"

"But yes, he opened the door and has poured me this excellent cup of coffee," said Jean-Louis, clearly not interested in either Ben or the coffee.

My curiosity rose. Jean-Louis was always courteous and generally quite serious about his coffee. As Ben passed me on his way to the living room, he dropped a kiss onto the top of my head and pointed at his watch. I reached up to caress his cheek.

I sat down at the kitchen table and pointed to the chair on the opposite side.

"Okay, Jean-Louis. Sit, and tell me what's going on. You can start with your dinner last night. When I peeked down from the office upstairs, things seemed to be going very well between you and Genna."

Jean-Louis's face turned red. I was fascinated. I'd never seen him lose his composure before. When I realized that he thought I'd witnessed much more than I actually had, I convulsed with laughter.

"No, no, all I saw was the two of you in your kitchen drinking a glass of wine. Why, did I miss something good?"

Images of what I might have missed chased themselves through my mind, and I couldn't stop laughing.

Jean-Louis's face turned even redder, but he grinned, waving his hands as though to brush away my words.

"Everything went very well, and I thank you for your help with dinner. The appetizers were fantastique, the main course was superb, and the crème brûlée," he kissed his fingers, honest to

260 · Sher Kyweriga

God, he kissed his fingers, "she was, oh I don't even have a word that is strong enough to describe the excellence."

"So, what's got you so wrapped around the axle this early in the morning?"

"Early? You think this is early? I did not sleep all night. I very properly walked my Genevieve home. Oh, it was very late when we finished talking. I almost knocked on your door, but the lights were out, and I wanted you to have your sleep. For the baby, eh?"

I choked on another laugh, and Jean-Louis threw me a look of disgust.

"I said I almost knocked, my friend, but I did not. I have waited until almost 7:30 this morning, a more decent hour, but now, now, Madame. Tell me what to do."

"Okay, if I can, I will," I said cautiously.

Jean-Louis reached into his pocket and pulled out a small jeweler's box. My eyes widened. He opened it and placed it in front of me.

"Voilà. You can see my dilemma."

My eyes locked on to the most beautiful yellow diamond I'd ever seen, flanked on each side, by what appeared to be flawless emeralds. I looked up at Jean-Louis. His face had the most comical expression of dismay.

"Uh not really, Jean-Louis. I don't see any dilemma. This is an engagement ring, right?"

"Yes," he said in a gloomy voice.

"It's the most beautiful engagement ring I've ever seen."

"Yes, it is that." If anything, the gloom in his voice deepened.

"Okay, I give. You have a beautiful engagement ring. You spent last night having a romantic dinner with the woman you say you love, and . . . "

Jean-Louis interrupted me with dignity. "I do not just say I love my Genevieve, I do love her. And, today? Today, I intend to ask her to marry me."

"So, what's the problem?" I asked gently.

"This ring." Jean-Louis's gesture was saturated with disdain. "This ring, it was my grandmother's ring, eh? It has been passed down to the eldest son for his wife upon their betrothal for, oh, many more years than I can count."

"What a beautiful custom."

"But that is the problem. Some people like customs, and some do not. What if Genevieve wants her own ring, instead of this old family heirloom? Leonie refused to wear it. She did not like my grandmother, you see."

Jean-Louis shook his head. "No, that is not fair. My grandmother did not like Leonie, and so she withheld the ring. I picked another for Leonie especially. Now, with Genevieve, I don't know what to do. What if she wants to pick out her own ring and not wear this old thing?"

I sat still for a moment, thinking. I reached over and put my hands over Jean-Louis's.

"You're not really all that worried about the ring, are you?"

Jean-Louis stared down at the table for a moment and looked into my eyes, panic in his own.

"What if she tells me no, Meg?"

"Oh Jean-Louis, do you really think she'll say no?"

He stood and stretched out his long arms, gesturing wildly. "But what if she does? Eh? My heart, it will break. I don't know what to do."

I saw a movement out of the window, and watched with amusement as Genna pushed her way through the hedge between our two houses. She carried a big basket over her arm, and my mouth watered, thinking about the possibilities that might be inside.

"Well, if I were you—and I'm not—but if I were, I'd just ask her, Jean-Louis. She's on her way over right now."

I pointed out the window.

"But no, I am not ready." Jean-Louis leapt to his feet, grabbing the jeweler's box and his coffee. He evaporated into the next room, just as Genna knocked on the back door.

"Come in, come in. Genna, if you've brought something to eat, you are a saint." I held the door open for her, taking the basket and setting it on the table.

"Out of food, again, eh Meg?" said Genna.

"Eh Meg? Gosh, I wonder who you've been hanging out with. How did it go last night?"

"You were right, Meg. Jean-Louis does care about me. Last night was wonderful."

Genna smiled, but her smile was not for me. I'd have bet a year's salary her smile reflected memories of the previous evening. Lovely memories.

In an absent-minded way, she started lifting things out of her basket and arranging them on my kitchen table. First, she pulled out a plateful of cheese and cherry Danish—my own personal favorite.

My mouth started watering.

She lifted out a casserole dish filled with something that looked like eggs and sausage. Next, she plunked a large plateful of waffles next to the casserole dish, followed by a large pitcher of orange juice.

"We'll need to warm things in your microwave, okay?"

"No problem. Genna, you're not just a saint, you're an angel from heaven. Now, I won't have to take Ben out for breakfast."

"What do you mean you won't have to take Ben out for breakfast? Ben is starving. Come on, Meggie. Why can't we go out for breakfast? You can bring along anyone you want," said Ben coming into the kitchen. He stopped short. "Wow, do you always have breakfast delivered?"

I couldn't stop laughing. "You'd be surprised, Ben. I know I have been. Only it's not only breakfast that gets delivered. Sometimes its lunch and sometimes even dinner."

I took a deep breath. "Genna, please meet my husband, Ben. Ben, meet Genna, my very dear friend." My eyes filled with tears as I said the words, but Genna just wrapped her arms around me and gave me a big hug. She turned and held out a hand to Ben.

"Ben, I am so pleased to meet you, finally."

Ben took her hand and looked from me to Genna and back to me again. His smile was gentle.

I pulled a tissue out of my pocket and blew my nose.

"Genna, you must have gotten up before dawn to cook all of this."

"Well," Genna's face turned that shade of rose that I always found so interesting. "I didn't go to sleep last night. That is, I couldn't sleep after I got home from dinner with Jean-Louis, and so I cooked. Now, I need someone to help me eat everything."

"No problem," said Ben. "Where are the plates and stuff?"

"Uh, not yet?" I flashed my eyes toward the living room.

"Oh, yeah. I mean, I'll be right back." Ben sent an anguished look toward the plate of pastries, but turned back into the living room. A moment later, I could hear the sound of low voices.

Genna turned to me in surprise. "Oh, do you have other company this morning?"

"No, not really, it's only that. . ." The telephone rang and I reached over and plucked the receiver off the counter. "Hello?"

"Meg, it's me. I need to talk with you."

"Oh, it's so good to hear your voice . . ."

"Wait, wait, don't say my name unless you're alone," hissed Sylvie. "Are you? Alone, I mean?"

"Uh, not exactly."

"It's Genna, isn't it? What did she bake this morning?"

"Danish with cheese and cherries."

"Ohhhhhh, it's so not fair that I'm stuck here in Chicago. Did she read my letter?"

"Yes."

"Well?"

"Well, what Syl . . ."

"No, don't say my name. She'll want to talk, and I don't know what to say to her, yet."

I turned to look at Genna, but she wasn't paying any attention to me at all. She had finished unwrapping the Danish, and she seemed to be focused on the voices coming from the living room.

For all of Jean-Louis's intentions to be quiet, the man just didn't have it in him. Genna knew who was in the living room all right, and I have to say she showed absolutely no interest in me or who might be on the other end of the telephone.

I turned my back and whispered, "Okay, listen to me. What you do with your life is your business. Genna knows that, and reading your letter didn't make her feel any differently about you. She loves you, Sylvie. She always has, and she always will. If I know that, for heaven's sake, you should as well. I'm going to give her the phone now, and I want you to talk to her . . ."

"Wait, no, wait. Meg, talk to me. I'm not ready to talk to Genna yet," wailed Sylvie.

"Well, as someone we both know and love once said to me, 'too bad, so sad,'" I set the telephone down on the counter, and I could still hear her tiny voice squawking away.

"Genna?"

But Genna wasn't listening to me. She was on her way into the living room. I followed, just out of curiosity, to see what would happen.

Jean-Louis was hunched over in one of the overstuffed chairs by the fireplace, his large hands resting on his knees, his coffee almost untouched on the table before him.

Ben, seated opposite Jean-Louis, rolled an empty cup between his two hands. When we walked in, they were deep in conversation.

"Jean-Louis, good morning." Genna's smile was open and filled with the kind of light that makes the world go round.

"Genevieve. You are here." Jean-Louis leapt to his feet. He stood there, saying nothing for the first time since I'd met him.

Ben looked back and forth between the three of us, except, every once in a while, he'd glance toward the kitchen where all the food was. Before any of us could say a word, I heard a loud knock on the door.

I tilted my head. "It's Rob, and something's wrong."

Ben looked at me. "How can you tell? Besides, isn't that the guy who always calls ahead?"

"Yes, that's how I know something's wrong."

I dashed back into the kitchen, Ben close on my heels.

Rob walked in as soon as he saw me enter the kitchen. I took one look at his face, pushed him into a chair, filled a mug with coffee, and slid it in front of him. See, I'm trainable.

Rob nodded politely at Ben and turned to me.

"Oh Meg, I don't know what to do. Jessie came over this morning. She's at the house right now, and I don't know what to do with her."

"Jessie, your ex-wife?"

"Uh huh." Rob took an enormous sip of coffee. "Pete's out with Ricky, taking Joey for a walk, so he doesn't even know she's here. I don't know how to prepare him. I don't know if I should let Jessie talk to him, if I should ask her to leave, or what. Tell me what to do."

"Does she seem to be okay today?"

Rob raised troubled eyes.

"Yes, she says she's been through treatment out at Hazelden. That's the program I told you about, remember? You know, the one we wanted to get her into a couple of years ago. I guess she looks okay. She looks better than she has in a long time. I'm happy for her, but I don't know if I can trust her. Thanks to you, Pete is doing so well right now. I'm afraid she'll confuse him if . . ."

Ben cleared his throat. "Excuse me? I don't mean to interrupt, but is that Jessie coming up the walk?"

A young woman with soft blond hair swinging to her shoulders marched briskly up to my door. She rapped on it twice before I opened it and invited her in.

"Hello," she said, looking past me to Rob. "I need to see him, Rob. I'm so sorry for the past few years. I can't promise I won't have any problems going forward, but I promise to do whatever it takes to stay sober."

I steered her forward to a chair and poured her a cup of coffee. Ben hovered between the table and the door, a smear of cherry filling on his lips from where he'd stuffed a whole Danish into his mouth.

My own mouth twitched in sympathy. Poor man, he was so hungry, and he was meeting all my neighbors at once. At least I got to meet them one at a time.

A tiny shriek echoed from the telephone receiver. I whipped around and scooped it up.

"Sylvie, I'm so sorry. It's a little crazy here . . ."

"Listen, before you put Genna on, I've got to tell you something about Ben."

"Ben? Oh, he's here . . .

"He's there? Oh good, I was so worried about how to tell . . ."

"Meggie, Meggie help me."

It was Pete screaming at the top of his lungs. I dropped the telephone back on the counter with a terse, "Sylvie, hang on for a minute longer," and grabbed a box of dog biscuits from the cupboard.

Rob leapt to his feet at Pete's cry, but at the sight of the dog biscuits, he grinned at me and sat back down again.

We'd been through this drill before. I grinned back at Rob and shot out the back door and down the path to the alley in two seconds flat. Ben was right behind me.

"Meggie, Meggie, help me," shrieked Pete in frustration.

I followed the sound of Pete's voice to the end of the alley. Sure enough, Joey had slipped his leash again, and the little twerp was dancing just out of Pete's reach.

Every time Pete would get close, the puppy pranced away, barking shrilly as Pete and Ricky tried to grab him. For such a young puppy, Joey was fast and remarkably good at staying just out of reach.

I didn't even try to grab him. I shook the box of dog biscuits. Joey stopped prancing, stood stock still, and watched me without a flicker of his eyelids.

"Joey, good pup. Do you want a cookie?"

The puppy tilted his head at me and trotted right over. He sat down in front of me. I immediately gave him a dog biscuit with one hand and reached for his collar with the other. It was missing.

Pete saw my look of confusion.

"It broke, Meggie. See?" He held up the remnants of the puppy's collar.

"Oh well," I leaned down and hefted Joey up into my arms, grunting a bit. He'd grown a lot over the summer. "We'll carry him home and fix the collar. Hey, guess what? Genna brought Danish, eggs, sausage, and waffles to my house. You guys hungry?"

"Are we hungry? I'm so hungry, I could eat a horse," said Pete dancing in a silly circle to reinforce his impending starvation.

Not to be outdone, Ricky started dancing around too. "Well, I'm so hungry, I could eat an elephant."

"Oh yeah? I'm so hungry, I could eat a whale."

"Oh yeah? I could eat a whole herd of whales."

"Oh no, you couldn't," screeched Pete with a note of triumph in his voice. "And ya wanna know why? 'Cause there's no such thing as a herd of whales, there's only pods of whales. Meggie told me about pods of whales, so there. I'm so hungry I could eat two pods of whales."

At that point in their conversation, I sort of lost the thread as they were racing back to my house to get their breakfast.

"So," said Ben. "How do you rate puppy duty?"

"I know the magic, that's why."

I tried to shake the box of dog biscuits at Ben, but Joey started wiggling, and I had everything I could do to just hang on and not drop him on his head.

"Here, Meggie. Give me that puppy. You're not supposed to be lugging heavy things around right now. What if you hurt yourself or our baby?"

Ben took the wriggling pup in his own arms, a look of delight on his face as he rubbed the small creature. Recognizing a master masseur, Joey settled right down in Ben's arms, cuddling close.

"Oh Meg, this is exactly the kind of dog I was always hoping we could get."

I strolled along as we made our way back up the alley to my house, watching his face as he rubbed his nose on Joey's soft, furry head.

"Well, let's get one. Our baby is going to need a friend, and it would be easy to fence in our yard."

Ben looked at me over the puppy in his arms. "Do you want to stay here, Meg?"

"Let's talk about it, Ben. Let's talk about everything. I don't know what's best. I just know one thing, and that's that I want to be with you. The rest we'll figure out together as we go along."

Ben hefted Joey so that he could free one arm and wrap it around me.

"Oh my gosh, I forgot about Jessie. Pete hasn't seen her in more than two years. How could I have forgotten? Pete? Pete?" I shrieked his name down the alley. A moment later, I saw his head pop back around the edge of my garage.

"Meggie? Are you calling me?"

"Come here a minute, will you Pete?"

"But I'm hungry, and you said Genna brought waffles."

"I know, Honey. I just need you for a minute, okay?"

Ben and I reached the corner of my garage where Pete stood waiting. Ricky had abandoned his friend and gone on into the house for his breakfast.

"Hurry, Meggie, hurry or Ricky's gonna eat all the waffles. He said he was gonna eat everything in sight if I didn't hurry up."

I sank down on my knees by Pete and pulled him around so that I could look into his eyes.

"Pete, remember how you decided your mama loves you a lot, even though she doesn't always do what she says she's going to do?"

"Yeah," Pete nodded his head. "You told me that even when she doesn't come to see me, she still loves me. I remember, Meggie. Now, can I go eat?"

"In just a minute, Honey. I wanted to tell you that your mama has come to see you this morning."

At my words, Pete's head came up, his eyes reflecting all the hope a small boy can hold in his heart. "She's here. My Mom is here."

"She's in my kitchen right now, Pete. With your Dad."

I reached out and touched his arm, and Pete threw himself against me.

"Oh thank you, Meggie," as if I had everything to do with his mother coming to visit. Then, he was gone, just like that.

"Does this mean we get to eat, too?"

Ben's words were light, but I could tell from the look in his eyes, that he was proud of me for some reason. That look brought a lump to my throat.

"Yeah, it means we get to eat, too. Come on."

We walked into organized chaos.

Genna talked on the telephone while she bustled back and forth between the stove and the dining room. Jean-Louis worked at her side, taking the dishes of food she filled and carrying them into the dining room. I smiled as I saw the flash of diamond on her hand. Ricky was already seated at the kitchen table, working on a stack of waffles.

Pete sat across the table on Rob's lap, facing his mother. Jessie leaned toward her son, and the yearning on her face was plain to anyone watching her. She was careful about initiating any touching, but even as I watched, Pete slid off Rob's lap and moved closer to his mother. Jessie wrapped one arm around him and started to cry. Pete looked up at me with a panicked expression, and I moved forward.

"Hey, I bet everyone's hungry, right?"

Pete nodded his head vigorously. Jessie wiped her eyes and smiled.

"I'd love to try one of those Danish, and if you have another cup of coffee, I'd be in heaven."

"You've got it, Jessie. Welcome, I'm glad to meet you."

I rested a hand on her shoulder, smiling into the uncertainty in her eyes. I turned to bring her both a Danish and a cup of coffee.

As I passed Jean-Louis, I stood on tiptoes and whispered, "So, what did she say, eh?"

"Yes. She said yes." Jean-Louis beamed.

Genna set the telephone down and turned to the room at large.

"Sylvie sends her love to everyone and her regrets that she is missing breakfast. I told her to come home next weekend and to bring her partner, Terri, and that we'd have breakfast all over again in their honor."

Genna turned to me.

"I put everything out on the dining room table, Meg. There are so many of us that I thought we'd fit better. Oh, I also made pancakes. Did you know that you have flour and stuff all sealed up tight in Tupperware containers? Here in this bottom cupboard."

"No kidding, you mean I could have been cooking all along?" I grinned. "Oh well, I guess I should have looked harder."

Genna got the boys settled with mounds of food at the kitchen table. She shooed the rest of us into the dining room, where someone had set the table, including a tall pitcher with orange juice and a small glass pitcher with what looked like maple syrup.

Ben pushed me into a chair, sat down beside me, and with a great sigh, he started passing bowls of food. Poor man, he really was starving. He'd just scooped an enormous pile of eggs and sausage onto his plate and raised his fork to his mouth when the front doorbell rang.

He looked at me and groaned. "I'm never gonna get to eat. So, who's that, Meg?"

"I don't know. No one uses the doorbell around here." I took a bite of cherry Danish and a sip of coffee—I was starving myself at that point—and pushed my chair back from the table. "Let's find out who it is."

My dining room opens into the front hallway, so all eyes were on me as I opened the door. A tall, slender young man dressed in a trench coat stood outside. In spite of the elegance of his clothes and grooming, he couldn't have been more than thirty years old.

"Mrs. Jacobi? Meg Jacobi?"

"Yes, that's me."

He looked past me into the house, no doubt hearing all the laughter and voices and smelling the fragrance of good breakfast food.

"I'm sorry to bother you, ma'am, but you never answered any of my calls or letters. I even sent you a letter special delivery. You should have gotten it on Saturday."

"Oh, you sent that letter. I didn't find it until yesterday." I looked at him, but I didn't have a clue who he was. "I'm sorry, you sent me letters and called? Who are you?"

He reached into his pocket and withdrew a business card. "I'm James Reddinger." He handed me the card with all the dignity of a foreign ambassador meeting the head of the country in which he was to reside.

"Oh, of course, you're the detective my Aunt Marion hired."

Ben pushed back his chair and joined me at the door. All the voices around the table hushed as everyone listened unabashedly for what came next.

"Yes, ma'am, that's me."

I nodded, waiting for him to continue.

"Your aunt hired me almost two years ago. I sent her a report every month. I don't know if you've read them or not?"

He hesitated, and I nodded again. "Then, you'll know that I got close a few times to finding your sister, only to discover that the contact I was seeking had moved or died."

I nodded again, a tiny flurry stirring in the middle of my chest.

"Well, I finally tracked someone down who remembered your sister's adoptive family. It was a niece of the woman who adopted your sister. She gave me Jenny's address and married name. Jenny lives here in Minneapolis with her husband, and I wanted to be sure that you understood we'd finally found her."

"Oh Meg," Ben put his arms around me, which was a very good thing, because my knees felt sort of wobbly.

"Jenny's here? In Minneapolis?"

"Yes, Ma'am. She's a graduate student at the university. I sent you her address in the special delivery letter. Didn't you read it?"

My eyes turned to the mantle, and I focused on the letter that I'd tucked behind the hurricane lamp the evening before.

"No, I didn't read it. I was kind of busy last night. Though, in all honesty, even if I had realized the letter was from you, I'd have thought you were reporting another dead end. I might not have read it anyway. I'm sorry."

The young man didn't look especially offended at my words.

"I never stop with a dead end. It's simply a matter of time and effort. These days you can find anyone, if you have a computer and an Internet connection. The only reason it took me so long to find your sister is that her adoptive father died, and her mother remarried. In fact, she's remarried twice, changing her name each time."

Suddenly the words he'd said a few minutes ago penetrated, and the flurry in my chest grew.

"You found Jenny? You really found her after all this time. How is she? Oh Lord, what if she doesn't want to see me? She may not even remember me. She was only four years old the last time I saw her."

Ben was a rock at my side. "Meggie, what do you have to lose? You've never stopped grieving for Jenny. What could you possibly have to lose at this point?"

"Nothing?" I whispered.

I looked into the dining room at all the faces that were watching me with concern. Genna looked as though she were about to leap to her feet and rush to my side. Jean-Louis nodded. Rob smiled at me, and Jessie just looked confused. I couldn't blame her.

Pete popped his head around the corner, "Hey Meggie, who's Jenny?"

Ben gave me a gentle squeeze. "See, what I mean? What have you got to lose?"

I looked around the room and smiled.

"Nothing," I said again, loud and clear. I would go to see my sister. Maybe she would remember me, and maybe she wouldn't, but I would do whatever I could to get to know her. That's all I could do, after all, right?

Shed pain, my darling, no regrets. Your life belongs to you.

I smiled at the young man. "Please join us for breakfast. We have tons of food."

I could see the young man wondering whether professional conduct included joining a client and her friends for breakfast. Professionalism warred with the good smells and laughter coming from my dining room. Guess which won out?